Phone M

"Office got a call," Detective Holdsworth said. "The guy said he saw me at the scene on Sunset this morning. Then he mentioned you. Described you to a T, Mr. House."

"So what?"

"So the caller said he was our man. The Slasher. Said he was cleaning up the boulevard."

"Crank?" I said.

"Was until he told us something he shouldn't a known. Said all the other guys were done in with a straight razor, but that the last one wasn't. It's the one thing we held back from the papers. Wasn't no way for the caller to know that."

"Good God," I said.

"Worse'n that, he's sane. No rantin'. The crazy ones make mistakes. This guy, goddammit, we still don't know why he's doin' it. He never said *that*."

"But he mentioned me. You serious, Jim?"

"Detail. Down to the pen in your shirt pocket. Said you should lose some weight."

"The hell with him."

Holdsworth sniffed, and ran a big hand over his perspiring brow. He fixed his heavy eyes on me. "And you ain't gonna like what else he said."

I waited.

"Said you should watch yourself."

Bantam Books by Crabbe Evers:

Murder in Wrigley Field
Murderer's Row
Bleeding Dodger Blue

Bleeding

Dodger

Blue

A Duffy House Mystery

Crabbe Evers

BANTAM BOOKS
NEW YORK · TORONTO · LONDON · SYDNEY · AUCKLAND

This is a work of fiction. References to real people, events, establishments, organizations, and locales are intended only to give the fiction a sense of reality and authenticity. All of the main characters, events and incidents in this novel are creations of the author's imagination, and their resemblance, if any, to actual events or persons, living or dead, is entirely coincidental.

BLEEDING DODGER BLUE

A Bantam Crime Line Book / October 1991

CRIME LINE and the portrayal of a boxed "cl" are trademarks of Bantam Books, a division of Bantam Doubleday Dell Publishing Group, Inc.

ISBN 0-553-29177-7

Published simultaneously in the United States and Canada

Bantam Books are published by Bantam Books, a division of Bantam Doubleday Dell Publishing Group, Inc. Its trademark, consisting of the words "Bantam Books" and the portrayal of a rooster, is Registered in U.S. Patent and Trademark Office and in other countries. Marca Registrada. Bantam Books, 666 Fifth Avenue, New York, New York 10103.

PRINTED IN THE UNITED STATES OF AMERICA

RAD   0 9 8 7 6 5 4 3 2 1

For Marjorie Braman—perfection!

Bleeding
Dodger
Blue

1

City of Angels

For years I always felt sorry for the West Coast. Oh, not because they were two and three hours behind the rest of the country—why, we were milking the cows and buying stocks before they were even out of bed—but because they were always in the minor leagues.

The Pacific Coast League was the best they could do. They reared guys like DiMaggio, then had to sit back and watch them go east to fame and riches. They even had a ballyard called Wrigley Field, owned by the same chewing-gum mogul, but it too was minor league. A puny version of the real McCoy.

Sure, the people in California had the movies and a lot of sunshine, and most of them didn't know a snow shovel from a rainy day. Yet they had to root for other folks' heroes. Bring their loyalties with them like old photographs when they moved from Brooklyn or Boston or St. Louis. While the rest of the country marked their lives by dropped pop-ups and ninth-inning rallies witnessed in official stadiums—some in that glorious October classic—Californians just retired to their lettuce fields.

Being from Chicago, where we had not one but two major-league teams for as long as I could remember, I felt sorry for the westerners. Didn't lose sleep over it, but felt sorry. Let them have Bogie and Bacall, we had Hack Wilson and Ernie Banks.

Those thoughts occupied me as I rode the DC-10

bound for Los Angeles International Airport. The plane wasn't very full, so I stretched out and put my handbag on the seat next to me. Mine is a handbag, not a brief-case; I've never composed a brief and never owned a case to hold one. Advanced age cries out for accuracy.

Inside were a couple of reporter's notebooks, a tape recorder, a proof copy of another paean to baseball written by a Washington, D.C. political pundit who didn't mind slumming in my bailiwick but would proba-bly fulminate were I to invade his—whose publisher begged for my kudos but would probably go on begging —and a volume of Raymond Chandler stories.

For my money you can take Chandler's opening paragraph of *Red Wind*—"There was a desert wind blowing that night. It was one of those hot, dry Santa Anas that come down through the mountain passes and curl your hair and make your nerves jump and your skin itch . . ."—and stack it up against just about any lead on the books.

Philip Marlowe, Chandler's shamus, has always en-joyed a suite in my mind's hotel. Hollywood has cast Bogart, Dick Powell, Robert Montgomery, George Montgomery, and Bob Mitchum among others in the role and, as far as I'm concerned, has still fallen short.

The more I read, the more my mind drifted off the page. My friend Mike Royko, the testy young Chicago columnist, has long referred to California as the "world's largest outdoor asylum." For evidence Royko points no further than the morning's paper. Every day there is likely to be a curious, cockamamy story of life on America's far West End, a place that remains one of the great magnets for the kooky, the out-of-sync, the flake.

Meet an old acquaintance on a street in Boston or Indianapolis or Dubuque, Royko has written, and ask, "Hey, what ever happened to that goofy brother of yours?" And the answer is always, "Oh, he went to California."

Sometimes you get the feeling that California, that big, rolling nation-state on the big, placid ocean, is a basin so immense that the whole country somehow flows into it. Land of wannabes, immigrants, dreamers, and drifters, of stars, of E.T. The Transient State where everybody comes from someplace else. State of Charlie Manson and Squeaky Fromme, of the Night Stalker, the Hillside Strangler, *Helter Skelter.* Land of the editorial "Where else?"—as in, "A man with inoperable lung cancer in California *(where else?)* sued to have his head frozen after he dies. . . ."

Everybody, it seems, has an opinion on California, especially Southern California. If you keep a camera on yourself all the time, that's bound to happen. And in this video age, even if you haven't been there, you've been there. I've been there many times. It's a pretty place, at least a lot of it is, especially in spring when the rainy season peaks—or is supposed to. Storms move from the northern Pacific and soak the coastal area and much of the valleys. The moisture reaffirms the land's remarkable tropical vegetation. The countryside blazes with pink and yellow hibiscus, freeway daisies, the yellow flowers of wild mustard. Ice plants bloom with explosions of magenta and lavender. There are the palms and cypruses, and hundreds of varieties of great, green eucalyptus trees so thick you can't see through them.

The rest of the year, rainfall in the southern part of the state is sparse, and the area, which is a desert, grows parched and vulnerable to fires. Southern California's fires, abetted in September by Santa Ana winds, devastate thousands of acres of brush and grasslands and devour millions of dollars worth of real estate. It is a harrowing phenomenon, and no one is immune. Yet in April, the season of my brief stay, there is no more lush and verdant place. And with the burning season seemingly remote, Angelenos casually pronounce their homeland the best place on earth.

While I have an eye for that sort of thing, I'm not a weather guy. I know that baseball is best played on green grass and in sunshine, but the two are not prerequisites for my continued merry existence. I'll take my share of eyeshade days, wipe sweat from my nape; but when the wind shifts and the seasons flip, I'll dig out the cardigan, give due reverence to a hard frost, and stoke the stove. Cold weather doesn't bother me a bit. For one thing, it stops insects and fleas in their many tracks, just hardens the soil like concrete and allows the pesky critters a bed for their larvae and nothing more. Somebody a lot sharper than I decided there is something to be said for dormancy and hibernation. They do wonders for golf courses. And the Muse, of course, thrives when there is sleet on the window.

The flight west was smooth and unremarkable, which made it remarkable, until an optimistic stewardess with shiny teeth asked me if I wished the chicken or the beef. When I asked her which she recommended, she said that she had not had either. "Young lady," I said, "you have a whole life ahead of you." She looked at me as if I had just removed my lower dentures. I took my chances with the chicken.

Riding that aircraft into Los Angeles from the east, I could see below me the uniform squares of tract housing—the cream and coral colors of little stucco homes with red tile roofs—on the desert floor and up the ravines and mountainsides. Suddenly the plane flew out over the infinite deep blue of the Pacific, did a loop, and hunkered in low for the landing.

With no relatives, wet-eyed loved ones, or limousine drivers holding a scrawled placard to greet me, I shuffled over to the inevitable stop of a West Coast visitor: the rental-car desk. I signed away my rights and my future for the privilege of navigating an Oriental flivver on Southern California's freeways. I had no choice. You do not cover this sprawling, fault-lined metropolis any other way.

My mission was simple: to put some flesh on my long-awaited memoirs. My two cents' worth, I'd always considered, was a publisher's gold mine; yet in order not to bore myself with mildewed anecdotes and mealy reminiscences, I decided to add some other opinions. California is a waiting room for a lot of old-timers in the horsehide crowd, good baseball people, to be sure, who knew the game as it was played in 1950 and have a choice thing or two to say about the way it is offered today. I'd look a few of them up and barber awhile, take notes, maybe learn something, and thicken the manuscript.

One of my targets was Jack Remsen, the glad-handing, tongue-wagging, fat, and current manager of the Los Angeles Dodgers. I knew him back when he was a stocky minor-league catcher whose path to the Dodger lineup was blocked by guys named Campanella and Walker. Why, Jack, who could block the plate and hit his weight, never had a chance. He played alongside Bobby Morgan, who batted over .330 one year at Montreal, the Dodgers' Triple A team, and still rode the big club's bench when he broke in the next season—because of Reese, Robinson, Cox, Gilliam, and company.

The Dodgers were on a home stand, and Remsen had said to come on the hell out here. So that's what I was up to, and why I was risking my life behind the wheel of an automobile on the concrete ribbons of the west. I'm a public-transportation person. I like the feel of subway tokens in my pocket; the goose of a turnstile makes me giggle. I can stand in the aisle of a hurtling train with one arm hooked around a stainless-steel pole and read a newspaper from front page to back. I understand garbled offerings of mass transit's public-address systems. I am immune to the irascible nature of the commuter and the crush of the crowd.

On the other hand, the freeway, the thruway, the underpass, cloverleaf, exit ramp, and turnoff frighten the bejesus out of me. I don't like lane changes, lane closings, merges, squeezes, or yields. Tailgaters haunt my dreams. Throw in a sniper or a freeway shooter, a swell in a Jaguar with a phone in his neck, or a dumb blond with a vanity license plate reading SPOILD 1, and my nerves bristle like those of a rookie crowding the plate against Don Drysdale.

Nevertheless, I nosed out of the parking lot of the car-rental agency on Century Boulevard like the little ol' lady from Pasadena. It was late afternoon, and I had plenty of time. There would be no San Diego Freeway, Number 405, in my immediate future. The good girl at the rental desk had used her yellow marker to highlight my journey, which sent me north along the ocean via

Lincoln Boulevard to Santa Monica. Do not think I drop
that or other Southern California locations like some
glib late-night talk-show host, either. I wince at the
usage "L.A.," and my oafish Spanish raises hell with the
street names. I simply read a good map.

My route of choice was Sunset Boulevard, the infa-
mous street that winds its way from the ocean through
Beverly Hills and Hollywood to downtown Los Angeles.
I had a reservation at the Biltmore, a castle of a hotel
that has offered me a plush pillow throughout the three
decades that I have come to town to write about a
ballclub. When I first began darkening its door, the
Biltmore had a midget redcap with a fire-bell voice who
became famous for crying, "Call for Philip Mor-rees!" in
radio and television commercials. That was back in the
days when people advertised cigarettes and a lot of
them smoked them and nobody apologized for it. Least
of all the midget.

So I slogged up Lincoln Boulevard. My old eyes
were stapled to the road, and my mitts gripped the
steering wheel at ten o'clock and two o'clock as if I were
ferrying an oil tanker through a reef. Somewhere to my
left was the Pacific. It would have to get along without
any gawking from me. There were folks on bikes, skate-
boards, roller skates, drivers in chattery Volkswagen
Beetles, Jeeps, convertibles, and sweep-finned 1957
Chryslers all around me, but I never saw a one of them.
I drove the car and nothing else. The windows were
closed. The radio was off.

Which is not to say that I was not mentally consid-
ering my surroundings. The City of Angels. The place
has a history, and I'm partial to that. It was one of the
few cities on earth to have been deliberately planned in
advance and ceremoniously inaugurated. The king of
Spain ordained it by royal decree—not that that meant
an especially auspicious beginning. In fact, despite in-
ducements of land, money, and livestock, the mission
honcho, one Governor de Neve, was unable to lure any
settlers from lower California. Finally, a poor and motley group of "nine Indians and one mestizo, two Ne-

groes and eight mulattoes, and two adults of Spanish origin" straggled in from Mexico.

Together with some soldiers, a few mission priests, and their Indian acolytes—a roster of forty-four people in all—on September 4, 1781, they established El Pueblo de Nuestra Señora la Reina de Los Angeles de Porciuncula, The Town of Our Lady the Queen of the Angels of Porciuncula. That makes the city older than Chicago, my hometown, and not a lot of people think about Los Angeles like that. The whole area has always seemed to exist only in the present, its population transient. If you live here, you had to have moved here. History knows otherwise.

But I came to California without blinders, much less a decent pair of sunglasses. In my mind the state will always rhyme with runaway franchises and expansion teams, two dubious developments in the world of baseball. I know it's been over thirty years since the Dodgers (with Horace Stoneham's Giants riding piggyback) came west; but in my mind, my imagination, and my memories, they will always be the Bums from Brooklyn. I spent too many golden hours in Ebbets Field to think otherwise. I sat at the feet of Mr. Branch Rickey, a wise, gentle, brilliant man, who came to the Brooklyn organization in 1942 and turned that dismal franchise into a contender. I watched Brooklyn become the zaniest member of the National League, and Ebbets Field, with Hilda Chester, the babe with the cowbell in the bleachers, become a landmark. I witnessed Jackie Robinson and Duke Snider.

Southern California, in my jaded perspective, is Walter O'Malley. O'Malley, that jowly, cigar-chomping autocrat, who blustered, bullied, connived, and jackhammered his will on professional baseball as few men before or after him have ever done. The lord of the lords of baseball, O'Malley was as savvy a businessman and politician as the game has ever seen. In 1950 he bought Rickey, his longtime rival, out of the Dodger organization and then forbade employees to even mention Branch's name.

It was O'Malley who seized—I use the term advisedly because other entrepreneurs wanted to go west before him—the fortune that was the California baseball market even though his Brooklyn franchise of the 1950s was the most profitable one in the National League. The old hustler's axiom states, "I saw my openings and I took 'em," and that's just what O'Malley did. He hoodwinked New York politicians and steamrolled fellow major-league owners in his planned escape from Brooklyn. Then he managed to keep all other clubs, including any American League franchise, out of Los Angeles. Along the way he picked up allies, but few friends. Bill Veeck, who admired a finagler as much as anybody, said of O'Malley, "He has a face that even Dale Carnegie would want to punch." And to Brooklyn, to the people in the borough, he was a Judas. Wrote Pete Hamill, "The three worst human beings who ever lived? Hitler, Stalin, and Walter O'Malley."

California, a land that had made fortunes for speculators who'd diverted water, drilled for oil, and pocked the hills and valleys full of houses, threw nary a jab at him. The City of Angels and its burgeoning metropolis were ready for the big leagues, and in 1958 O'Malley delivered. Thus the citizenry, those folks who venerated the likes of Howard Hughes and Louis B. Mayer, who tossed around the term *mogul* without shame, embraced Walter O'Malley as if he were a prophet.

Of course, he brought with him a veteran ball team—Reese, Hodges, Snider, Furillo, for crying out loud—and a manager named Alston. He brought Emil "Buzzy" Bavasi, who was probably the smartest general manager in baseball at the time. He brought those white home uniforms with the inimitable Dodgers logo stitched across the front. The blue caps had to have *LA* instead of *B* put on the front, but that was a minor, relatively inexpensive problem for the ever penurious O'Malley. Carrying steamer trunks with "Brooklyn" painted on them, Walter's minions unpacked the rest of the team's equipment, and the transition was complete.

They gave him parades and let him play in an oval-shaped arena modestly named the Coliseum, which normally hosts a college football team whose mascot dresses as a centurion in a crimson toga and circles the playing field on a snorting steed. It was a joke of a baseball park. The left-field fence was only 251 feet away from home plate and threatened to make Pee Wee Reese a home-run hitter. Still, latter-day Dodger fans in sun visors and reeking of Coppertone packed the place. On opening day over seventy-eight thousand of them showed up. Joe E. Brown, a comedian, introduced the opposing managers. On other desert days as many as ninety thousand fans, almost three times the capacity of Ebbets Field, would pay to get in. And in 1959, only a season after their arrival, O'Malley's Dodgers brought the World Championship west by winning in six over the White Sox.

In the meantime the city of Los Angeles ceded O'Malley a choice chunk of public land called Chavez Ravine on which to build a new ballyard, and threw in carte blanche as the player to be named later. Despite the delays and the lawsuits pressed by some silly local goo-goos who thought eight hundred acres of prime Los Angeles real estate might be used for something other than a donation to a private individual with a ball team, O'Malley got his way. He got the Bums out of Brooklyn and ensconced in a terraced, bougainvillea-draped playground with the appropriate address of Elysian Park Avenue in Los Angeles. It was the smoothest piece of highway robbery baseball style since Jake Ruppert snatched a kid named Ruth from the Red Sox.

So no, I don't see Southern California through O'Malley's wire-rimmed, rose-colored spectacles. A pox on progress. The Dodgers should have stayed in Brooklyn. There were plenty of struggling franchises that could have and should have moved here. Having said all that, and hoping that I have not infuriated greater Los Angeles, all 14 million souls—perhaps including the Orange County mortals who have the Angels to infuriate them—I should hasten to add that I'd be more of a blathering old fool than I usually am if I did not recognize the triumph that is the Los Angeles Dodgers. It is a golden—in every overused sense of the word—franchise; its fans are as blessed and as loyal as any east of the

Mississippi. And well they should be, for in three and a half short decades the Dodgers have won remarkable titles in dramatic fashion. There is a glow to the Dodger uniform—the one worn by Garvey, Lopes, Russell, and Cey—to the very *wearing* of it, an aura comparable to the mystique that once resided in Yankee pinstripes. Now that's saying something.

By this time I had taken a left on Santa Monica Boulevard and reached the corner of it and Ocean Avenue. Here was the western end—or beginning, depending on your point of view—of Route 66, the most fabled of American highways and one of my vintage. In fact, the other end of Route 66, that "colossus of roads," is in Grant Park in my burg of Chicago.

I turned right when I reached Sunset Boulevard and swung northeast over its winding, mountainous route. Its up-and-down curving feel was green and rich, and it was lined with thick trees and wide lawns in front of expensive residential real estate. UCLA popped up on the right in what may be one of the loveliest campuses anywhere. If ivy and architecture could recruit a kid, UCLA would have a lock on every high-school senior in the land.

When my bumper nosed off Sunset and into Bel Air, I was nearly suffocated by the exclusiveness of the neighborhood. The streets said No Outlet, and many of the cars—Mercedeses, Jaguars, and classic Thunderbirds—were covered with tarps. Private drives led past stone entryways. The specter of security was everywhere; below the security company's name on the signs were the ominous words Armed Response. Behind these walls and the thick, manicured shrubbery were familiar faces who wanted to be seen only on their terms, the maps hawked by roadside vendors pinpointing the stars' homes notwithstanding. I edged past the private Bel Air Patrol at the bottom of the hill, a posse formed to keep riffraff like me out, and welcomed the sight of Sunset once again.

At Rodeo Drive appeared the Beverly Hills Hotel, a pricey inn known for its lounges and dining rooms and the aura of the deal. An old, wafer-thin woman in a blood-red dress, a woman so frail she seemed held together with Scotch tape, minced her way up the drive of the pink hotel. I swear it was the ghost of Bette Davis.

The green lights came fast on Sunset Boulevard, in a few miles Beverly Hills gave way to the splash of West Hollywood commerce, and the boulevard became the strip known to the rest of the world through television and cinema. There is no more need to describe Hollywood than there is to detail the taper of the Eiffel Tower or Durante's schnoz. Only the Japanese take photos; the rest of us—even we who were not raised on television— have the street's postcard scenes burned into the flaky outer layers of our brains.

Talk of the Japanese, and you'll hear of how, during World War II, artists from the motion-picture studios were employed to camouflage the rooftops of the huge Douglas defense plants near here. They painted them to look like big pastures and farmyards, complete with cows. Amazing!

Traffic was more frenetic now, and even though it was the stop-and-go variety that I'm used to, I drove like a chicken. It was getting into early evening, and the sun's long rays colored the boulevard true to its name. Over my shoulder were Hollywood's hills and the famous white wooden sign on the cliff.

On I drove, winding beneath the Hollywood freeway and into central Los Angeles. In almost no time the street lost its gloss. Its six lanes became crowded with buses, those belching animals Los Angeles is not known for, and bus stops full of dusty faces with the price of a fare and little more. At intersections with streets named Descanso, Silver Lake, and Coronado, there was not even a hint of tinsel or romance. Towering fan palms still cut the sky overhead, and the street still rose and fell, occasionally slicing through rocky cinnamon-brown cliffs seeded with jagged century plants. Yet the famous boulevard had become a grid of grimy tire shops and body shops, and the hotels, theaters, and comedy shops had given way to the ubiquitous strip malls with their laundromats and taco stands, tax accountants' offices, furniture stores, tattoo parlors, and liquor stores

with wrought-iron doors. Corner buildings were laced
with graffiti, the tedious, modern-day script of young
street hoodlums who huffed and puffed in the stucco-
tough bungalow neighborhoods just off the drag.

At a stoplight in front of one of these strip malls, I
realized without any profound insight that this stretch
of Sunset Boulevard was now just another gritty street
in the guts of a big, tough, sunbaked city. A row of
haggard old-timers, some of them wearing unmatched
shoes with yesterday's clothes, sat along a low wall in
front of the mall's parking lot. What we called a bum in
my day, but is now referred to as a homeless person,
pushed a grocery cart full of aluminum cans and plastic
bags against the light and held up traffic. The bum's face
and neck were sunburned, he limped badly, and I could
not have guessed his age if good money depended on it.

Billboards with Dodgers on them told me I was
getting close to Elysian Park Avenue when I got cut off
by a bullying sedan that thought it owned the road. I
swore out loud and bellowed a bevy of blue expletives
that discolored the windshield before I realized that the
auto, barrel-assing in front of me, *did* own the road. It
was a squad car, a black-and-white that served and protected on its good days and mopped up on most others.
Now it was in a hurry, its red Mars lights flashing, its
engine groaning and tires hissing like something out of
the movies. Cars and pedestrians stopped where they
were. Some watched the path of the squad car, and
others looked around for the production crew.

Pulling over to the curb just in time to keep from
getting clipped by yet another squad car, I craned to
see what the draw was. I didn't have to crane too far, for
the commotion seemed centered at the corner of Sunset and Mohawk, only a half block ahead. Traffic wasn't
going anywhere, so I got out and walked. I may be
retired, but my reporter's nose is far from cold.

At Mohawk I looked north and saw a half-dozen
squad cars parked chockablock near an alley. No movie
set this, but a crime scene buffeted by the crackle of
static on two-way radios and the migraine-inducing

blipping of squad car lights. Officers in ink-black uniforms moved about the rear of a *taqueria* and its fetid trash containers. Their concern lay on the oily, stained pavement. It was a still, apparently lifeless body. When I looked more closely, I saw that it was that of a slight man, a pensioner with silver hair and dressed in a lime green long-sleeved shirt and baggy brown slacks, legs akimbo, a pair of old sneakers pointing up at the darkening sky.

But it wasn't the fellow's age or clothes that held my eye, not the awkward collapse of his body with the right arm pinned beneath it, but the gaping wound to the man's neck. In what looked like a gash made by the maw of an ax, his gullet was sliced open almost to the bone and from ear to ear, a bloody salad of tissue and cartilage. In my youth I worked Novembers for my grandfather, who operated a live poultry shop on Adams Street on the west side of Chicago. I slaughtered turkeys for Thanksgiving. In a few swift, mechanical motions, I grabbed one fatted bird after another, raised a razor-sharp boning knife to the soft flesh of its crop, and slit it. I then pulled the nearly severed head through a large funnel, and while its torso shuddered and its legs peddled, the dead bird's tepid blood drained to the floor below.

The wounds I inflicted as a boot-clad boy against dumb holiday fowl were no different, and no less effective, than the one I was looking at. The vital and complex food, breath, and nerve tube had been cut and exposed like that of a newly slaughtered turkey. But unlike my quarry, the victim in the street was lying in his own blood. It soaked his collar into a crimson ring and radiated in a burgundy puddle beneath his white-haired head. His eyes were open, and his tongue hung out like the tab of a zipper.

I silently stared, transfixed, the sights and—most vividly—the smells of my childhood washing over me. The old man's blood was everywhere, sticky, red, more ghastly than anything in my memory. And no one made any effort to blot it, or cover the source. I was sickened by it, and sad for the old guy. Then in midgape it struck me: the indignity! What the hell? Was this Bogotá or San Salvador or some pissant banana republic where a leaking corpse in the street is just another piece of terrorist carnage? Was this just a quick piece of TV news footage? A few minutes of cinema?

"Cover him up, for godsakes!" I barked.

It was the least I could do for somebody of my vintage so ignobly displayed on the pavement. A young policewoman looked at me evenly and repaired to her car. By now people were crowding around in order to see. Adults lifted children on their shoulders as if they were in a zoo. I heard the phrase "Another one?" uttered more than once. Another what? I wondered.

"Happy now?" the policewoman said to me, and I saw that she had covered the corpse with a blanket. She seemed to want a response.

"Who is he?" I asked.

"Number five," somebody behind me said.

"Sunset Slasher, man," came a tobacco-laced gust from over my shoulder. It belonged to an out-of-work movie extra who mimicked the looks of Bob Dylan in his subterranean homesick blues days.

"Dude zaps old guys. Lays 'em out up and down the strip," the actor said, then added a few guttural sound effects, as well as a pointer finger across his neck. "It's bullshit, man."

The policewoman bumped into me as she cordoned off the area with yellow plastic tape strung from the nearby dumpster to the light posts and back again. It *was* bullshit, I decided, for want of a better explanation. From time to time, police, now suit-clad detectives, came over and lifted the blanket and studied the corpse. They jostled photographers and camera crews who rinsed the area with bright camera lights and served as a magnet to passersby. I could feel the crowd pressing against my back.

Through the gathering crowd of cops and photographers, my eye caught a last glimpse of the heap. Blood had seeped from beneath the blanket, soaking its edges. Blood, so much blood, now black in the artificial light, a viscous, seeping liquid too awful to associate with a human being late in his years, who only hours ago could have spoken of Dewey and Truman and Lana Turner.

I had to get the hell out of there.

2

Jack Remsen

"You wanna talk to me, Duffy, you gotta bring along one of Ike Sewell's deep-dish pizzas and a New York strip from Gene and Georgetti's."

That was Jack Remsen yakking, and at a volume level somewhere between a harpooned walrus and a freshly ejected Leo Durocher. I lagged the phone receiver two inches from my ear and still didn't miss a word. Remsen never paused.

"That's just to get your big Chicago butt in the door, Duffy. You wanna stay awhile, then bring along a chucker. A left-hander who can give me six respectable innings twice a week and a couple dozen pair of fresh legs. I need good *legs*, the kind that can beat out a bunt without snappin' a hamstring, for cryin' out loud. We're so wracked up on this team, Duffy, our man at Blue Cross–Blue Shield got his number unlisted. I got more injuries than Custer. Hell, my trainer's got hisself pulled muscles from workin' on everybody else's pulled muscles. You wanna get into my training room, you gotta take a number. My whirlpool baths are in the shop from overwork. My guys don't wear Old Spice, they wear Ben-Gay. I go to mass the other day, and even the priest is limpin' with a charley horse. My own doctor says he don't read the *New England Journal of Medicine* no more, he reads my disabled list. The other day Sinatra called for box-seat tickets. 'Box-seats!' I said to him.

'Hell, if you ain't wearin' an Ace bandage, you can sit in the on-deck circle!' "

At that he belched and took a breath. I'd done no more than dial his private line, chimed in with a howdy-do, and Remsen started in. But never mind. Jack and I went way back, so there was no need for small talk or euphemisms, which he wasn't much good at anyway. He had time to see me if I came out to the West Coast, hell, I didn't even have to ask, he said.

I asked because there was always a parade, an entourage, a mutual admiration society, a waif or two, as well as one of Jack's rehabilitation projects—the guy can't say no to anybody—and an old-timer's reunion going on around the Dodger skipper. And it had been that way from the day he took the job. There was no more popular manager in baseball, and no more visible, voluble Dodger.

On the plane I tried to count up how many times I'd gone to Remsen's well while I was writing my column. "Need a column?" he'd say. "Stop by and I'll give ya three." How many times had I gone over to his office when the Dodgers were in town, opened the notebook, and let him rip? How many times had I called him just for a quote or a bit of background and gotten enough material for a whole piece? And I was no exception, no one special.

Jack Remsen ate and slept baseball and the Dodgers, and he had time for just about anybody as passionately involved with the two as he was. He was tireless, boundless, infectious, and loud, the proprietor of a year-round courtship with the press, TV, and radio. Perhaps nobody but Bill Veeck was better at it. Army Archard, the guy at *Variety*, which is a sheet they read like Scripture in Los Angeles, used to say that Remsen was more popular in Hollywood than the term *gross*. His mug popped up in more commercials, variety shows, and comedy shows than Soupy Sales in his prime.

"Get over here before nine," Remsen said. "We'll have a bite and tell some lies."

Even though it was a weekday, the schedule had the Dodgers with a one-thirty start, one of those April quirks they throw in just to give codgers like me a squirt of the old days. You wouldn't see many players in the ballpark before nine, but Remsen would be there at seven A.M. Earlier than the clubhouse boys and any of his coaches. He'd sleep in Dodger Stadium if his wife would let him, and Nina, bless her heart, wouldn't let him.

As for me, I considered Remsen a friend and a valuable chapter in my current ramblings. When I can get away from the commissioner of baseball and his penchant for making me play gumshoe for the game, I am putting together my memoirs. Broken-down old farts and sportswriters like myself usually do so after a lifetime on the beat.

The last thirty of my years on the Chicago *Daily News* found my furrowed brow atop a daily sports column called "On the House." So it wasn't all that original a title, given my name is Duffy House. The memoirs will probably be called *One More On the House,* which ain't too original either, but why start now? My late friend Jack McPhaul called his scrapbook *Deadlines and Monkeyshines,* which pretty much described his half-century on the city desk. Yet when a paperback house reprinted Jack's book, they called it *Chicago, City of Sin.* Understatement at its finest, and Jack shrugged.

As for the tag on my column, Charlie Miller, my editor on the *News* back then, came up with the title on his way to a gin mill after work one day because he didn't think the column would last two weeks. He also thought Bobby Franks was murdered by Terrible Tommy O'Connor. A lot he knew.

Nevertheless, I'm not just putting a net around a bunch of the old "On the House" columns and delivering it to the fish house for wrapping and a double-sawbuck cover charge. It's called double-dipping, and too many washed-up columnists do it, God knows. Personally, I have no itch for the rehash, and I certainly don't wish to spread chum on the waters for all those bullheads who used to ring me up at the paper to argue about Burleigh Grimes.

No, I figure I'll attempt one more feeding of the

goat—the affectionate name we scribes give the sports-reading public—and do so with something substantial. I'll look at the game with some kind of perspective, maybe even dig up a few things about it that people didn't know. I'll put some spin on the old stuff, talk to people who've been around the game as long as I have, tell some yarns and compare the game of my early days—some forty years ago—with the game today. Then I'll step back and let the cow chips fall where they may.

That's where Jack Remsen came into the picture. He and I go way back. To ten-thousand-dollar salaries, fifty-cent bleacher seats, and ten-cent hot dogs. To Burt Shotton, Ralph Branca, Van Lingle Mungo, and White Owl Wallops. Way, way back.

"I'm still doing things by my two favorite rules, Duffy," he said to me before he rang off.

"Let me have 'em, Jack."

"There's the Kiss Rule and the Hellmann Rule. The Kiss Rule stands for 'Keep It Simple, Stupid.' Okay? That ain't very original, is it? All right, then try the Hellmann Rule: keep cool but don't freeze. Got it from the side of the mayonnaise jar. Whattaya think? Should I keep 'em in the repertoire, or are they minor-league stuff?"

"Wear 'em out," I said, knowing he would.

Call him what you will: cheerleader, hot dog, motivator, bullshitter, strategist, backslapper, genius, buffoon, or caterer—as in food—Jack Remsen didn't give a shit as long as you called him a Dodger. Simply, grandly, a Dodger.

Remsen worshiped the club that Branch Rickey built and Walter O'Malley transported. When it came to bleeding Dodger blue, nobody besides Tommy Lasorda ever hemorrhaged more of that cerulean stuff than Remsen. When it came to invoking the powers of the Big Dodger in the Sky, nobody since O'Malley had a more direct line.

Remsen was one of those stubby, cactus-eared kind of guys who came up through the organization and never left. Forty-four years ago he was a stocky, low-slung kid out of Philadelphia with a good fastball that he wasn't afraid to throw inside. When he was in high school, the old scouts used to tell me, Remsen stood on the mound and shouted at hitters, daring them to dig in. Then he'd throw chin music so loud and so often that fights broke out like junkyard fires.

His arm was good enough to get him into the Brooklyn farm system in the fifties. Unfortunately for him, that was the time when the Dodgers finally had some talent upstairs. Guys like Podres, Newcombe, Loes, Erskine, and Labine were ahead of him, throwing good stuff and winning pennants, and Remsen didn't stand a chance. But he could swing a bat, and he was built like a boxcar, so they turned him into a catcher. It was his only hope, and a slim one, what with Campanella, Roseboro, and company up ahead. He'd accumulated only a few September call-up games in Ebbets Field, the proverbial several cups of coffee, by the time he retired and in fifty-eight signed on as a scout. A few years later the Dodgers offered him a job as a manager in the deep minors.

"Ogden. That's in Utah. Thanks to Rickey, God love him," Remsen used to say. "Full of mountains and dust and long bus rides. I can tell you more about the countryside in that state than a Mormon can. But hell, for me it was heaven. I'd have managed in Siberia with a bunch of one-eyed Russians and a hermaphrodite batboy as long as the Dodgers were signing my paycheck."

From the moment he planted his spikes on the dugout steps, Remsen was a manager, one of those full-of-shit/full-of-wisdom guys made for the game. He either hugged his kids or kicked them in the ass and always seemed to know the right time to do one or the other. He pushed and goaded and spat. He scolded and taught and inspired. He devised a method of creative lying, a technique, he once explained, that came in handy during pep talks and team meetings.

"Shoot, Ted Williams once went oh-for-July in the minor leagues," he once said to a struggling new kid. "The best pure hitter in baseball never got a hit in the longest month of the summer." Of course, Williams never did any such thing, but Remsen's charges never knew it. "Why, the 1927 Yankees, the greatest team in baseball history, once lost nine in a row," he said in the middle of an Ogden losing streak. Said it with a straight face even as Gehrig and Lazzeri flipped over in their graves.

If that didn't work, he threw tantrums and towels. He once heaved a half-chewed plug of tobacco at the home-plate ump. It hit the arbiter in the shoe and cost Remsen a suspension, a fine, and the price of a shoe shine. More than anything, Remsen kept his kids' heads in the stars.

"This train stops at Chavez Ravine," he'd scream. "Dodger Stadium. The greatest ballpark on earth."

And then he'd add, "If God lets you become a Dodger, start singin' hymns, 'cuz you've made it half-way to heaven."

His minor-league teams won for him, taking flags or coming close. He sent dozens of kids up the ladder before he himself made the climb. He also had success turning guys around, that is, reversing the fortunes of players who'd been cut from the parent club's roster and were free-falling through the minors on their way out of baseball. Rem called them Judes, as in St. Jude, the patron saint of hopeless causes. Their problem, he insisted, wasn't talent or luck but confidence, concentration, or one of those sticky intangibles that keep capable athletes from succeeding. So he worked with these guys like a missionary, talking to them, stroking, kicking them in the butt, trying to rekindle the flame. And there was nobody better at it. If you couldn't get up for a game playing under Jack Remsen, if you didn't bleed Dodger blue and goose bumps didn't erupt all over you at Kirk Gibson's homer in the '88 Series, well, then you *were* a hopeless cause.

From Utah he went to Spokane, then Albuquerque, always with the same balderdash and the same success, and no one among the Dodger brass, an organization that, since the days of Rickey and O'Malley, was famous for developing its own talent, was unaware of it. He

finally joined the Dodgers as a coach under Walter Alston, the man who managed for twenty-three years and
seemed as if he could have gone on forever, and stayed
on when Tommy Lasorda took the job. But Remsen's
ascendancy was in the cards, and soon the Dodgers
would offer him the first of many one-year—one year
and only one year, as Walter O'Malley himself ordained
—manager's contracts they were famous for.

I agitated all that and more of Jack Remsen's bio
around in my brain early the next morning as I drove
out to the stadium. I drove carefully, because though
the Biltmore had given me a Swiss chocolate on the
pillow and a quiet night, I didn't sleep worth a damn.
Now while I've always believed slumber to be overrated, I give it its due because I'm a grouch without a
reasonable dose. The lack of sleep doesn't bother me as
much as the reasons I'm awake, and last night I was up
because of the murder on Sunset Boulevard. The old
guy. Hell, his body was on my lap. The blood—dammit,
I could *smell* it.

I went four decades without tripping over corpses
or chasing ambulances. I was a sportswriter, a merry
inventory clerk in journalism's toy department. Death
for me came symbolically in the bottom of the ninth.
The genuine, inevitable article occurred intermittently
in the form of my beloved, stricken Wilma, expired
friends, relatives, and colleagues laid out in funeral
homes with the requisite amount of embalming fluid
and makeup to fend off the dull, inevitable rot. It wasn't
pleasant, but it was part of life. I don't fight ashes-to-
ashes.

Yet in this, the brandy and cognac hour of my life,
I've suddenly kicked upon more foul play than a cock-
fight. My gilded eyes have glommed freshly killed ball-
players, owners, even petty hoodlums whom I'd jawed
with over a beer. Mucus seeped from their noses, and
their blood ran at my shoes. And I can only say that I
don't like it. I hate it. It affects me. Murder is a scabious
rat peering at you with pink eyes in a dank basement.

There is no place to turn, no club, no light to scare it off. Don't let any cheap TV drama tell you otherwise.

So I counted on some fresh-squeezed orange juice and the citrus morning air to clear the midnight demons. The sun was shining, and I got an early start. In no time I made a right turn off Sunset onto Elysian Park Avenue and drove up the rolling asphalt drives that wind through the endless parking grounds of Chavez Ravine. The tiered roads were Walter O'Malley's idea and, as usual, a shrewd one. They ring the ballyard and lead to multilevel parking lots that allow fans to park close to their seats and not have to drag up and down miles of ramps, escalators, and stairways. O'Malley knew back in fifty-eight that the car was king out here, and he catered to it.

From the dusty, brown-clay hills and the stalky palm trees of its perimeter, to the tended, technicolor plantings on its different parking levels, the ravine offered panoramas usually reserved for desert scenes in cowboy movies, not stadiums set in the middle of a metropolis. Dodger Stadium was gorgeous in the morning, a sight not even the smog of the day could mar.

I parked near the Dodgers' main office on the far upper left-field side of the stadium. There weren't many people around yet, and park personnel seemed full of yawns and good nature. They waved me inside as if I were an old friend and directed me down to the clubhouse. Dodger Stadium, I should mention, has a reputation for being a friendly, breezy place, and these smell-the-roses types I met that morning didn't sully it. The Dodger offices are two levels above the field level, so I took the elevator down two floors to the clubhouse and Remsen's den.

Stretching on a line from home plate to just past third base, the Dodger clubhouse is like one long railroad car. The white light, blue carpeting, and blue-and-white director's (what else?) chairs of the players' dressing room sit at one end, and I padded inside on the off chance that I'd see Nobe Kawano. Nobe has run the place for years, almost as long as his brother Yosh has silently presided over the Cubs' clubhouse. Of course,

Nobe recognized me and gave me a smile that said nothing that matters had changed.

From the dressing room I passed the video room, a new staple of big-league clubhouses that contains video equipment so sophisticated a player can run in between innings and view his just-completed strikeout. Or he can play a video game or catch a few minutes of a comedy show. Oh, for the days when a player ducked into the tunnel for a drag on a Lucky Strike.

Remsen's office was ahead on the left, the doorway in line with the ramp leading down to the dugout. I knew that from memory, but today the noise reminded me.

"Just kill the damn bugs, I don't care how," came the bellow. It was Remsen's. He was sitting in his underwear behind his desk, running one hand over the short nap of white hair that bristled on his stout head, and blistering the telephone. He was steamed, and it was unlike him to be so over anything but a questionable call on a balk. Bugs? I considered, then remembered all the problems Tommy Lasorda had with critters in his restaurant in Pasadena.

Then the phone was down, and Remsen was onto me.

"Get this, will ya, Duffy? I start up my car the other day and turn on the heater to take off the chill, and the smell just about drives me out of the thing. Rotten, whew! Stunk like something crawled up there and died! So I take it over to the dealer and tell him to give whatever's up there a decent funeral, and just now he calls me and says a whole family of mice—*mice*, for pete's sake—got up by the power steering and the heater right behind the dashboard, you know? And then the little buggers went and died. Was it somethin' I said? But hang on, that ain't the worst of it. The guy says now the whole thing is full of maggots! Maggots! Crawlin' around in there like it's a fresh delivery in Forest Lawn. Like to have gagged the mechanic when he found 'em. How's that for Mr. Goodwrench, huh? Gonna cost me four hunnert bucks 'cuz they got to take out the housing and everything just to get at it. And top it off—now listen to this—he says he can't guarantee it won't smell when he's all done, for cryin' out loud! He can't guarantee it won't smell! I'm drivin' around Southern California in a maggotmobile. Can you top that, Duffy, and how in hell are ya?!"

He stood up and let gravity have its way with his belly. It was a good pot, a proud, sloping bloat on which Remsen could rest his folded hands and still have room for a bowl of Häagen-Dazs. I was still enjoying the maggots when he got to me and clopped my shoulder. By underwear I mean that he had on a Dodgers T-shirt and a pair of white midthigh briefs that accentuated his ample behind and hugged his skinny, parentheses-shaped legs. Rubber shower thongs flapped against his heels. And Jack was grinning like a Dodger manager.

"So whattaya think? Things changed any?" he asked, sweeping his arm around his office.

Normally I don't write about offices. It's an old rule of journalism: if you have to describe the office, you're in trouble. But Remsen's office defied the rule. Its paneled walls were choked with more black-and-white glossies than the inside of a celebrity delicatessen. And every one of them had Remsen in it. Remsen with his horsey grin, his gut, his Dodger hat or his clipped haircut, his big arms and glad hands looped over shoulders and around backs of anybody who had cracked a joke or made a name for himself in the world overseen by the Big Dodger in the Sky. There was Remsen with Sinatra, Oral Roberts, and Michael Jackson, with Gina Lollabrigida, Jackie Onassis, and Rula Lenska. There was a whole wall of Remsen with Buddy Hackett, another acre with Sammy Davis, Jr., and countless other frames holding the mug of just about every comedian, actor, and show-biz personality who called himself or herself a Dodger fan. There was Remsen with a pope and a president—no, two presidents.

I could go on and on. The place was an interminable *Ed Sullivan Show*, a hemorrhaging Bob Hope special, a salute to Hollywood. Then again, behind Remsen's metal desk was a big painting of Jesus Christ and a bigger one of Hank Aaron, which may have meant something and maybe not. Of course, there were photos of former Dodgers everywhere, the Hall of Famers and the bench jockeys, as well as shots of their families. Remsen had a thing about families. He could remember kids' names better than a pediatrician.

"Turn off the set, Jack. The press is here," I said, nodding at the forty-eight-inch TV in the middle of the room. It was stacked with mail—boxes of mail—knick-knacks, souvenirs, and every kind of keepsake and curio somebody in Cucamonga might think appropriate for the manager of the Dodgers.

"No sound. Just the picture," Remsen said. "Like the silent movies in our day, Duffy, you old hemorrhoid, you."

"Not me. I'm a picture of health. Marvel of Medicare," I said, and shook the hand that shook a million hands.

"Fruit. It's all in fruit," Remsen said. He grabbed a banana from a hefty fruit basket and stuck it in my pants. There was room.

"Who eats all this?" I said, eyeing a table full of enough bagels, jellies, cream cheese, sweet rolls, cold meats, hard-boiled eggs—enough calories to feed Guatemala. Forget the fruit; Remsen loved the hard stuff.

"Freeloaders. Bums. Guys on convention. The Sisters of Mercy. People like you. This office is Hollywood and Vine. I get no privacy here. I can't think straight. So I figure give 'em a bite and send 'em away happy."

He could go on like this forever. He was the king of palaver, a schmoozer, a small-talker with no cork. He'd never met a digression he didn't like. If you let him, that is. For my purposes I wanted Remsen to crank it up a notch, talk baseball then—forty years ago when we both broke in—and now.

"Hey, grab a bagel and turn on your machine," he said, as if to read my mind. Then he closed the door. He thumped a finger against his temple.

"I loaded the old think tank up here," he said, "after you told me what you were interested in. Hear me out."

He dressed a bialy for doom and let his false choppers have at it as he paced in front of me. Managers think and talk on their feet.

"You're lookin' at a guy who had a fastball and a slider decent enough to win more'n thirty-five games in high school after the war, and I come to the minors and they make me a *catcher*, for godsakes. Had to 'cuz there were so many good arms back then. That's a difference between now and then, for starters. I looked in the mirror and saw Preacher Roe, and they saw Joe Pignatano!

"But I'd've pounded sand up my butt if they told me to. Baseball was the only game in town. I put on the shin guards, and before you could say Jackie Robinson, I had a peg to second like a sniper rifle. Gunned 'em down. I could also hit a little—I had a stick, Duffy, you bet your ass!

"But it wasn't good enough to get me but a hello–good-bye with the big club, not with Campy and Rube Walker up there. Then Roseboro, hell, even Norm Sherry was ahead of me. Today I'd be startin' for a half-dozen teams, makin' three-quarters of a million and bitchin' about gettin' that. You wanna know how the game's changed, Duffy, that's how it's changed.

"Guys like me were lined *up* to play back then. We had guys in the bushes hittin' three-eighty, and they couldn't break in. Couldn't break in! Now a kid comes out of college—and hey, who went to college back then, huh?—and hits his weight in the minors, and by September he's brought up, and his agent is talkin' a three-year contract. No-cut. Got pitchers go three-and-eight in the bushes, and they get called up.

"Of course, it's the money. Here's something for ya: during the off season, hell, we didn't work out, we worked. We had to. Guys like Johnny Klippstein were mailmen. Guys painted houses or butchered. Lived in little cold-water flats around the ballpark. Didn't have time to go to the gym much. Didn't condition. Winter ball was for Puerto Ricans. We couldn't afford it. Spring training came around, and you had to get in shape. Serious. You remember how it was, Duffy. Guys came to Florida with fat on 'em. Had to work it off. Not today."

I didn't interrupt. As long as he could keep the lox, cream cheese, and onions inside his chops as he jabbered, I was a fool to even think of jumping in.

"Course, a lot of the guys then didn't get into shape. They were thumpers, those big boats like Hank Sauer and Roy Sievers and Harmon Killebrew. Look at where they lived. I mean you had a lot of little parks, Duffy, the bandboxes. Guys like Sauer and Kiner used to feast off them parks. Crosley Field, the Polo Grounds, Ebbets Field—you know 'em all. Ebbets was two ninety-seven down right. Even Mantle and Maris had the porch in Yankee Stadium—course I ain't takin' nothing away from those two. But a lot of guys back then would suffer in the Astrodome or St. Louis or Cincinnati today. They'd hit those big rainmakers, and they'd die about ten feet from the warning track—just big, long outs.

"I could go on. It was a different game back then, Duf. Wasn't better—oh, maybe it was 'cuz there wasn't the money and free-agent bullshit—and it sure as hell wasn't worse. Just different. Different parks. Day ball. Not as much TV. Now you can't say bleepin' shit without the camera countin' the pimples on your nose. And one more thing: no fuckin' agents. We didn't have 'em, and I think we were better off. So there. Just you and me on this. Otherwise I get my ass blistered in arbitration. Arbitration—there's a crock of shit for ya.

"But you know all that. We're talking between the baselines now, right? That what you want? Oh yeah, one more thing a lot of people forgot. Between you and me now, Duf, this whole free-agent thing started way back with O'Malley. Walter. He was the one who didn't sign Andy Messersmith. Walter was pissed. He didn't sign him for the whole season and just about guaranteed that he'd test the reserve clause. The other owners jumped in like monkeys at a buffet table, and *kaboom!* the roof was blown off.

"But I'll tell you this, Duffy, you won't hear me complaining about the big money. I'm glad all over about what these kids make. I make it too, in case you didn't know. No, now I'll take that back. The big money's bad on account of it screws up the basics. Play the game right, and you got to sacrifice a little, hit behind a runner, swing at a bad pitch when the steal sign's on, that kind of thing. Red Schoendienst used to deliberately shorten a sure double into a single so they couldn't walk Musial behind him. Guys don't wanna do that today. Eats at their statistics, that's why. And statistics are money. Numbers. You got me? That's why you see guys stealing third with two outs and five runs down. Keeps me up at night, Duf, 'cuz how can you manage over that?

"Money distracts 'em. I come through the locker room the other day, I hear these guys talking real-estate portfolios, orange groves, all that kind of shit. They got stockbrokers and investment counselors. Everything's long term, short term. Capital gains. What can you say to that kind of talk? Huh? Makes you yearn for the old days when the locker room was a place you talked about gettin' laid.

"Hey, we were laughin' about it the other day, the coaches and me, about what we used to tell 'em on the farm. We spent all our time keepin' 'em away from pussy. Capital P. Especially the older stuff, those women with boozy voices and beer-breath perfume. Those small-town vamps, you know, the women who smoke cigarettes and have big, empty beds in their house trailers and would screw these kids silly the first time around. Hell, I all but put a clamp on my guys' dicks. I told 'em the older broads carried syphilis and the clap and that they'd get a case of the blue balls so bad they couldn't fit 'em in a jock. I told 'em the young chicks had crabs and herpes, AIDS—did they have AIDS back then?—hell, I'd throw leprosy in there once in a while. I'd *invent* a goddamn epidemic if it kept my boys from getting preoccupied and diverted and what we used to call 'clammed.' The game's tough enough, you know that, without poontang draggin' on your bat. The old line: it ain't gettin' it that wears you out, it's chasin' it all night long that tanks you. Don't let anybody kid you—you got an eighteen-year-old kid away from home and his mother, and he's lonely and horny as a two-peckered goat—it became the challenge of the century to keep his mind on the short hop instead of the short hairs. At least it used to be. I ain't sure anymore.

"Which reminds me, I gotta get dressed and make a day out of it. My pitchers are hitting, and I gotta get a look-see at a couple guys."

With that he went to his closet and got a fresh uniform. The blue long-sleeved undershirt. The linen white Dodgers blouse with its blue script and crimson number over the heart. It is a classic, a look as well-known as any in baseball.

Remsen put the uniform on like a priestly vestment. His chest swelled automatically, taking some attention from the expanse below. He pulled on his pants and cinched the black belt, then slipped into a pair of rubber-soled Dodger blue spikes.

"Onward," he said, and led me out into the clubhouse proper. The players had shown up by now, and a half dozen of them and assorted Dodger personnel jawed with Remsen before he made it down the hundred feet of runway to the dugout and the playing field.

There he paused. He grasped the handles of his front porch and exhaled lox and bialy fumes into the morning air.

"*Ahhhh*. The Garden of Eden. A wonderful bleepin' day for baseball," he said, and smiled at the green grass and the cinnamon red clay of Dodger Stadium, the gymnastics of the young men who ran and threw, the smack and whistle of bat and ball.

"If you can't get it up for a scene like this, Duffy, you're ready for the nursing home," he exclaimed. "No shit. I'm a guy who remembers back when the L.A. club was the Angels, and it played in Wrigley Field out here. How 'bout that? Remember that little dance hall? Every fly ball gave you a heart attack."

I stayed with him as he went behind the batting cage and watched the choppy swings of his pitching staff. He put his fingers in the screen and kibitzed.

"Look at Ruffin there," he said, nodding at a rookie pitcher laying down bunts. "Big as a tree—goes two-forty—and he can outrun some of my outfielders. There's another difference between now and then, if you ask me. We had a few guys like Dick Radatz in the league. Or Newcombe—Newk was a horse. But you didn't see the size that you see today. These kids are big. Real big."

At that a foul tip stung the cage and missed his knuckles by a hair.

"Let's get outta here. These guys can't hit horse-shit."

We made our way around third base and moseyed into the outfield. Only pitchers and utility players were out this early. Most of them were loosening up. A few were working out on their own, raising a sweat, trying to heal an injury. It was easy in this setting, this mani-cured field under a desert sky. In my eyes this was the stuff of reverie; it was business for Remsen. Jack's eyes were everywhere.

"Biggest job I have is basics. Kids come up too fast. They don't get the time in the minors that we had. You see 'em throwing to the wrong base, missing the cutoff man, missing signs, swinging at no kinda strike zone. It's stupid, undisciplined stuff. Shoulda been coached out of them before they got here. Makes me wanna pull my hair out."

"That why you keep it so short?"

He stopped and pulled his cap from his bottle-brush scalp.

"What? You don't like my hairstyle? What are ya, Mr. Blackwell?" he yelped.

We kept walking toward the outfield wall. The rip-pled canopy over the outfield loomed in front of us. The canopy has always reminded me of a carport, one of those bad ideas for people unable to afford garages. I'm no ballpark architect, but I never thought it did Dodger Stadium justice.

"We're all right this year. We got Geer from the Royals. He's a bat, or he better be. And watch this kid Terrio. Adonis Terrio. Like that name? From a little town in Mexico. Greatest arm since Nap Rucker," Rem-sen said, and threw me a glance.

"Nap Rucker?" I asked, searching the files.

"Look that one up," he said.

At that our shadows were crossed by a sprinting, huffing player wearing a nylon windbreaker over his uniform. He pulled up near us. His purple-black face was rinsed with sweat, and as he gulped for air, I was reminded of a young Willie Davis. Davis, that gazelle, played when blacks wore thick Afros, and his bobbed like a tumbleweed as he ran. This kid's scalp was cut so short he looked bald. His cranium glistened.

"How's it feel, Tommy?" Remsen asked.

"Ready. All set and ready," the kid replied.

"Don't give me that shit. You hunnert percent? You feel any twinge? Come clean with me now."

"It's ready, Skip. No excuses."

"Duffy. You ever met Tom York?" Remsen asked, turning to me.

"Read about him," I said, and shook York's sweaty hand.

"Man's written a million words about baseball. Get healthy, Tommy, bust your butt, and he'll write about you," Remsen said.

York shot me a look, a nod, one I could have painted as confidence or fear. There's less difference between the two than most people think. Then he ran off again. I watched him lope, looking for the injury Remsen was getting at.

"Kid's twenty-eight years old, Duffy. In pro ball ten years. Been up for a cup of coffee two or three times, then back down. Can play any place in the infield, won't embarrass himself. Problem is the bat. Hits four hundred one month and one-sixty the next. You never know.

"So this spring he's a flash. Hit six-oh-two in Vero Beach. *Six-oh-two,* Duffy. Couldn't get him out. Stole bases. Some home runs. He made the squad, fair and square. Couldn't keep him off. Fifth infielder. Then a day before we come west, he pulls a groin muscle. Pulled the shit out of it. You could see tears in his eyes. By rights he should be sent down until he's healed. But I know this kid. He goes down now, and he won't make it back. He's got a wife—sweetheart of a gal—pair of twins look just like him. Named Toby and Roby.

"If he stays up with us, he could make a season of it. Stay in the groove. Help us out. If he goes down, well . . . 'cept I won't play him hurt. Nothin' I hate more. York knows that."

"He a salvage project for ya, St. Jude?"

"Don't think of it that way. Tom's good."

"Twenty-eight is old nowadays," I added. I needn't have. Not after all the years Remsen had spent in the minor leagues watching kid phenoms turn into old journeymen.

We had started walking back toward the dugout. The rest of the squad was coming onto the field.

"What amazes me, Jack," I said, "is how you can remember the kids' names. The missus, the whole family tree."

He smiled and clapped his hands, applauding for the hell of it.

"Hey, we don't wear masks in this game. Not like football or hockey, where you can't tell who in hell anybody is. Everybody knows who you are, and you gotta recognize who they are. If I get to *know* Tommy York out there, he'll conquer the world for me. Go to *war* for me. So what's it take to remember his wife's name? Play pepper with his kids, huh?"

He broke into a trot, a duck-waddle sort of thing that didn't put much distance between him and me.

"Let's get out of here while the millionaires warm up," he said within earshot of two of them. They tossed a ball at his knobby ankles.

By the time we got back to the clubhouse, the popular herd had begun to assemble. The carpet was covered with press, the fondlers of TV and radio microphones, the feature writers, the card collectors, and the cable-TV producers. People from publicity and marketing were chaperoning tours of wide-eyed sponsors and their relatives. There were clumps of former players and visiting raconteurs from the radio booths. Known faces from prime time appeared wearing Dodger caps. And all of them wanted at Jack Remsen. His office was must-see. He had time for everybody. A joke, an autograph. New glossies were waiting to be taken. The red light of Dodger air time was aglow.

"You got your ducats?" he said to me, which was code for the end of our interview. I didn't mind. He'd given me plenty.

"Obliged for the wisdom, Jack. As always."

"And thank *you*, Mr. House," he said, and gave me that veteran grin.

Then he turned and was devoured by the hubbub. His Dodger uniform shone; his barker's voice echoed. Jack Remsen was the happiest man on earth.

3

Joe Start

Talk has a curative power for me, words a balm of a sort, so much so that the rambling, memory-drenched gab with Jack Remsen succeeded in washing the image of that wretch on Sunset Boulevard out of my mind for a few hours. I watched the game in a section of box seats just behind the screen where the visiting scouts sit. Just in front of us but out of sight was Mike Brito, the Dodger scout in the white hat who holds the speed gun on the pitchers.

The Padres were in the visitors' dugout, and nobody around me thought much of their roster. A few scouts were iffy on the Dodgers too, so things evened out. I like scout chatter, so the game passed easily for me. At my age you appreciate anything that passes easily. The Dodgers won it with a three-run sprint in the seventh, and the home folks, who filled two-thirds of the stadium, seemed pleased. Out here, when the afternoon sun bakes, it is often hard to tell. Dodger fans are good and plentiful, but not loud.

It was late afternoon as I exited the stadium and fumbled with the dashboard gizmos of my rented Japanese car. Traffic flowed swiftly out of the Ravine, as if Walter O'Malley had ordained it. I turned left onto Sunset and fought my way back downtown to the Biltmore. I was tired and could have used a nap, but I had an appointment with a glass of some rich elixir capable of strangling a few brain cells, and with an old friend, if the two aren't one and the same.

I parked the car beneath Pershing Square and made my way up to Olive Street across from the hotel. I've always been fond of the little square and have spent many an idle moment with pigeons and the statues of Beethoven and General John himself. It's a lovely place full of eucalyptus and palm trees, a rose garden, and the stunning orange flowers of the birds of paradise. You can just about feel the homage, the crack of twenty-one-gun salutes, the folded flags, and the tears of war widows. Old soldiers do die, and so many young ones too.

But I didn't tarry in Pershing Square this day. Much of it had been taken over by sleeping bums and transients. They littered the grass like discarded rolls of carpeting, some balled up under a bush or a small ficus tree. Other park spaces were occupied by street types: hustlers, grifters, people with fishy eyes and dirty fingernails. Most of them were young, some female, with weathered, itchy looks. They paced and smoked and dropped cans, cups, and cigarette butts at their feet. Some prowled around trying to bum a smoke or a hit of residual firewater from anybody who had a bottle.

I paused and absently watched as pigeons alighted on, shat on, and flew off Beethoven, and I felt for the guy—the greenish white excrement rolling down the lapels of the great composer's waistcoat.

Generally I like people in city parks. I enjoy the eccentrics and the chess players, and I tolerate the babblers. I even admire the practitioners of three-card monty. But I didn't like these people. I didn't like the way they grimaced in the sunlight. The way they fidgeted and looked from side to side and down the block, generally expecting somebody or something, I didn't know what it was. And I had the odd feeling that if the light was right and the cravings were severe enough, they'd slice my wallet from my pants. And gut me like a rabbit.

Maybe I was crotchety. Maybe my neck was sore from looking over my shoulder too much lately. Maybe I needed sleep. Maybe I had to give the Sunset Boulevard episode a rest. The cooled air of the Biltmore felt good against my forehead, and I smelled furniture polish.

I followed the oak floor's angled arrows over to the Grand Avenue Bar on the other side of the Biltmore, a sleek watering hole that caters to jazz. Any saloon with a picture of Anita O'Day on the wall is okay by me. And Dizzy and Miles, Art Blakey and Carmen McRae. I camped on a stool at the marble-topped bar. Some late-afternoon souls had similar persuasions at a few tables in the center of the place. On the low, carpeted stage off on the far end of the room a mixed-race jazz quartet and a deep-toned female singer were getting warm amid the triangular neon art. They nibbled on Brazilian fare, softly with lazy smiles, their music lilting like smoke. It was enough to let the effects of the day—a decidedly warm spring day for this midwesterner—and the California sun drip out of me.

I tapped a caramel-colored I-V and replayed my session with Jack Remsen. He'd given me everything I'd hoped for, told me things new and things even I had forgotten, and I was elated over what it would do for the book. No one, not the barmaid who forgot a napkin and did not apologize for an empty nut bowl, or the saleswoman who was crying in her beer far on my right elbow, paid any more attention to my mottled mug than they would to the face of an old clock. For which I was grateful.

After uncounted moments and refreshed images of Wes Parker and Tommy Davis, I swirled the ice against my glass and turned to look out into the joint. A hardwood dance floor glistened, but it was empty. Somebody sooner or later would be moved to cut the maple, but it wouldn't be me. The group was still in Brazil—the part of the country that wasn't burning—doing a very romantic, very sad song. The sentiment that went with the tune, at least in my head, was that love is the saddest thing in the world when it has gone away.

I'm a sucker for that kind of lyric, and I thought of my niece, that sobered young lady back in Chicago. I had seen much of Petey throughout the winter—nothing could interrupt that—but she wasn't the same kid, wasn't the streak hitter I knew. The weight of a crushed New York romance and the battering her psyche had endured—well, it roughed her up pretty good. The bleakness of it returned to me as I sat there, and again the thought of a murdered old man started crowding in, and I had the leaden feeling in my innards of being very old.

For some not very mysterious reason, I started thinking about Wilma. How, when I came back from Guadalcanal a bundle of exposed nerve endings, there she was, like out of a dream, in Kroch and Brentano's on Wabash Avenue recommending a book of poetry by Wilfred Owen. Poetry instead of foxholes, meter instead of mortar shells, and a smile that made it heaven to be back home.

The singer had switched to English now, and I pricked up my woolly ears to hear something about love returning after an "infinite" sorrow. I had known that infinite mixture of sadness and romance, but I wondered what kind of popular song, other than a hymn, would use the word *infinite*?

Wilma, why did you have to die?

Time puts scar tissue over old wounds but doesn't necessarily heal them. Touch the scar, and the pain is still sharp. That woman introduced me to some of the world's great art and literature and stretched my cultural perspective from the minor leagues to the pros. She also put up with a lot of baloney and smoke, too much traveling, and a valise full of dirty clothes when my plane landed. The woman was a saint. But not so much of one that I wasn't panting to get home from a road trip to her soft skin. God, how I loved her.

When I lifted my head and stared across the dance floor at nothing, my eyes were swimming. They weren't dripping; they were just full enough so that images were slithering all over the room. *Dammit.* I shook myself, got out of the proverbial batter's box and knocked the dirt from the cleats, and remembered, apart from the cocktail, why I was here. I had put in a call to Joe

Start, a one-time colleague and longtime crony from the salad days of the *Daily News*.

Now there are probably a half-dozen old friends and former colleagues that I could bother out on the coast, but most of them are sitting in the shade comparing cholesterol counts and setting up tomorrow's foursome. Joe wasn't one of them, not a transplant or a retiree. After a stint as copy boy—why, he'd gobbled up reams of my prose when I was covering high-school football games—and then as a cub reporter with the *Daily News*, Joe decided to follow Horace Greeley's advice when it was worth following. He'd gone west at midcentury, when Los Angeles was still charming, when the halo was still on the seraph.

Today he was still here and still a newspaper jockey for the mighty *L.A. Times*. He'd moved after, oh, I'd say a twenty-year tour of the sports beat, to rewrite on city side. It was no mystery to me that folks said he embodied the tradition of that unseen but invaluable skill of combining the bleatings of many reporters into one coherent story, and that there was nobody alive who was any better at it. Now he was an editor.

When I called him at the paper, he barked harried but not inhospitable.

"I'm swamped with this Sunset Slasher madman, Duffy," he had said.

He'd meet me at the Biltmore, however, for a long drink and maybe a bite before he went back to the paper. Start was a bachelor and knew the dictates of no time clock when he worked the desk, and, I suspected, no more so than in these violent days.

So I blotted my eyes with a suddenly available cocktail napkin and made sure they were not playing tricks on me. That's when I spotted his familiar mug across the lounge: nobody had those ears, that same high forehead with the widow's peak and a haircut that hadn't had any coaching in forty years. Not to mention a lantern jaw and a pair of thick bifocals that probably drove him nuts but were necessities for eyes that had scanned untold thousands of inches of copy through the years.

He seemed headed my way but had stopped midway to chat with a fellow, and I recalled the last time I'd seen him. It was an easy recall: the 1965 World Series between the Dodgers and the Minnesota Twins. Joe was the beat writer for the *Times* then, and he had sat right next to me in the press box at old Metropolitan Stadium in Bloomington. I'll never forget the look on his puss when the Twins' Mudcat Grant hit a three-run homer off Howie Reed to win the sixth game for himself and tie the series 3-all.

"Wouldja look at that, Joe?" I had said. "The pitcher!"

Old Mudcat had waited on a hanging curve like a good T-bone and spanked it into the left-field bleachers.

"Aw, shit," moaned Joe, who had become a true Dodger partisan by that time. "Alston shoulda seen it coming."

I chuckled to myself as I remembered, and Joe was suddenly close enough to see my smile.

"What's so funny, House?" he barked, then offered both hands and a grin.

"Well, Joe, to tell you the truth, I was laughin' about the last time we shared a press box," I said as we both situated ourselves on bar stools.

"Say no more. Bloomington, Minnesota. Dodgers and the Twins. Sixty-five Series."

"Grant's homer in the sixth game."

"Yeah. And Walter Alston had Frank Quilici walked to get to the pitcher."

" 'Member that smile on Mudcat's face as he trotted the bases?" I said.

"Got a better one for ya, Duf. You remember who was coaching third for the Twins?"

"None other—Billy Martin."

"Damn! You don't forget a thing. Boy, it's good to see ya, you old scribe. You look good, and your glass is empty."

"What can I buy you, Joe?"

"Anything. I'm just glad to get away. Haven't had a minute to take a shit much less call up the old days," he said.

He ordered a dark Anchor Steam, and it sounded so good that I dittoed him. We clinked bottles and toasted each other and our mutual memories of the likes of Junior Gilliam.

"Schnozz to the grindstone, huh?" I asked.

"So what else is new? And how 'bout you? I heard all about your adventures as Dick Tracy for the commissioner of baseball."

"Ahhh, that's what I'm afraid of. I spend my whole career chasing deadlines, and people forget about me. I chase a few crooks, and that's all people want to talk about."

"This is Hollywood, Duffy. Hooray. In no time you'll be reading the trades and taking meetings with the studios."

"Joe, you talk funny."

He laughed and quaffed.

"Look, you snagged murderers in Wrigley Field and Yankee Stadium, for pete's sake. Big deals out here have been made on a lot less."

"Get Swifty Lazar on the phone," I said. "In the meantime I'm done with the gumshoe beat. I'm out here to put some piss and vinegar into my memoirs. Did a little reprise with Jack Remsen this morning."

"Good. I'd hate to see my old mentor in a new line of work," Joe said.

"Don't worry about it. Tell me, how long has it been since you last saw the Chicago River dyed green?"

"Nineteen fifty-three. I was twenty-two and just back from Korea. Hell, I never even lived there with a Daley as mayor."

With that Joe refreshed my memory about his tenure in Los Angeles. He'd come west in fifty-four, a time when Southern California represented a paradise to many Americans, when thousands of newcomers were happily settling into the canyons around Los Angeles. It was a land blooming with commandeered water, acres of orange and lemon groves, and plenty of oil derricks bobbing up and down. The smog was negligible. The mountains that rim the metropolitan area were clearly visible in the morning sun. A soul could walk down

Whittier Boulevard in East Los Angeles with blithe unconcern for his personal safety.

Joe and his wife Rosalie were among the new settlers, newly married and soon to have a child. Joe, the hotshot kid who'd cut his editorial teeth in Chicago's hardscrabble newspaper wars, was a fast-rising star of the *Times*'s fast-improving sports section. Two decades and several three-run homers hit by pitchers later, he had left the baseball beat for a year-round desk in Editorial.

"My wife got real tired of me being on the road. Especially during the season. I came in from the cold in seventy-four after the Bums lost the series in five to the A's.

"But hell, I was forty-four," he continued. "Otis Chandler had turned the paper into a first-class operation, and they offered me what I wanted cityside. I've been there ever since." He started in on another Anchor Steam.

I kept my peace. I'd never met Rosalie.

"So in one of those ironies that life specializes in," he went on, "Rosalie left me not two years later. Couldn't stand me home or away, I guess. Whew, things were sour. As Ring Lardner said, 'There's nothing on earth more depressing than an old baseball writer.' Present company excluded, of course."

"I should hope so, dammit. And I don't even want to speculate on how Wilma put up with it," I said.

"You didn't have kids. That had to help."

"How is—"

"Eddie. I should say Ed now. He's a big shot in P.R. with the Angels. So at least he's still carrying the torch. He lives close, and I see him often. It's good."

"I know what you mean," I mused. "My sister's girl came to town last year, and she all but moved in with me. She's a hell of a kid."

"I read about her, didn't I? She's your Lois Lane on those gigs for Chambliss?"

"And then some," I said. "She came along on the Wrigley Field thing and turned the case inside out.

Same thing in New York. Now she's on the mend from a broken heart and bound for law school."

"She's what—twenty-three? Four?"

"Too young for you. Twenty-three. Gorgeous— why I can't walk down the street with her without the cabbies honking like geese. And brainy too. How do you like that?"

"Why didn't you bring her along?"

"Like I said, she's recuperating."

"Horseshit," Joe said, and I remembered how much I used to like the guy.

We sat and barbered for a while. Joe stayed with his dark beers and sopped up a bowl of chili. I had a sandwich and moved into some brandy. We talked about the newspaper business, and we shared guff about guys we both knew and had lost track of. He gave me a nice handle on what it was like to be out here when Walter O'Malley showed up with the Dodgers. As I had expected, Joe brought up some stories and some memories I had forgotten about, and I found myself scribbling in my notebook. He was still a good baseball man, with a great eye for detail and a memory for the anecdote, and I considered asking him for an hour or so on tape.

After a while our talk turned in a bunch of directions, how our lives differed since his departure from the Midwest. Joe took life in Los Angeles for granted pretty much the way I did in Chicago. Boosterism wasn't our style. We wore our hometowns like old coats, knowing there were newer, sleeker models, but none as comfortable. Neither city was what it once was in our eyes, no longer the place you could leave the car unlocked or take a walk in a park after dark just to cool off in the summer. Or was that the world in general?

But we didn't dwell on it. We weren't a couple of geezers grumbling about the universe over soft food and too much booze. You don't navigate both leagues as long as the two of us had without learning the ropes and building up some calluses on your mitts.

"Joe," I said suddenly, "I'd appreciate it if you'd pinch this Sunset Slasher. I don't like his choice of victims, and from what I saw last night, I don't like his style."

"Whattaya mean?" Joe said.

"I mean I stumbled in on the mop-up. I was driving on Sunset Boulevard on my way back to the hotel when I just about got broadsided by squad cars over by . . . by wherever—"

"Mohawk."

"Whatever. So I got out and gawked the whole thing before the crowd showed up. Blood all over the street. Guy's throat was sliced open like a coho salmon, for chrissake."

Joe perked up.

"No kidding, Duffy. You were there? That was the messenger. The old fella who rode the bicycle. Fifth one in two months.

"The worst for me was the second one," Joe went on. "A guy named Pop Corkhill. Little mick. Reminded you of Charlie Dressen—had a newsstand just catty-corner from the paper. I bought papers from him every day just to hear what he had to say. Smart little guy, could give you a rundown of what was going on all over the world. I wanted to hire him and put him on the op-ed desk, he was that good.

"Next thing you know they find him on Sunset, near Coronado, throat slashed, the whole business. That brought it right into my lap. *Goddammit.* Pop couldn't have put up much of a fight. He'd have argued with the bastard, but he couldn't have fought him off. Son-of-a-bitch. That got to me, Duffy.

"I been on this thing ever since. Head the desk on it. I'm going back tonight to check in. Guy hits a little after sundown. Nice touch, huh? We got a crew full-time on the thing feeding me everything they got. Victims are pensioners, old farts like us, Duffy. Two of them were bums, which, I gotta say, happens more than you'd like to think. But the other three, like Pop, were men still working for a living. It's a damn shame."

I'd pushed a button.

"You're going against one of Fred Allen's maxims," I advised.

"What's that?"

"He once said that to a newspaperman 'a human being is an item with skin wrapped around it.'"

"Not this time," Joe said with a slow shake of his weary head.

With that he put his hand over his mouth as if to wipe away any residue of the hops, and looked down at his shoes. They were scuffed.

"You ever meet my brother?" he asked softly.

"No," I said.

"He came around the *Daily News* office once in a while. You probably don't remember. Fought at Inchon. Came back shell-shocked. Bad case. El train sparking on the tracks overhead would set him off. He'd panic, you couldn't calm him down. Now they call it posttraumatic stress disorder, and there's lots of help available. But not then. So he drank, and his drinking got him thrown out of the house and just about every place else. He was one of the reasons I came out here; I couldn't face him anymore. To make a long story short, Duffy, he became a stumblebum. Always loaded with rotgut—the cheap stuff that packs more alcohol than the good stuff. Last time I saw him he was thirty-five and looked sixty-five. Took him about ten years to age forty. Weighed maybe a hundred twenty pounds. Didn't have any teeth left. Lost three fingers to frostbite. They finally found him in a lot on Clark and Ontario. Remember that liquor store with the big sign, "Last Stop Before The Expressway." Stabbed to death. Cops got some project bastard who rolled drunks for quarters. Figure he stuck Rich when he put up a fight. Who knows? I just know that he was my brother. Could've been me. Damn well could've been me."

He stopped and looked for something to wet his chops and didn't find it.

"So I'm sitting on this Slasher case," he said. "I'm sentimental."

He said it without a single glint of humor in his eye.

"Okay," I finally said.

"Say, I gotta get back," he said abruptly, pushing off

from his stool. "You wanna come along? Stick your nose in a newsroom again?"

"I would, except I'm in no condition. I'm worn out, and I need a shower."

"How long you out here?"

"A couple more days."

"If it's longer, stay at my place. I've got plenty of house and nobody in it. And I know you're not on the commissioner's tab."

I picked up the bill, tipped the barmaid far too generously, and walked with Joe to the sidewalk.

"Say hello to some of those old war-horses for me," he said. "What'd Casey used to say? 'Tell 'em I ain't dead yet.'"

"That wasn't Casey," I said. "That was me."

4

Suicide Squeeze

I let the Ks wake me up. K as in KCBS, KNBC, KABC, and the rest of the television stations on the West Coast. They filled my screen with chuckles and guffaws, great heads of hair, and big teeth. They were pretty and pretty blithe, a chewing-gum crowd with names like Bree and Jess and Wendy, all of whom were extremely hopped up for morning and seemed to be having the time of their young lives. Banter is the art of these morning shows, I decided, an ability to report a kidnap and rape with the same lilt as the weather. In fact, the weather seems to get a home team's share of concern. And that smog, well, what can you do about that smog?

My A.M. needs were modest. Was God in his heaven? Had the country gone to war? Was the Constitution intact? Did the stock market trade? How did the ball teams fare? By the time I emerged from the bathroom showered, shaved, and talced, I wasn't sure. The heads were still bantering—which was a positive sign—and commercials were hawking goods like a Turkish bazaar, but they had told me squat. I needed a newspaper.

I bought the good gray *Times*, the Chandler version, and parked myself at a table in the Biltmore's elegant lobby restaurant. It was not much past eight. The April morning seemed innocent, the coffee was black, and the English muffins were lightly dusted with seeds. I once read about a fellow whose job it was to count the sesame seeds on hot-dog buns. He randomly grabbed a bun from the line and counted the seeds with a tweezers. If there were too many on a bun, his job justification said, the cost over the long count of millions of buns could mount. "A million here, a million there," said the congressman, "and after a while you're talking some real money."

I kept that nonsense to myself and finally made my way to the sports pages. All my adult life people have asked me if I read the sports pages first. Of course I do not and never did. Not even when my column ran. The front page is in front for a reason, for crying out loud. What kind of a citizen would go to the amusement section first? Nevertheless, the pennant races were getting off. There were some surprises out of Boston, Texas, and Seattle. Remsen's Dodgers, after yesterday's win, were in the middle of the pack, which is where he said he wanted them. Jack never liked front running. Said it didn't suit a team well. Pick your openings and exploit 'em, he said. That was a lot of baloney. If he could be in first place, he'd be in first place. Like everybody else.

After covering the globe with the *Times* and filling my bladder with coffee—like beer, you only rent coffee—I was ready to get away. I had a late-morning appointment with another old-timer who lived in Claremont, some thirty miles east and a little north of the center city. His name was Frank Larkin, but they called him Terry, and he once played for the deadball Dodgers back when home runs came in clumps of one. I wanted to talk to him because I never had, and I'd been told he could tell a story. In fact, I think, it was Larkin himself who had told me that.

That had been in a phone chat a few years back, and since I was going to be out here with not a lot on my plate, I double-checked Larkin's number with information once I was in Los Angeles and gave him a call. A voice that wasn't Terry's told me to come out—"if I wanted to." I wasn't sure what that little kicker meant. I was soon to find out.

Like a white rat sniffing his way through a maze, I

drove off from the hotel and onto freeways named Hollywood and San Bernardino. The signs told me I was passing through Alhambra, San Gabriel, El Monte, and West Covina. If the signs lied, I was in Cucamonga, for all I knew.

Traffic was all around me at all times, and I watched my front and tail. Yet I wasn't so preoccupied that I did not notice what my fellow navigators were up to. If my old eyes did not deceive me, I saw drivers talking on not one, but two, telephones, tapping on computers, watching dashboard TVs, taking papers from fax machines, inserting discs into stereos, taking drinks from refrigerators, and shaving. I am certain of it.

After about an hour of that—an interval that passed like the dancing wieners at the intermission of drive-in movies—the Foothill Freeway came to an end, and I closed in on Claremont. To my left, appearing very close, was the dramatic outline of the San Gabriel Mountains, with one snowy peak, Mount Baldy. It was rugged canyon country, beautiful in its largely uninhabitable state, which is saying something for California, where people inhabit just about any place.

Larkin's neighborhood, just off Indian Hills, wasn't hard to find. Streets in Claremont are flat and wide, on the square, with parks just off the main streets. There are a number of good little colleges here that suffered badly some years ago when Californians passed their bare-bones tax propositions. The houses sat on subdivided lots with asphalt driveways and lemon trees in the backyard. A single story, with plenty of stucco and tile, was all anybody seemed to want. The walls, I was told, were so thin you could put your fist through them and feel no pain. A lot of homes were for sale—something, I was also told, which meant nothing. In California you did not measure the good times or bad times by For Sale signs, because everybody was always moving and always selling. If you want roots, find yourself an oak tree.

I rang the bell a long time. That should have told me something. Larkin finally appeared behind the screen door wearing a bathrobe and little else. He was as scrawny as a guinea hen and older than Ebbets Field. His cheesy white legs had veins as blue as two-lane highways on a road map, and skin so translucent you could trace the bones.

"Jerome?" he said.

He looked at me with a pair of milky eyes that focused somewhere in the neighborhood of Dazzy Vance, and I knew nobody was home upstairs.

It was all downhill from there. I introduced myself and tried to revive his memory as to our past conversations. I didn't get through. The geezer was not only going deaf, but he had a memory like an old catcher's mitt. Nothing stuck. I don't know what had happened to him between the time he'd contacted me and now, but it had happened fast. Larkin's mind was playing night baseball before lights were installed.

A young fellow came out of the kitchen and looked at me as if I were there to read the electric meter.

"Lemon head! Lemon head!" he shouted, and the old man started to hop like his puppies were on fire. Just hopped all over the room while the kid grinned like a baboon. I didn't know what the hell was going on.

"Knock it off!" I yelled at the kid.

I'd had my fill of cruelty to old-timers, dammit. Terry Larkin had been a two-fisted pitcher in baseball's major leagues seventy years ago, and the grinning shithead from the kitchen didn't deserve to carry his jock. Then or now.

The kid scowled and backed off.

Larkin touched down and grinned at me, a grin with some mustard on it, which made me wonder if a circuit or two in his brain might still be intact.

"I saw you strike out Tris Speaker," I said, which was a lie. Speaker quit the game when I was five years old.

"Wanna hot dog?" Larkin replied.

"How about Ruth? Could you get the Babe out?" I tried.

I swept my hands in front of me in a passable rendition of Babe's swing, and Larkin started hopping again.

"Hold it, Terry! Time-out," I said, and he stopped.

There was no chance. I had arrived too late. Whatever memories Larkin may have had were scrambled eggs. I shook his withered pitching hand and wished him the best.

He liked that. Then he cupped his hands around his mouth and croaked, "God bless Mommy! God bless Daddy! God bless Babe Ruth!"

I smiled, thinking of Waite Hoyt, and turned to leave. From the kitchen came the shout, "Lemon head! Lemon head!" Behind me came the thump-thump of an old man's feet on the rug.

My drive back was unhurried and unbothered. You don't always get what you want in this business, especially when you prowl the dustier vaults. Had I been on deadline with Larkin as my payload, I would have been furious and a little frantic.

It was still early afternoon by the time I trespassed the Biltmore, and I settled in with a glass of something aged in a southern state and the prose of Raymond Chandler. I'm always amazed when I read books in which you never catch the protagonists sitting down to read books. Except Holmes, of course, who was often perusing a volume or a magazine in Number 221B, Baker Street, when desperation interrupted.

The Dodgers had a seven-thirty start that night, and I had a pair of seats waiting for me. Joe Start was going to meet me there if his work habits did not prevail. Remsen, of course, had invited me down to the clubhouse before the game, and I wanted to take him up on it. Jack's booster club was meeting, and I had a temporary membership.

My parking pass put me near the team lot just beyond the bullpen in left field. It was just after four and the sun was still healthy as I entered the stadium and ducked into a long corridor beneath the stands along the third-base foul line. This was the way the players and coaches came to work, passing a laundry room, a batting cage, and a deserted locker room dubbed the "California Angels" dressing room because the Angels had lived in it when they played home games here one season. Now it is used for special games—celebrity games, Old Timers, and other publicity affairs Dodger Stadium stages like reprises of "Your Show of Shows."

I was within shouting distance of Remsen's office, but for once there was no shouting. The manager himself was a few steps inside the players' dressing room, half-dressed in his uniform pants and a straining gray Dodger T-shirt. He waved me in when I caught his eye. He had one bare white foot propped on a chair and was bending the ears of a coach and three of his regulars, who sat in director's chairs nearby.

In all my years as a clubhouse observer, I never forged a boilerplate conclusion regarding player-manager relations. I've seen managers from John McGraw and Joe McCarthy on down who were dictators, aloof strongmen who ran their clubs like slave ships. I've seen other managers, such as Chuck Tanner and Tommy Lasorda, who were just one of the boys, the head elk in a benevolent and protective order. I saw Durocher bellyache and malign; I saw Walter Alston leave well enough alone. I've seen managers who came in kissing the boys on the lips and left communicating through their coaches, and vice versa.

Different tacks alternately succeed marvelously and fail miserably. And every manager with a half a wit remarks at one time or another on his pure genius when his team is winning, when his clutch hitters hit in the clutch, his starters finish, and his closers do just that. Throw in luck, no injuries, and a weak division, and bingo! you're Casey Stengel. Of course, the next year, when his stopper can't get out of the whirlpool, his power hitters go Oh-for-April, and his Gold Glove infield turns to tin—well, the poor skipper wonders how he got so stupid so quick.

Remsen, of course, was a players' manager, a holler guy, a fanny slapper, schmoozer, and confidant. To see him fraternizing with them inside their den was no surprise. He was the Skip, to be sure, around longer and better known than most any one of them, and the guy who stopped the buck, yet he was still one of them.

"Duffy, say hello to Jack Cassidy, Dave Foutz, and Joe Visner, a sore-armer, and Bill McGunnigle, my coach, who's forgot more about baseball yesterday than these birds will ever know," Remsen said.

I caught a nod from McGunnigle and the players.

"Duffy House," Remsen went on, "in town from Chicago, where he owned the sports pages for thirty years. Now he's out here sucking up to me and eating off the franchise."

"Sums up my entire career, Jack," I said.

The players chuckled, some a little too sincerely.

"Jack here was just talking about real estate in Santa Monica. Foutz wanted my advice on a limited partnership. And these two guys just listen and steal our ideas. How 'bout you, Duf? Where'd ya go?"

I told him about Terry Larkin.

"Whoa, now you're going *way* back," Remsen said.

"A little too far," I said.

"Hear that, fellas? Duffy tried to talk to an ol' guy used to throw for Brooklyn in the Rube Marquard days. What, he's gotta be ninety if he's a day. And he's lost it, you say?"

" 'Fraid so. Not too many stubs in the ticket box," I said, and hated myself for it. An old man who'd lost his facilities would have sufficed.

"Lord," Remsen cried, looking heavenward, "take me on a road trip. Take me in the seventh game of the World Series. Take me in the saddle, for pete's sake, but don't let me linger and get nuttier than a fruitcake!"

"Hey Skip, how's he gonna know?" said Cassidy, and the others cracked up.

Remsen scowled and led me off down the hall.

"They're all right, Duf. They're loose. They wanna play. Hardest part of my job is convincing 'em they gotta *want* it. They look at me, Mr. One-Year Contract, like I'm blowing bubbles makin' maybe one-eighth their salary, and they all but tell me to kiss off! Club'll get rid of my ass a lot quicker than it'll risk fuckin' with a player who's got a ten-million-dollar contract. And they know that, whew boy! Look me straight in my big bloodshot eyes, and I can see it every time."

"Heard that before, Jack," I said.

"Yeah, and if I want security, go buy savings bonds, right?"

"Was that true? Were you talking real estate and limited partnerships?" I asked.

"Not really," he said, "but close."

We kept walking past his office and the video room until we got to the weight room.

" 'Member what I was telling you yesterday about conditioning?" Remsen said. "Look at this place."

All around us were exercise bicycles, rowing machines, stair climbs, treadmills—the gleaming Nautilus equipment that isolates and challenges specific muscle clusters like a chiropractor—and dozens of cold, intimidating free weights. The place was as well equipped as any in a health club, and players used it year round. Two of them dressed in sweats and apparently rehabilitating from injuries were stretching and pushing the iron around as we came in. A radio played something loud. At the sight of Remsen, a pair of T-shirted young attendants hustled over.

"This is Butt and Bogey Slasser," Remsen said.

"With the 'ass' in the middle, where it belongs," said one, and the other laughed like he'd never heard that one before.

Remsen liked it, nevertheless, and grinned. The two grinned back at him. Remsen looked into the training room just beyond us and saw that it was empty. The training room is the last area of privacy in a professional clubhouse. Off limits to everybody but trainers, players, and coaches, and often a healthy but sulking player will hole up there. If he can get away with it.

"Billy Geer been in here?" he asked the two.

Butt and Bogey stiffened at the sound of the Dodger center fielder's name.

"No, Jack. Ain't seen him," one said.

We turned and retraced our steps. I didn't ask what that was about.

"Gotta get dressed," Remsen said, and I left him alone.

I wandered off, minding my own business, and nobody looked cross-eyed at me. By now Remsen's coaches, the only ones besides Jack that I was interested in barbering with, were out on the field. In no time, however, the clubhouse began to fill up with the night's pass list, a collection of former Dodgers, restaurateurs, reporters, a few sponsors, actors, and cops. When I say cops, I mean cops, because the place was lousy with them.

"Arrest that man, officer!" I heard Remsen shout above the din.

Now in full uniform, a Dodger hat on his big head, he clopped a meaty hand on the shoulder of a uniformed member of the Los Angeles Police Department, one of a dozen officers, all solid, strapping young guys who looked like Don Drysdale in his brush-cut days. They wore pressed, immaculate black uniforms, patent-leather shoes, and they wreaked of law and order. Tonight was Police Recognition Night, I was told, and these were the recognizees. Talk about central casting, these officers were straight arrows right out of the police manual. The word *incorruptible* sprang to your lips.

Right now they were being regaled by one of Remsen's personal tales of police run-ins. Jack larded the story with hyperbole, a salacious reference or two, a bad joke about salami, and a choice punch line. Nobody stocked a better line of bullshit, and the officers' laughter rolled through the clubhouse like rifle fire. Their silver badges and pins caught the bright dressing-room light.

I made my way into Remsen's office, where a couple of former players were picking at his buffet table and jockeying their black-and-white photos into better positions on his walls. The television was tuned to *Wheel of Fortune*.

"You think my job is tough? Hell, my job ain't *shit* compared to those guys!" Remsen announced, waddling in a few minutes later.

"Hey, you assholes, get your cotton-pickin' hands off the food! Watch Duffy here. Show some class," he said, and jabbed the two players in the back.

"Say hello to Duffy House. Best damn writer out of Chicago since Jimmy Cannon." I winced, both for me and Cannon, who never set foot out of New York.

"Bunce and Burdock. 'Member these guys?" he added.

I did. They were Dodgers of a decade before, Jack Burdock, a pretty fair second baseman, and Josh Bunce, an outfielder who always looked like the franchise in April and the farm club in June. They hadn't changed much, even though their hair was longer and thinner, and their midriffs were cinched. They were both wearing loose-fitting sport coats and loud shirts, slacks that had to be let out in the thighs, and expensive loafers. And they were shorter. I have always been amazed at the shortness of retired ball players in street clothes. Ron Cey, the penguin, had hustled by me in the hallway earlier, and I swear he'd shrunk a good six inches.

"You know what I mean, Duffy?" Remsen's patter interrupted my thoughts. "We play a kid's game here while those guys out there play for real. Wear bullet-proof vests and pull babies out of burning buildings, for cryin' out loud!"

The phone rang, and Remsen picked it up. More people came in and hung around, some of them worthy of a Remsen shout even though he had the phone in his ear. The office was like campaign central, with food and chatter and a microphone and a reporter's notebook or two. With Remsen everything was on the record—hell, it was on tape, compact disc, and video.

I kept to myself, content to observe, spotting a few familiar faces, mostly former Dodgers and a few regulars on *The Ed Sullivan Show*. As for the latter, Remsen never forgot a name on a marquee. If you had once grasped the brass ring and kept in touch, if you loved the Dodgers, told a good joke, and didn't make a pest of yourself, you were never nudged from his guest list.

As for the former, once you made the club and wore the Dodger uniform, once you worshiped in the house of the Big Dodger in the Sky, you were a life member. It didn't matter if you had left the club, if you had been traded away, or even went as a free agent. Once a Dodger, always a Dodger—at least in the eyes of Jack Remsen. It didn't matter if you had starred or subbed. He treated utility infielders who hadn't worn a uniform in ten years as if they were Steve Garvey.

I averted my eyes from the flash of a camera and refocused to take in the beaming countenance of Bombo Carillo in the doorway. The room tilted his way as he entered, partially because Carillo had been one of the Dodgers' best Latin pitchers before Valenzuela and also because he was now as big as a taco stand. His chest heaved and his wide, molé-brown face glistened.

"La Bomba!" he yelled, and before you knew it, he and Remsen were bear-hugging each other.

"El Toro, you big lummox!" Remsen said, pulling back.

"How 'bout this guy, huh?" he said, drawing everyone's attention. "Out of baseball five years, and he's still in shape—for sumo wrestling!"

The place erupted. The gold chains danced around Carillo's enormous neck like strands of lights on a Christmas tree. There was no mystery behind the mutual admiration between manager and former player. Carillo had been one of Remsen's gems, a rough, pimple-necked kid out of Mexico whose screwball moved a half foot. Remsen treated him like a son, used him magnificently, and watched as Carillo put together a great career. Bombo became a hero to Los Angeles's Mexican population and had been so for years. His picture adorned the cash registers of every bodega in town.

"I come to see thees keed. Thees Adon-ees," Carillo said, his words heavily accented, though he'd lived in the States for twenty years.

"A keeper. Makes you look like *la cucaracha*," Remsen said, and slapped Carillo's wing.

"Hey, Josh! Jack! Look who's here. The gay sombrero!" Remsen yelled.

Again the crowd hooted. Bunce and Burdock, the two ex-Dodgers I'd seen earlier, were now on either side of Bob Ferguson, another one of Remsen's former charges. Ferguson had been one of the first free-agent millionaires, a reliever who'd parlayed a career year with the Cardinals into a fat contract with the Dodgers. The three of them balanced drinks and grinned as if they'd just won a play-off game.

Just then Remsen moved through the crowd and nudged my elbow.

"Enough of this saloon," he said. "I got a ball game to play. Go upstairs for some real food, why don't you?"

"I will, Jack, thanks. Say, that kid pitching tonight?" I asked.

" 'Thees Adon-ees,' " he laughed. "Terrio. Give him a good look-see. Greatest arm since Dutch Leonard."

"Which one?" I quickly replied.

Remsen winced.

"Look that one up," I said.

Remsen chuckled.

"Wiseass," he said. "And hey, if I don't see ya, Duf, take care of yourself. You ain't gettin' any younger, kid."

He trumped that with a clap of his hands and toddled down the ramp, the big Dodger blue number 2—the same digit Durocher and Lasorda had worn—standing out on his back like an escutcheon.

I made my way up to the press box and the media dining room directly behind it. There I spotted Remsen's wife Nina with a bunch of her friends. Nina was as gabby as Jack was, and she was working the room, basking in her own notoriety as the First Lady of the Dodgers. She gave me one of those Don't-I-know-you? looks, then decided against it. I smiled back but let her go about her rounds. She was an ample but handsome woman whose trimmings told you that she threw good money at the hairdresser and haberdasher. A Louis Vuitton handbag swung from her elbow, and her fingers were spaced with ice clusters the size of macadamias. After years of bush-league towns and lean household budgets, you couldn't blame Nina for the splurge.

Dinner fare for the press was short ribs, and they were excellent. I sat by the windows and looked out past the press rows to the slowly filling stadium. I could have watched the entire ball game from my table. Just down the hallway, behind a door marked simply with the number 7, was Peter O'Malley's private box. It held about fifteen guests, all of whom dined with the Dodger heir at a tiered group of tables set with linen, roses, and crystal. Each setting was provided with a pair of field glasses for better viewing.

Game time finally approached—it seemed as if I'd been here since dawn—and I found my seat behind home plate. Before the first pitch was thrown, however, LAPD's finest were introduced to the fans. With withering prose ripped from the lips of Jack Webb, Vin Scully recounted the heroic acts of each officer—men who had shielded downed comrades with their own bodies and plucked injured motorists from flaming automobiles—over the public-address system. Then each man strode from the dugout and stood like a piece of granite, feet slightly spread and hands crossed at the waist. The fans cheered. It was dramatic, stirring, and altogether corny, but it played beautifully. Every crook in town must have felt about two feet tall.

Just between an account of deadly cross fire and a kidnapper with a grenade taped to his chest, Joe Start wedged himself into the seat next to me.

"This the ballpark or the police academy?" he asked.

"Straighten up," I said.

Finally we watched a little baseball, which soon became a lot of baseball. Adonis Terrio, the new kid from Mexico, was everything Remsen had promised. He was skinny and meek—I don't think he shook off his catcher once—but his fastball snuck in on the hitters. He had good stuff, great control, a change-up that just about stopped in midair, and good defense behind him. Problem was, San Diego had a pitcher named Click Groot who was just as effective. After nine innings both teams had squeaked out a single run and worn out both starters. Terrio got a nifty standing ovation when he walked from the hill—oh, how these Dodger zealots appreciate their flingers—and headed for the steam. He had pitched a whale of a game and wouldn't have anything but a lower ERA to show for it. It was worse than kissing your sister—something, by the way, I always thought was kind of nice. Anyway, we were headed for extra frames and a parade of relief pitchers.

Joe and I watched and talked, enjoying that rocking-chair rhythm of a good baseball game. The night was warm, the peanuts well roasted, and I didn't care if I ever got home. A lot of fans disagreed with me. Several thousand of them had already left the ballpark. The old in-by-the-second-inning-out-by-the-seventh handle was holding true.

"It's after ten, and you don't know how far some of these birds have to drive," Joe said. I didn't, and I never would.

Into the eleventh inning the crowd leakage had become a gusher. No more than a third of the stadium was full when a Dodger cracked a drive that could have ended it but fell short by the length of an outfielder's glove. In the fourteenth a Padre did hit one out; but in the bottom of the inning the Dodgers' Geer did the same. We were still all tied up, and I noticed that even Joe was fading. His chin sagged into his collarbone when Remsen took an eternity to make a pitching change.

Both managers were trying anything to nudge the game into the showers. When the Dodgers didn't score after loading the bases in the fifteenth, the exits were once again jammed. Going into the sixteenth, with the big outfield clock passing midnight, there couldn't have been five thousand people left in the place. And the contest had become painful, giddy. When a game goes that long and that late, you almost beg someone to win it, or lose it. Even if you happen to be playing.

In the top of the inning the Padres put together a rally that left men on second and third and, with the pitcher at bat, tried a squeeze bunt of the suicide variety. I've always liked the concept. The runner from third bolts with the pitch. If the batter gets the bunt down, the runner scores effortlessly. If the batter misses, the ball is waiting for the runner like a cream pie.

Everybody from the press photographers to the hot-dog vendors saw it coming. Everybody except the Dodgers. Remsen must have been downright unconscious, dreaming, occupied by the call of nature, or shelling a peanut not to have called a pitchout. His pitcher offered a change-up instead, and the Padres' pitcher laid it down like a quilt on a baby. The runner from third scooted across the plate. There was a groan from the crowd, but it was an anemic, almost relieved one that could have been mistaken for a sigh.

In their at bat the Dodgers went down like weary children. I felt sorry for Remsen, but not too sorry. He should not have lost one like that. A manager has got to read the other guy's book; Remsen would be the first one to tell you that. Had I been working the game, my lead would have been: "A suicide squeeze bunt is just that. Not for you, but the other guy. Last night, however, the Dodgers took the kill."

Joe and I went off in separate directions, and in minutes I was in my car and back on Sunset Boulevard. The pillow was all I wanted. When it finally cradled my heavy head, it was like a mother's lap. No dreams, no churning, no gas. I was out, and I slept hard.

Then my black sleep suddenly exploded. A clanging, dissonant jolt to my eardrums. Had it been minutes? hours? What in hell—! Suddenly I was conscious and groping for the telephone. It rang like a fire bell—the howling device!—and it would not cease.

"Who is this?" I rasped into the receiver.

"Duffy, it's Joe," came the voice.

I swallowed, snapped my fuzzy brain into focus, and then listened to words I never dreamed I would hear.

"The goddamn slasher hit again. This time it's Remsen, Duffy. *Remsen.* Jack Remsen's dead."

5

One More On the House

Aw shit.

It was not eloquent, sentimental, or particularly creative, but I said it over and over again as I sat in the tangle of sheets and the ruin of the night. The red digits on the alarm clock declared 4:10 A.M. I was anything but rested, but sleeping now was a ridiculous proposition. *Jack Remsen dead.* Murdered, his throat slit like a turkey's. That big, happy jamoke, that barrel of warmth and bullshit, that Dodger of Dodgers. *Aw shit.* The guy who only a few hours before had told *me* to watch myself. That blustering, gobbling old catcher, knuckles mangled, a crawful of dust and bad hash. A pure character with juice beneath the skin, blood running blue. *Aw shit.* Jack Remsen, the guy who never made a buck outside of baseball. And what he made he gave back to the game fourfold. Was still giving, dammit. No natural, no kid, no shooting star. Just a piece of gristle with pine tar and bear grease and lamp black. Taste of leather in his mouth. World championship ring on his finger. *Aw shit.* . . .

I said it as I stumbled from the bed and stood in the shower, the hot spray bringing me to, my head clearing to the reality of Remsen falling prey to this maniac. I found no way to couch it, to explain or rationalize it. I found no way to deny it, which is the way ordinary minds like mine tend to react. No, Remsen's death just made me mad; my head throbbed, and my eyes hurt. To say it gave me a sense of my own mortality was like saying Roy Campanella would never again throw out a careless base stealer.

Before he rang off, Start had added a few specifics. Remsen's car had been spotted in a parking lot behind a taco shack on Sunset Boulevard only a couple miles from the ballpark. Jack was in the front seat, his throat slashed. He'd bled to death. *Bled* to death. There it was again. Draining down his chest, over those gnarled hands, onto the leather of his car seat, blood running like water down the tiles of a shower. My knees buckled, and I grabbed the towel bar for support.

Room service brought hot coffee, and I drank it black while I dressed. It was good coffee, I think. Start had told me to come over to the *Times* if I wanted. He'd been there most of the night and had no plans to leave. A few minutes later I passed through the main lobby and walked out onto Fifth Street. I waved off the offer of a cab. The Times-Mirror Building at First and Spring streets was but a few blocks away, and I needed the walk and the air.

Dawn had cracked the sky, and downtown was beginning to get off its ass. I had not walked but a few yards when I was approached by a wild-eyed old bird in a white straw cowboy hat. He looked like a rodeo hand who'd lost his way or a fugitive from the Pershing Square wine colony. Under the hat were flowing, unruly locks of shoulder-length white hair, plus a white goatee and mustache. If you didn't think of Buffalo Bill at first sight, you weren't conscious. I remembered e e cummings's line, "How do you like your blue-eyed boy, Mr. Death?"—which doesn't make me some kind of aesthete in the red eye of morning. The Grim Reaper was just on my mind. The cowboy swept by me without a glance, no doubt having bigger broncs to break.

In no time I had come upon the *Times.* On a normal day I'd remark on the daunting romanesque architecture of the Times-Mirror Building, the gray stone facade, the terraced third and fourth stories sprouting with trees and shrubs. On a normal day I'd genuflect to the memory of Harrison Gray Otis, the *Times* founder; his son-in-law Harry Chandler, the Walter O'Malley of Los Angeles journalism; Harry's son Norman; and Norman's kid Otis, who enhanced the theme, and consider the ways in which these men and their *Times* left any and all rivals in the dust. On a normal day I'd take pause in the building's stunning lobby and point out the marble and the inlaid brass, the magnificent globe centerpiece, the stirring words cut in stone about freedom of the press, the gallery of photos and broadsheets outlining the history of the paper, artifacts including linotype machines and their hot-lead slugs, accordion-style cameras, typewriters as old as the century.

But this wasn't a normal day, not for me and not for the forces that ran this sheet. I could no more linger like a museum patron than I could go back to bed. I had lost a kindred spirit; Los Angeles had lost part of its soul. Still, as I stood in the Times-Mirror lobby, I could fairly feel the hum inside the place. A big story had broken, a tragedy as stark and cruel as any, and newspapers set their daily tables on tragedy.

It was just a little after six A.M. when I told the security guard I had a date with Joe Start, and he looked at me like I'd said Rita Hayworth. But his phone call confirmed me, and I had entrée in the form of an alligator-clipped visitor's badge. I wasn't sure what good that was. I belonged in the newsroom that morning about as much as I belonged in Jack Remsen's office yesterday, for what it's worth. But it was better than sitting alone in a hotel room watching those hairdos on the Ks.

Start's side of the city desk was a hive. A half-dozen editors, from the bow-tied big fish to the hands-on managing editors, were knocking heads on the Remsen story. The overnight edition had already been held, and its front page remade. DODGER MANAGER REMSEN SLAIN raged the headline. It would go unchanged with each new run. Subsequent editions were being thrown together with new photos, updated stories, and whatever features could be created at this time of the morning. Everybody was working the phones. Start, looking like a guy who'd been up all night fighting a grassfire, was in the middle of it.

I stood on the edge, feeling the heat and the energy, temporarily engrossed at the spectacle of pros covering a big one. In my mind's eye they were all working in slow motion, like horses bobbing on a carousel. Actually the production was going in cut time, with copy passing directly from editors' and reporters' terminals into the computers of the composing room and then into the data banks of the printing presses themselves. Trucks were being stacked with bundles of papers containing stories that had been written not hours but minutes earlier. The ink smudged your fingers.

And Jack Remsen was still dead, I reminded myself. All this technology, and murder was still murder. The guy's throat was slit. And that was not modern at all.

Start noticed me and came over. He handed me a paper. It was still warm.

"Read all about it," he said. "Poor bastard."

Start had saucers under his eyes and coffee stains on his shirt. He was hostage to this story, and he *looked* like a hostage. There was no more tired man in the hemisphere.

"How about you?" he said. "Can you put something together for us?"

"C'mon, Joe," I said.

"Money's no object, you know that. The scene in Remsen's office you were telling me about last night would make a hell of a sidebar. You knew the guy."

"Everybody knew the guy."

"Don't be so sure," he said, and moved off toward the fray. After a few steps he turned back to me and said, "Use the terminal in my office."

I lifted a cheek on a desk and dug into page one. The details were straightforward, arranged side by side by the *Times*'s baseball writer and the paper's night police reporters—an unlikely tandem—like suspects in a lineup. After the game Remsen had been rankled by the Dodgers' loss. He groused to reporters in his office,

chewing out himself and his coaches. Stadium security
said it was just after one A.M. when he left the park. He
was wearing a thin pale-blue Dodger sweater and
brown casual slacks. He drove off alone in his white
Cadillac Brougham, presumably headed for the Pasadena Freeway and the thirty-minute trip to his home in
the San Rafael Hills near the Rose Bowl.

His whereabouts for the next hour were unknown.
He was next seen by the taco vendor, a twenty-year-old
kid named Alejandro Madrid, at the joint on Sunset and
Lucile. The kid said he did not recognize Remsen. Jack
had ordered three soft-shell beef tacos with extra hot
sauce and a side order of guacamole. Nothing to drink.
The tacos were still in the bag on the seat when he was
found. Detectives speculated that the killer had
climbed into the backseat of Remsen's car while he left
it running unlocked in the lot behind the shack. His
throat was slashed with a single cut. There was no sign
of a struggle. Remsen's wallet had been cleaned—and
Jack was known to carry cash in his wallet. He'd paid for
the tacos with a double sawbuck and told Alejandro
Madrid to keep the change. Madrid said he still did not
know who his customer was.

That was pretty much all the police had, or all they
said they had. Like the other Sunset Boulevard
murders, nobody in the area seemed to have seen anything or anybody. If any evidence had been discovered
inside the car, the cops weren't talking about it. Remsen
was discovered by a pair of patrol officers who'd pulled
into the lot to check on the laundromat next door. One
of the coppers recognized Remsen's license plate,
DODGER 2, and went over to investigate. It was
2:12 A.M.

The rest of the story was padding, most of it background material on the Sunset Slasher murders. It
didn't make the reading any easier. If Jack Remsen had
been killed by the Slasher, the police seemed to be
saying, then this maniac was far more dangerous than
the one who'd previously preyed on derelicts and frail
pensioners. Only Remsen's age and the locale of the

murder fit the profile. Otherwise he was of sound mind, strong, and as tough as a rattlesnake. And still he'd had his throat slashed.

The *Times* ran a photo of Remsen's car taken from an angle that gave only a slight outline of his body as it slumped in the front seat. That was enough. Start told me the rest of the photographer's portfolio was graphic and horrifying. It had been a gruesome, bloody crime, a true indignity to a guy like Remsen who believed in appearances, who insisted on crisp white uniforms and polished spikes. In death there was no modesty or decorum, no uniform. Jack could only rely on the standards of others, and in this town, where the camera, the paparazzi, and the tabloids rage like banshees, he would get scant regard. I told Joe to keep the photos to himself.

Then I hunkered behind Joe Start's desk. The keyboard drew my idle hands and my scrambled thoughts like a siren. I was as useless as a bat bag out in the newsroom, and I didn't want to get in Start's way. Writing has always been a living to me, words strung together for the benefit of the ordinary person who had not been there. I did a good job of it and collected a paycheck. Let the ivory-tower boys see the artistry in it; I simply sat down and put together prose clear enough for a tuck-pointer to read over his coffee. Hell, I know all the tricks. I can exhort the Muse and vamp the Thesaurus. I can throw my voice as well as Lardner and Sandburg and Granny Rice and all those other ink-stained wretches who toiled back in the "Front Page" days. You want fertilizer, I can cover the barnyard. Did it five times a week for forty years and can still do it.

But I was writing this one for myself. I felt damn grieved for Jack. I was sick to my stomach, mad, and altogether weary of this whole mess of death in Los Angeles. I needed something to quilt. I needed a chord, a fuse that might tie things together in my old, unsettled brain. And writing was the only way to get at it. Or so I thought, because when I sat down at the chiclets in Joe Start's office, my fingers trembled like a schoolboy's.

*. . . lie in the backseat, you gutless bastard,
and spring upon the good kid like a viper on a
child. Jack was about to pound a taco, for
chrissake, ply the gut, which is what you do
after losing one the way he did. Suicide
squeeze in the sixteenth inning. Damn. Do you
know how hard it is to lose one like that? Jack
Remsen knew.*

*Hear this, you son-of-a-bitch: every one of
those cops, the real nut-busting LAPD cops
who came to the ballyard and shook Jack Remsen's hand only hours before you made it cold,
will hunt you down on his own time. Won't
sleep until you are handcuffed to a ring on the
wall. Take Jack Remsen, and you have taken
one of their own. Our own. You can walk down
the street and not look over your shoulder, and
you turn out the lights when you go to bed if
you want, but I wouldn't. . . .*

I pulled back and reread that. It made me feel
good, like the first minute of a good scrap where you
blow off steam and throw the wild punches. My chest
was cleared. Then I pressed the "delete" key, settled
down, and let the professional take over.

*A few hours earlier, in what seems like a
lifetime ago, Jack Remsen was entertaining the
troops. The guys in the offices upstairs had
scheduled Police Night, and Remsen bought
into that like he bought into everything else. It
was part of being the Dodger skipper, best job
in baseball, he said. He said that when he woke
up every morning. And Jack didn't just show
up the last minute to say howdy but was there
when they walked in the door. Showed the officers the clubhouse. Had them in his office,
where they gawked at the pictures on the
walls. Shook every hand, asked every name,*

then told them Jack Remsen stories they'll never forget.

Then he came over to me, and he said, "I play a kid's game. Those guys play for real." That's what he said. That was Jack Remsen.

All the stories about Jack will be retold. Some will be true and others not a bit true, and it won't make any difference. I knew Jack when he was filling out rosters with a three-inch pencil under a bare light bulb in a mildewed clubhouse. I knew him when he scuffled with minor-league skippers named Spud, Sparky, Knucks, and Hoot. Don't be fooled. The real name of those cussed, dust-eating, bus-riding, rednecked critters is Longsuffering.

Just ask Jack Remsen, who suffered long, who endured untold numbers of seven-hour, red-eye, axle-grinding bus rides through miles of sagebrush and cactus, who managed raw-boned kids with dirty socks and bad habits on uneven fields in front of 175 fans. Before his eyes lit on Tipperary, before he gazed on the blue Dodger script and the shimmering grass of the Ravine, he had languished in Ogden, Spokane, Albuquerque, and all points in between.

It didn't matter to Jack. He was a son-of-a-gun from the first inning on: squeezing, stealing, hit-and-running, playing every game like a play-off game. When he wasn't managing, he was coaching, showing his kids how to get their butts down on ground balls and hit behind the runner. Kids. "It's a kid's game," he reminded me.

Then he showed them how to load a plug of tobacco in their cheek or a pinch of snuff inside the lip. He wanted his kids to chew and spit and chatter and cuss. There was no better bench jockey. He'd cup his palm around his mouth and bellow like a foghorn. His pitchers *threw with two-day beards. "If you feel dirty and nasty, you pitch that way," he said. His players got into fights, and Jack Remsen usually joined in.*

Mayo Smith, the old manager who coached against Remsen in the majors and minors, once told me about a game in Spokane when Remsen's team was down by five runs and sleepwalking.

"Jack turned to his pitcher and told him to start a fight. I swear it," Mayo said. "Next thing you know there's two guys beaned, and everybody's swingin', including Remsen. They ended up beating us by six runs."

But he nurtured the young players coming up, and he was tough on the overpaid narcissists. He helped guys who had dropped out of the game, who had lost it because of blown-out rotator cuffs, or whose careers had taken a nosedive. He held onto them, kept them intact. He was a father confessor, a counselor, a baseball therapist. He was what we used to call "a good influence" on the game.

And this was the guy who sat in the front seat of his car about to scarf a taco when a maniac came up from the rear, up behind that famous bristly head, the only place Jack had no defense, and slit his throat.

"Take care of yourself, Duffy." That was the last thing Jack Remsen said to me. Manager of the Los Angeles Dodgers, best job in baseball, about to embark on sixteen tortuous innings and take a fateful ride down Sunset Boulevard. And he told me to take care. That was the last thing he said.

You too, Jack. You too. . . .

Joe Start ran it on the front page. Didn't change a word. By the time I was finished with it, the shakes had gone away.

. . .

The next time I looked up at the clock, it was just after nine, which meant Chicago and New York were already in the middle innings. I called a familiar number and got a wonderful voice in a Park Avenue office. The pleasing pipes belonged to a young wonder named Marjorie. Without her the commissioner of baseball, Granville "Grand" Canyon Chambliss, could not function.

"He's been looking all over for you," Marjorie said. "This place is a bunker. Where are you?"

"In the snort of the volcano," I said. "Los Angeles."

"You're remarkable, Mr. House."

"No, I'm an old jackass who just lost a good friend," I replied.

"I'm sorry," Marjorie said. "We can't believe it here. The boss is socking the walls."

Then with a few clicks and the sound of a garbage truck in the background, she added, "Hold on, the commissioner's on the line."

"Duffy? You got anything on this?" Chambliss bellowed. "Jack Remsen, for godsakes. A great baseball man—Mr. Baseball. This is an American travesty, a crime against the Game itself!"

I exhaled through the bluster. "You talking to me, Grand, or you got a fistful of microphones in front of you?"

"Take it easy. Where are you?"

"Los Angeles."

"Come on—"

"Came out here two days ago to talk to Jack Remsen."

He held the line and considered some.

"What a damn shame!" he finally said.

"That's exactly it."

"What in hell happened, Duf? Is it really this Sunset Boulevard Slasher thing the wire services are saying. I thought he went after bums. How'd Remsen get in there?"

"Good question. He lost a ball game and stopped

for a taco, the fat jerk, and he never made it out of the parking lot. Nobody out here knows any more than that. Including me."

"So now what? You stickin' around? This office'll pay for it, you know."

"If I do decide to stick, it'll be on my own tab. I think I owe Jack that much."

"One more on the House?" he said.

"So to speak."

"Still got the legs for it?"

"No," I said. "This one comes from the gut."

Chambliss had four calls waiting for him, I knew, but he did not seem in any hurry to ring off.

"Where are you now?"

"At the paper. The *Times*. Joe Start gave me his office. Remember him? Used to cover the Dodgers. He's a big city editor now."

Chambliss coughed. "So I don't have to talk you into anything. Just stay in touch, will ya? Check in with Marjorie. I'll be out there in a few days for the wake.

"And one more thing, Duf. Nina. Jack's wife. She's a favorite of mine. If you get a chance, pay some respects to her for me and this office. It would mean a lot."

Then he paused once again, and the two of us felt the silence. Grand was an old friend. The less said, the more.

"This is a bad one, Duffy," he said. "This one really hurts."

I ran a paw over my face and gently hung up the phone.

Joe Start had entered the office and was standing in the corner watching a television. In just about every editor's sanctum there was a television, and just about every one of them was turned on this morning. It was a fact of today's newspaper offices, like reading the competition.

"I'm goin' home. My batteries are dead," Start said. He had the latest edition folded under an arm.

"Hell, I'm fresh as a choirboy," I said.

"Good, 'cuz you look like shit," he said, and then he smiled wearily. "It was a hell of a piece, Duf. Thanks much."

"We don't write 'em," I said. "They write themselves."

"Bullshit," he said. "There aren't a handful of writers in the land could give me what you just did."

I let it stand. In the country of the young, it's nice to score once in a while. I tried to stand up, and my bones shrieked.

Start stopped. "I almost forgot. You're a popular guy around here. We got calls—wasn't minutes after your piece hit the street."

He fished in his shirt pocket and pulled out a pink scrap of paper.

"Two you might wanna get back on. One's from the widow."

"Nina Remsen?" I asked.

"Mrs. Jack, she said. Liked your prose and wanted to tell you so. Here's her number. Then there's a copper wants to talk to you. This is his phone. They're buttonholing anybody Remsen ran into yesterday."

"If they want to talk to me," I said, "they're already in trouble on this thing."

"You be the judge. Cop's name is Holdsworth. Jim Holdsworth. Ring a bell?"

"The old Laker?"

"That's him. Big detective now. I run into him every once in a while. I told him you'd call him."

Joe motioned me out of the office, and I followed him through the city room. It was still a hubbub. We walked outside, however, to a day bright and breezy. Traffic was going in both directions on Spring Street. Despite what screamed from the newspaper boxes, life went on.

"You gonna stick around?" Start asked.

I hesitated.

"You should," he went on. "This is a hot new potato in this town."

"Forget it. Hollywood's seen it all."

"Consider it, Duf. Actors land in the obits all the

time. Goes with the territory. But not baseball players. That's who the movie people go to for diversion. Dodger Stadium is the only script they can't buy. With Remsen you got part baseball, part *Entertainment Tonight*. They don't get much bigger."

"You're talking like a producer, Joe."

"I'm an editor. I know a good story when I see it. And you're the guy to write it. My boss told me to buy anything you come up with, if that makes a difference.

"I'll tell you what," he continued. "Check out of that millionaire's hotel and stay with me. I got a big empty house in Alhambra, and you can take your choice of two extra bedrooms. It's a good base. Come and go as you please. Use my car. Zero in on this thing.

"Unless, of course, Chambliss is paying the tab. Don't tell me he won't want you to stay out here."

"Chambliss thinks I'm his personal agent."

"There you go. More work than you can ask for, Duffy."

"Aw shit, Joe. I appreciate your offer—don't get me wrong. But I'm a grizzled old scribe. I'm tired and retired. I'm too old to keep renewing the gumshoe license."

I sounded about as sincere as a stockbroker.

"On the other hand . . ." Start began.

"There's no other hand."

". . . Jack Remsen's been murdered. Tell me you can walk away from that."

With Nina Remsen's phone message in my pocket, I couldn't walk away just yet. I was exhausted, weary to the bone, but it felt good to be worn out by a column once again. Red Smith, who never stopped writing them until his heart stopped pumping, used to talk about the old spark, the spirit, the enthusiasm. He said that if he ever lost it, he'd quit. He never did. Maybe I did, I don't know. But I do know that in Joe Start's office in the infant hours of that day and the sting of Jack Remsen's murder, the pilot light glowed and the burners fired and the piece on Remsen came to life. Red

Smith's son, Terence, wrote that when Red learned that his wife Phyllis had cancer, he broke down and cried. Then he wrote a column. I know about that too.

So I called Nina once I returned to my room, and after several rings she answered. I immediately apologized for bothering her.

"But I called you," she said. "I wanted to thank you."

"No need," I said.

I relayed the commissioner's condolences.

"I should be doing this in person," I said uncomfortably.

"Why don't you? I've got the time. The Dodgers are taking care of everything," she said, and without a moment's hesitation gave me directions to her home.

After a long shower and a few slaps on the jowls, I summoned a second wind and took on the freeways once more. The Remsen abode was almost due north of downtown, near Pasadena and its freeway, in an area called San Rafael Hills. And hills they were, winding, rising, falling, giving me fits. There were golf courses all over the place and rich real estate tucked in them like fairway bunkers. An infant's first word in these parts is "Fore!"

And then I found the asphalt drive leading up to the hacienda, a meandering, split-level piece of Spanish architecture that was as open and uncluttered as Jack Remsen's office was a sardine can. This was obviously Nina's domain.

There were several vehicles in the driveway, and I parked next to a floral truck. A young woman in blue jeans answered the chimes. She led me through a front room filled with so many bouquets that it smelled like a meadow. Nina Remsen was sitting with a group in the kitchen, but she quickly arose when I appeared.

"It's so nice of you to come out," she said softly, patting the back of my hand and leading me off to a screened-in veranda.

A plump, stylish woman, she was as I had remembered her from our brief encounter in the clubhouse. She seemed to have herself together in these aftermath hours, looking as fresh in a loose-fitting pastel outfit with pants as could be expected. I noticed only that the makeup seemed a little heavier, and who could blame her for that?

"Cocktail hour," she said, and matter-of-factly put in my mitt a tumbler of cold gin that matched one of her own. I did not rebel.

We chatted some. She said the outpouring from family and friends was overwhelming. She thanked me again for the column.

"It struck a chord," she said.

In the background I heard the door chimes and the telephone ring again and again. Nina was subdued, doing her best, relying on the sacred gin and a lot of old-fashioned strength to get her through.

"I've always been a Dodger widow," she said in passing. "Just never thought it would be permanent."

"Can you manage?" I said.

"Of course. I always have. You don't know what it's like being married to baseball for forty years," she said.

"Yes, I do," I said, and shrugged. She reconsidered.

"Except for the books. The money," she went on. "It's a mess, you know. He gives money away like autographs—all you have to do is ask. And the restaurant— what a *disaster*. They're stealing us blind, if you ask me, but Jack wouldn't pull the plug. Now George, our accountant, says we got tax trouble over that. Then there's the preacher, the Right Reverend Billy Harbridge, who thinks he's tapped into a gusher. He just keeps coming and coming, and Jack keeps writing checks."

I flashed back to Remsen's office, mentally scanning the photo wall across from his painting of Jesus. One of the shots was of Jack and a fellow with brilliant silver hair, aviator glasses, and a flawless smile. In the background was an edifice that looked like a plate-glass museum. Reverend Billy.

I was surprised at Nina's outpouring. She was tired and grieving.

"But Rem was bringing it in . . . ?" I said.

She smiled thinly. "Sold everything from cars to TV

dinners," she said. Then she sighed. "And the more he made, the more he gave away. Mr. Soft Touch—that's what I called him. It didn't bother him a bit. Not a bit . . ."

She stared off. It was a digression, a momentary spasm of frustration and anger. Yesterday she was living with a lovable fool. Today she was trying to figure out how to live without him. Her gin was gone before mine.

6

Long Jim Holdsworth

It took me three tries to get in touch with the detective. Which was fine, because in the meantime I went to bed and slept out the early evening and the rest of the night. It was not the weak deposit of sleep and the running around that downed me—though that did not help any. It was the writing. Writing is not brain surgery, and it is not throwing 147 hardballs over nine innings, but it *is* physical work. Flannery O'Connor, the Georgia lady who kept peacocks, wrote like an angel and died too early of lupus, used to say that after a few hours of writing in the morning, she was so exhausted she had to rest up for the next day's stint.

As for the detective, Jim Holdsworth, it was a good sign that he was not at his desk much. If you're in the office, you're not out catching fish. When we finally connected, he told me he'd come over to the Biltmore. I told him to save it, I'd show up in his dugout the next morning instead. He worked out of police headquarters on Los Angeles and Temple, and I knew that it was only a few blocks away from the hotel. I used to do a lot of strolling around downtown Los Angeles back in the days when I had time to kill before heading out to the ballyard. The city is older than a lot of people think, and the landmarks came back to me in a hurry. Come to think of it, I have always done a lot of walking in this town. And how long could it last?

It was not yet eight o'clock the next morning when

I trudged up Olive Street, turned right on First, and walked past the county building. It is a postcard structure, a white brick beauty built in the Depression, when West Coast baseball was bush league. I've always admired it. That morning, however, its sloping lawn was a barracks for vagrants and free-lance transients lying all over the grass like railroad ties. Now I'm all for the underdog, and I've lived through hard times, but how often do you have to watch one of these guys taking a leak on a palm tree to say enough already? And every time I talk like that, I sound like Ronald Reagan and I want to kick myself.

I continued down First, passing the Times-Mirror fortress again, the bail-bond joints, and the "kosher burrito" stand, until I got to Los Angeles Street, where I spotted city hall. Across Los Angeles Street stood police headquarters, a squat, modern building about eight stories tall with the architectural appeal of a paddy wagon. The lobby was uninviting, no matter how much had been spent on the mosaic off to my left. To my right a bunch of ordinary people of all colors sat in folding chairs. On their faces was the glum look of wasted time, fatigue, and a relative who had been pinched overnight. I did not want to know their stories.

The keepers of this den, the half-dozen uniformed cops and clerks behind the high front counter, seemed to be having a gay time in their bailiwick of pushed papers and duplicate forms. They called upstairs and told me to linger. Holdsworth was coming down.

In a minute I was in the shadow of a black string bean, a towering man who made Don Newcombe look diminutive. He was six foot seven if he was an inch, maybe fifty-five years old, with skin almost Nigerian black. He reminded me of Willie Crawford, but a head taller. His beige business suit, a powder blue shirt, and navy tie made him just about the best-dressed, best-looking guy in the building. He fielded looks like fungo hits from the female cops behind the desk and lobbed them back.

If you had to guess about him being Long Jim Holdsworth, former Laker, the Minneapolis and Los

Angeles version, you'd hesitate on sighting Minnie Mouse. I did not know a whole lot about his career or his abilities—basketball being a game I followed only casually—but I did know of his stature in black sports history. He was one of the first black men to break into the NBA in the 1950s, along with guys like Ray Felix, Sweetwater Clifton, Walter Dukes, and of course Bill Russell. I have a great respect for ground breakers, and Holdsworth was one.

I guessed only on how few pounds he'd put on—he couldn't have carried more than 210 of them—since he'd quit the boards. He was a skinny man. Age showed on his forehead, something hard to control, which had backpedaled some. Yet even that was hard to gauge because Holdsworth's hair was clipped to the skull in the style a lot of black fellows seem to favor nowadays.

He never broke stride, extended a great, two-toned paw, and motioned toward the door.

"Mr. House, I take it? Jim Holdsworth, detective lieutenant, homicide division. A pleasure," he announced. "Catch a bite on me while we double-clutch this thing."

I hurried along next to him like a towel boy during a time-out.

"Can't talk up in the shop," he said. "Phone is merciless. This is the only thing on the platter right now."

He went on. "That piece of yours in the *Times* was gospel. Why didn't you ever write about me?"

He smiled when he said it, one of those cover-the-globe smiles that serene, smug guys pull out just before they get thrown out of a ball game.

"Wrong sport, Lieutenant," I replied. "Your game's too fast, and the ball's too big."

"Shoot, that's no excuse. I read *your* stuff all the time. When I could. You probably didn't know that."

I liked him already. He didn't have a doubt in his body. He walked so fast I had to trot occasionally to keep up, his giant brown wing tips devouring the pavement, hands in his pants pockets, tie flapping. We headed up Spring past the Criminal Courts Building and over to Broadway.

"You had a good line once, I'll never forget," he went on. "Said a guy was a 'credit to his race.' And he was *white*."

He guffawed like Paul Robeson and clapped his lobsters together.

"You a baseball fan?" I asked.

"Not so much now as before," he said. "Junior and I were real close. And I miss him."

He didn't have to explain. Junior was Jim Gilliam, the Dodgers' one-time classic second baseman and later a coach. One of the Bums from Brooklyn, Gilliam was so good he forced Jackie Robinson to third, then into the outfield. Out west he had a half-dozen good campaigns before he quit in sixty-six. He died of a cerebral hemorrhage just before the 1978 World Series, and everybody grieved.

"He taught me the game. Taught me the attitude. Man was indomitable," Holdsworth said, his words carrying to me despite a tailwind.

"That's the word," I said.

"So yeah, I met Remsen. I knew he owned that side of the town. That side, 'cuz you know show biz *owns* the town. Always has. Always will. Remsen was shrewd because he *was* show biz."

I sensed more was coming.

"I admired the guy," he went on. "His teams won. Can't do better'n that. But I didn't kiss his ring. He was too much of an industry for me."

We passed over the Hollywood Freeway, crossed Sunset Boulevard, and moved into a dense low-rise strip of Chinese stores and markets. People were gawking at us from the moment we hit the sidewalk—the old guy huffing to keep up with the Sears Tower—and when we hit Peking Central, we became a spectacle. They looked at Holdsworth like he was King Kong. The Chinese may be able to feed us well, but they'll never be able to guard our pivots.

"These Chinamen love me," Holdsworth said, ducking into a little greasy chopstick called China Garden.

Holdsworth ordered chicken dumplings with an-
gel-hair noodles and a junk-sized container of fried rice.

"I don't eat breakfast," he said.

"I do," I said. "How do you say *bagel* and *nova* in
Chinese?"

"Noju," he said, and laughed too loud.

I drank hot tea. Holdsworth sipped the iced variety.

"Two things, right off," he said. "I got a friend in
New York named Bill Devery. Pretty fair cop. He told
me about you. That's number one."

No preliminaries. Go right to the hole.

I toyed with my tea. "Devery. Big white guy with
hair about as long as yours?" I asked.

Holdsworth grinned.

"He said they're wringing the city dry after the big
Yankee gets zipped last summer and you come up with
somebody new. A cat nobody'd tagged. Broke the thing
wide open, that's what he said."

I knew what he was talking about and shrugged.
Given that I had put up with his choice of menu, he
could do the chatter. His food came, the dumplings
steaming like hot rocks, and he dug in with a fork that
was too small for him. Holdsworth looked like a man
visiting his kid's nursery school.

"We got every dick in the show on Sunset Strip. A
dragnet'd make Jack Webb look lazy. Anybody on that
street so much as stops to pick his nose, and our guys are
on him. We don't find this ringer that way, then we go
flood the neighborhood. House to house. Saturate the
hills. People gonna be real sick of us.

"I figure we get a break in a day, maybe two," he
added, "and we slam this bastard. Try anything. Put out
a hundred cash on Sunset, and people start tellin' you
things. That's how it is."

"Good," I said.

"Course, it wouldn't hurt if you give me what you
gave Bill Devery. You're in on this, aren't you? You're
the point guard for the baseball commissioner, right?
Like in New York. If that's the situation, I'll take a perp
from ya anytime, Mr. House. Take him in a minute.

Give you a parade on Hollywood Boulevard too. No chip off my shoulder. My ego's been checked at the door ever since I took this job."

He slurped and fought with the noodles. He took great divots out of the mound of fried rice.

"What's the second thing?" I asked.

He bobbed his head up and down. Then, without saying anything, he held the bottle of soy sauce out in the aisle. It was empty, and in seconds a full one was slapped against his palm. It was a clean pass; Holdsworth had played here before.

"You read anything between Jack Remsen's lines? Anything make you wonder?" he asked.

"How's that?"

"He seem preoccupied? Look like something was eatin' him?"

"Not before the game. Clubhouse was mardi gras. After the game, I don't know. I suspect he had red ass worst case."

Holdsworth ate. Occasionally he lifted his black eyes at me just to make sure I was paying attention.

"We don't know what he was up to after he left the Stadium. More'n an hour. Big gap. Nobody saw him. Nobody saw his vehicle. Maybe from one-fifteen to two-fifteen, until the squad found him. He musta gone somewhere, maybe met someone. That's what I'm after," he said.

"What'd Nina say?" I asked. "She ever know him to ride around, let off steam, before he came home?"

"She said no. Which don't mean it didn't happen. She just said he wasn't a loner. I can buy that."

Suddenly Holdsworth was finished with the meal. The noodles were gone, and the floor of the fried-rice platter shone.

"You got appointments?" he asked. "If not, come tag along. If anybody asks, I'll tell 'em you're a suspect."

"Thanks," I said.

With a sweep of a napkin and a sawbuck under the plate, he was on his feet. I momentarily calculated the freight. This joint's day wasn't made by Holdsworth. Then again he had paid, and cops are not known for paying. He used the bathroom and a public phone, and a few minutes later we were picked up by a black sedan driven by a black man in a black suit. I sat in the backseat, which I wasn't crazy about. If you know anything about police vehicles, you don't want to sit in the backseat.

"Duffy House, Sam Kimber. Mr. House wrote the article," Holdsworth said.

Kimber reached over the seat and shook my hand but didn't say a word. He was as light-skinned as Holdsworth was dark, maybe ten years his junior. He looked as if he'd strayed from the FBI.

"We'll show you what we got out here," Holdsworth said.

We drove up Sunset, following its winding path, past Elysian Park Avenue, stopping for streetlights and merging buses. As we approached Silver Lake, traffic thickened.

"Instant tourist attraction," Holdsworth said.

Kimber shook his head and tried to muscle the car through. Finally we pulled up and parked in front of a fire hydrant. The asphalt lot between the taco stand and the laundromat, an area normally good for maybe a dozen cars and a pair of dumpsters, was clogged with people. At least fifty of them, concentrated near the side of the taco shack, some of them still, others milling about. As we approached, I could see the attraction.

A memorial of sorts had already been created where Remsen had died. It was a ragtag collection of flowers—single roses and bunches of daisies, forget-me-nots, and birds of paradise—and Dodger memorabilia. There were Dodger hats, photos of Remsen, baseball cards, souvenir bats, T-shirts with his caricature, and almost anything else that had to do with the deceased number 2. There were even several tacos, still wrapped, lying in the jumble, and onlookers had to shoo the birds from them.

The crowd was a slice of the stadium, except that there was no cheering, and little chatter. A couple young ladies in Dodger hats and Dodger jackets sat on their haunches and cried like widows. The street's normal stragglers, the hustlers and the vagrants, wandered in to see what the glow was on. More people came and tossed additions onto the pile. Somebody laid in a pair of blue spikes that looked brand new, then had to keep a bum from grabbing them.

"Been like this since yesterday," Holdsworth said. "Taco guy's doin' good. Laundromat guy's pissed."

"John Lennon. Bobby Kennedy," I said.

"Tells you somethin', don't it?" Holdsworth added.

I followed him and Kimber around the edge of the crowd until we were near the back door of the taco shack. Two picnic tables for the on-premise eaters stood next to empty produce boxes. A few yards away were the dumpsters. The odors commingled and made you want to double the hot sauce. As Remsen had with his three takeouts. Behind the containers was a steep littered hill, and what looked like a small garage or house about twenty feet up.

"If he's a street type, he could have been camped out here," Holdsworth said. "You find 'em in cracks like this all the time. Having their garbage-can buffet."

"Our people found some small stuff, a few bottles, some bags. Usual stuff. Somebody was here—could have been an hour, a day, maybe two before—we don't know. Mexican guys in the stand don't give us shit. They see people back here all the time."

"Jack could have been an accident. Wrong place, wrong time, and your boy took him," I said, thinking out loud.

Nobody paid much attention to us as we nosed around. A few people eyed Holdsworth, but people probably always eyed Holdsworth. I noticed Kimber was off to the side watching everybody else. I hoped he was seeing something. What I saw was a stone-faced young man who looked like a police detective, acted like a police detective, and would not fool a blind man.

As I riffled through those uncharitable thoughts, a slow low rumble hit my ear.

"Pea-nuts. Pop-corn. Cold be-er. Hom-i-cide," it went.

It came from a little woolly guy, a five-foot-high

fellow with coal gray hair all over his head, a bushy beard, a walrus mustache, a mop of a scalp, even a mat of gray on his neck. Only the top of his cheeks and his bleary eyes weren't growing something. He was probably fifty, but he could have been thirty. He smelled like last week's eggplant and wore a bulky sweater so dirty, it grew on him. For all I knew he may have crawled out of the dumpster.

And yet he had a voice. Basso profundo. A walking public-address system.

"What's on your mind, pal?" Holdsworth said.

"Take me out the ball game, copper" the guy said, then he laughed like Iago. For a moldy guy, he had a larynx that belonged in an opera house. He also had on gloves with the finger tips cut out. His nails were licorice.

"You know about this?" Holdsworth said.

"Gimme fi' dollah," the guy said.

"Gimme something first," the detective said.

The hairy one shook his head back and forth like a collie. I swear I heard something rattle inside.

"How's the weather up there, long john?" he said.

"See ya around, pal," Holdsworth said.

He nodded at me to follow and started back toward the boulevard. The hirsute bum turned on me.

"Gimme a buck."

"For what?"

"What ya don't see, that's what. The killer. Can't get the killer. Ya don't know what to look for. He ain't what ya think. Now where's the buck?"

I fished for some change.

"What is he then? You tell me," I said.

The little guy's eyes widened.

"A Dodger fan!" he hooted.

Then he laughed, just doubled over and busted a gut. People gawked at him. I kept the silver in my pocket. My elbow was nudged, and I turned to see the beckoning stare of Detective Kimber. Holdsworth was already in the front seat.

"That's half the problem here. Nut cases. Wine

heads. Lice pots," Holdsworth said once I got back into the car.

Kimber got us off the curb, and we drove away from the scene.

"Hit the garage," Holdsworth said. He turned to me. "Let's see what they got off the car."

The car, I said to myself.

As we drove, Holdsworth looked straight ahead, seemingly preoccupied. I thought out loud.

"You still on the street with this? One killer. Remsen and all?"

"So far, yeah," he said. "I'm bright enough not to count nothin' out, but when it happens on the boulevard, with a knife, well, you know. . . . Wrong time a day, though. First one in a car. That's two different strokes. But yeah, I'm still lookin' for the Sunset Slasher. He just bagged a bigger kill, that's all."

We stayed on Sunset until we got to Elysian Park and the entrance to Chavez. Then we turned left and went up Academy Drive, so named for the police academy located there. Elysian Park was all around us.

Kimber parked in front of a low windowless building that I soon realized was a police garage. There were vehicles everywhere, including a new white Cadillac with vanity plates in the center. All its doors were open, revealing a beige-and-brown interior. The seats were soft leather. Nobody was inside. The car apparently had already been tumbled.

A handful of police personnel hovered nearby, and they eyed us as we approached. They were not a cheerful crowd. I stayed with Holdsworth as he walked up to the Cadillac as if he were about to rent it. Then the smell hit me. Blood smell. Body fluids. Urine. It was all there in a putrid wave that hit me like a slap.

I sunk to one knee and tried to shake it off. A technician, a young woman, came over.

"Are you okay?" she said. She was wearing a slight perfume, and the backdraft helped considerably.

It took a few moments of concentrated breathing before I regained some equilibrium. Whatever flush my puss may have had when I arrived was long since gone,

I was certain. The young lady patted my back. Holdsworth and Kimber were leaning inside the front seat of the car, oblivious to my vertigo.

I finally joined them but questioned the wisdom of it. The front seat of the car still had too much of Jack Remsen in it. Blood was spattered all over, on the inside of the windshield, on both doors. The sliced jugular had spurted like a garden hose. It was dried and clotted on the dashboard and steering wheel. It was smeared on the driver's-side door. It was dark red, coppery, and scabbed purple. The rich, milky leather of the front seat was a stew of crimson. The brown carpeting had been stained black.

And again, the smell, the rotting, acid-sour smell. It hung like a damp curtain over the vehicle. I clamped a palm over my nose and mouth. I tried to hang in there. Jack Remsen's life had not ebbed from him, it had gushed out in a fatal frenzy. He'd been gutted and drained.

"When he was cut, he lurched," said one of the evidence officers. "Struggled and flopped around. We got blood prints on the windows and dash. They're all his. We got some fibers and some hair in the backseat. No prints."

I backed off. I had heard and seen enough. For these detectives the car was a laboratory. Let them sift through it. Let them dust and paint and scrape and weigh the residue. For me it was a horror. I knew the man who'd bled, and I wanted to remember him as he was when he breathed. I wanted to see him that way, and only that way. The gut bucket that was parked here sickened me, moved me not to anger or revenge, but revulsion. Jack Remsen's spirit was enough to keep me afloat. His earthly remains belonged to the grave digger.

At that Holdsworth peeled off from the group and went into a nearby office. He was looking at his beeper. A few minutes later he reappeared and came over to me.

"How you feeling, dad?" he said. It was blather, and I shrugged. "Office got a call. Guy wanted to talk to the big colored detective. Guess who? They toyed with him for a while until the guy said he saw me at the scene on Sunset this morning. Then he mentioned you. Described you to a T, Mr. House."

"So what?" I said.

"So the caller said he was our man. Said he was the Slasher. Said he was cleaning up the boulevard. Or something like that."

"Crank?" I asked.

"Was until he told us something he shouldn't a known. Said all the other old guys he'd done in with a straight razor, but that Remsen wasn't. Damn, we listened when he said that, 'cuz it's the one thing we held back. Didn't give it to the papers. Coroner said Remsen's cut had serrated edges to it. Serrated. Like a good bread knife. You know what I mean? Wasn't no way for the caller to know that."

"Good God," I said.

"Called from the street too," he went on. "We locked in the number when it hit our system. Pay phone not far from the taco place. Sent a team there in a hurry, but it didn't help us none."

"He's good. Boy, is he good."

"Worse'n that, he's sane. No rantin'. No horoscopes or voodoo. The crazy ones make mistakes. This guy, godammit, we still don't know why he's doin' it. He never said *that*."

"But he mentioned me?" I asked. "You serious, Jim?"

"Detail. Down to the pen in your shirt pocket. Said you should lose some weight."

"The hell with him."

Holdsworth smiled, but not much.

"Could have been the hairy bum with the big mouth," I said.

"Shit. I seen him before. He's bats. Wouldn't know a straight razor from a toilet plunger."

Then Holdsworth sniffed and ran a big hand over his perspiring brow. He'd already put a lot of hours into this investigation. He fixed his heavy eyes on me. He was a big man, a presence.

"And you ain't gonna like what else he said."

I waited.

"Said you should watch yourself."

7

A Driver

"Stay low. Stay close. Stay cool. Cat like Remsen can get it, don't think *you* can't. You ain't Superman. We got a dare thing here. Killer saw you. Likes your looks. You want a shadow, I can arrange something. Otherwise, watch yourself. You poke around, take somebody with you. Pack something—I'll slide a permit through for ya. And don't go quiet. Call time out once in a while and ring old Long Jim. Your pal. You got a better track record snaggin' bad guys than anybody around here since Sam Spade. And I'm your best buddy till death do us part. Wait a minute, I didn't mean that."

Those were Holdsworth's parting lines. They could have come from Estelle House, my dear mother, may her worrying soul rest carefree. Back then her cautions concerned streetcars and stray dogs, panhandlers, bullies, thugs, and any other ne'er-do-well who might threaten harm against her knickered little lad. That was back in Chicago when the Cubs ruled the National League and the cream of the Dodgers was Zack and Mack Wheat.

My assurances to my mother had been full of blithe unconcern. I was a scamp. I could pitch pennies and dodge streetcars on the red brick streets of Al Capone's Chicago as well as any gamin around. I could bait the tough nuts and run like hell. I would never die.

To Holdsworth I returned no such bravado, false or otherwise. He offered his direct telephone line, the beeper that sent him scurrying to the nearest horn, and I took it.

"This ain't no city of angels," he reminded me.

Cops are paid to admonish. They scrape too many underbellies to be idealistic. To them every human being is a bogeyman, the city is a hellhole. Their world is divided into those who should be handcuffed and those who should be doing the cuffing.

Now I've lived in a tough city all my life, and I've traveled to many more. I've walked down a few dark streets, and I've been mugged more than once. Twice, to be exact. You don't forget that total. In St. Louis a hopped-up kid with a chrome pistol that shook in his hand like an electric toothbrush swore at me for not having more than twenty-five bucks in cash. Yet without puffing myself up as some tough guy, I never felt like giving up an inch of the sidewalk. I never felt afraid.

Until now.

The city of Los Angeles had a rotten taste to it. Sunset Boulevard gave me the creeps. Its denizens were either predators or prey; there seemed to be nobody in between. The neighborhood of the Dodgers, that baseball family living in that flower-draped ravine, had been ravaged by a madman. The sky was dirty, and the air smelled not of orange blossoms but of a friend's caked blood.

Back at the Biltmore my phone light flashed. Two messages—one local, one long-distance—and I recognized both numbers.

Each one could wait. I dialed one of my own first. What I got was an answering machine, but that was okay. Its voice said, "This is Petey. You know what to do." Then it beeped. I smiled. Recorded or real, her voice always made me smile.

Some people my age get transplants, bypasses, or valve jobs. Some people tuck the eyes, bob the nose, or fool with tissue once lofty but which has long since drooped. Some folks just dye the rug. I got Petey. She had tap-danced into my life almost a year ago full of seltzer and had lopped a good twenty years off my psyche.

Petey is short for Petrinella, an old, quirky family name that she could have shortened to Nel but never did. Petey always fit better. She is my little sister Betty's girl, last name of Biggers, a kid with rich red hair, neon green eyes, and a great brain. She also freckles up something fierce in the summer, which drives her nuts. Betty had called me last year to ask if Petey could bunk in until she was ensconced in Northwestern's law school and her own apartment. Before I knew it, she was on a first-name basis with my doorman and had turned my spare bedroom into, if I can use the term loosely, a boudoir. For reasons I have documented elsewhere, she did not make it to law school on opening day. And it took her a few months to move out of my place.

But that was all right. I loved having her. Surprised even myself. As you age, the concrete tends to set. It's not easy having your musty, doily-draped domicile invaded by a twenty-three-year-old rookie with a portfolio of strange music and a predilection for bare feet, Dr Pepper, and peanut-butter-and-banana sandwiches at midnight. On the other hand, she also brought along the personality of Pee Wee Reese and a baseball head better than that on the shoulders of guys I used to share press boxes with. And on top of that, I say with all modesty, she adored me. She hooted at my jokes, pinched my giblets, and dropped references to columns I'd written in the Middle Ages. My place had not known her kind of hurly-burly in a long time, and I liked it.

That was then, before some of the fizz had been shaken from her by an aborted love affair in Gotham. She was deflated, a schooner in the midst of doldrums. She was also on her own in an overpriced apartment and ready to succumb to lectures on torts and contracts at the law school, which still wanted her. She had not asked to come west with me. She had not hollered at the news of Jack Remsen. She hadn't even called since I'd been here.

"Petey," I said to the machine, "this is your uncle.

Your old, cocksure, life-by-the-sack uncle. Veteran scribe, rich man's shamus. I'm out here in what you used to call Hollyweird and Lala-land. The weather is fine and the fruit is fresh and the baseball is played on real grass. The agave are said to run for a century, but who checks?

"I've met some old friends and churned the nostalgia waters. The tapes in my machine are packed with lies and exaggerations. Great stuff for a book, perhaps the one I'm supposed to be completing, but who knows if I ever will?

"See, Pedro, I've also gotten a stomachful of death. The raw version known as murder. I've seen more blood in two days than in a lifetime. At first it was a stranger's, an old guy on the sidewalk, then a friend's, and each time the blood was just as red, just as thick. You read the papers, so you know what I'm talking about. Jack Remsen's blarney still rings in my ears, God love him.

"Look, I've been around. I've counted out more colleagues, cronies, and crumbums than anybody. Written my share of tributes and eulogies for absent friends. I buried my wife. And each time plenty of tears stained my lapel. But that's okay. You don't challenge the tilt.

"But hell, Petey, none of that prepared me for this damn carnage out here. I walked right into some kind of first act where the bodies are flopping like tuna and everybody's got the shakes. Only this isn't a drama, no moving-picture production where the scene board will clap, and we'll all break for lunch. It's real. It's what they're living with out here on the famous Sunset Boulevard. Did I say they? How about I? Me. I'm right in the middle of it. And I don't like it. It doesn't feel good, and I want to leave.

"That's why I called you, Petey. Because I can't leave. I can't just go back to Chicago and call back here now and again to see if Jack Remsen's murderer still roams. I should, but I can't. I can't just say thanks to the guy when he was alive but no thanks now.

"So it should be easy. Grand Chambliss has already said go get 'em. Big police detective told me he'd help me all he could. So what's the problem, Unk, you say? Well, this one's different, that's what. This isn't Chicago, where I could make some calls and touch all the bases. This isn't New York, where the commissioner did the blocking. This is California, Petey, and I don't know where in hell that is.

"Which is to say that I need you. I never thought I'd hear myself say that with regard to this business. But I need you. Call me. And I hope your tape gizmo got all this, because I'm out of wind. I love ya, now bye-bye."

I don't know if that made any sense or not. I do better behind a keyboard than into a phone machine. But Petey would get the idea.

The other calls were easier. The long-distance one was Marjorie, the office commander and right hand of the commissioner of baseball.

"His nibs touches down at seven-ten tomorrow night. LAX. The Czar Suite in the Biltmore. He wishes breakfast with you at seven. Number fifteen-twelve. Sound like fun?"

"I may be late," I said. "This is the West Coast, Marjorie, things are more relaxed out here."

"I'll put a call in to your room," Marjorie said, and she meant it.

"Is this just a social breakfast?" I asked.

"You kidding? He wants chapter and verse on the case. C'mon Duffy, you have a reputation to live up to."

"Uh-oh."

"Come again?" she asked. "What's happening?"

Anybody but Marjorie, a terrific gal who had once treated my niece like a daughter, and I'd have rung off.

"Little," I replied. "A dragnet on Sunset Boulevard. A lot of cops trying to figure out what Jack Remsen did after he left the ballpark that night."

"Do they still think that slasher madman did it?" she asked.

"Sixty-four-thousand-dollar question, Marjorie. Right now it looks that way."

"My God. I remember Son of Sam. People were so scared around here."

"Here too," I said.

"You be careful, Mr. House," she said.

I thanked her for the sentiment, without saying who else had recently suggested that.

"By the way, is there a Czar Suite in the Biltmore?"

"That was a joke," she said, obviously disappointed in me.

"But there should be," I added.

I hadn't put the receiver down long enough to go to the bathroom when it shook anew.

"So what did Holdsworth, the cop, give you?"

Joe Start wasn't one for introductions.

"A ride. Went to the scene on Sunset. Monument Park, Los Angeles style."

"Yeah, we got a photo, color, page one, early edition. They really got tacos on that pile?"

"Yeah. Then the car. Over in the garage near the police academy. Don't photograph that."

"Already did."

I could hear the office din in the background. If Start had gone home, he had not stayed there long.

"Holdsworth is quite an operator, isn't he?" Start went on.

"We got along. What kind of a cop is he?"

"The best. Smart. Cool. If he had a political bone in his body, he'd be chief now. Then again, if he were a politician, he'd be a lousy cop. Where'd he leave it with you two?"

I hesitated on that one. Start was on the record.

"What'd you get from the autopsy?" I asked.

"Whattaya mean?" Joe said, his voice rising.

"Anything on the weapon?"

"Nothing jumped out, that I remember. Long blade. That's all."

"Have your best cop guy check out the weapon," I said. "That's on the record."

"You're shittin' me. There's something there? Goddamn, Duffy, you're good."

"Nothing a cub wouldn't have kicked up."

"Okay, now what's off the record?" Start asked.

"You know, Joe, in my journalism there still is such a thing," I said.

"Mine too," he replied.

"Okay," I said. "The bastard threatened me."

Start held his breath, or at least I didn't hear any lung action on his end.

"He threatened *you*?" he finally asked.

I exhaled. Joe Start was a newspaper man, a colleague, a guy who breathed ink fumes and smelled a bouquet. I didn't have to go over the rule book with him. So I told him what happened according to Long Jim Holdsworth, the phone call, the caller's description of me. And then told Start he had to sit on it. At least for the time being. He had no choice—or, at least, that's what he told me.

"Do me a favor," I said. "Let me take you up on the key to your front door. Right now the city of Alhambra sounds like home to me."

"Done," he said.

We made the necessary arrangements. I told him the commissioner was coming into town, and he told me of other anticipated arrivals among the baseball crowd. The Bums from Brooklyn would be there, including Campanella.

"And hey, Duffy," Start closed, "with that knife business—you're still damn good."

"Save it," I said.

On an offhand chance, I cracked the phone book and ran a finger down the page in search of George Pinckney. He was the George that Nina Remsen had mentioned. Behind his moniker would be CPA, those charming little initials that stand for "where the money is." What Nina had said about Jack's cash outflow nagged at me. I wanted a second opinion from somebody who'd had a look at the spigot.

Base hit. Boldface type, Bank of America Building, only a few blocks from the Biltmore. I called first. It was almost two weeks past tax season, so this guy would have his feet on his desk. But that didn't mean he'd jaw with me about a client.

"Got your column under my blotter," he said. "Right here next to Murray. Downey—he wrote sweet. Rapoport in the Valley. He's good. My sister saves him for me."

I'd tapped into a reader, that voracious animal who reads every word and then rings you up and wants even more. I'd made a living off appetites like his.

"Let me swing by," I said.

"I gotta call Nina."

"Then call Nina. I'll be in your office before you get off the line."

I wasn't, but close enough. Pinckney was pretty much a one-man bean counter. His suite was a shoe-box affair with no waiting area and a lone secretary who sat behind a partition with a sliding glass window. She was a small woman who looked like she admired the writings of S. I. Hayakawa. With an almost imperceptible nod, she sent me back to ledger central.

"Word meister," Pinckney said as I entered. He was a short guy with a white shirt and a wide tie, a thin head of hair, and a thick pair of sideburns. "Word meister, word meister," he continued. I got the drift.

He pointed me to a chair that faced his across from a double desk. It was a big thing, cluttered with files, folders, and, of course, ledgers. A computer hummed behind him. I half expected to stub my elbow on an abacus.

"I read sports. I do. Can't help it. Statistics. Hey, say no more. It's me. Boxscores, need I say more? Here's one for ya."

He went over to a bookshelf full of spiral binders.

"Score books. Every home game. Personally scored. Pencil. Number-two lead. Twenty-three seasons. It's all in there."

I wanted to take out my hanky and signal surrender.

"Amazing," I said, reaching for breath. "And when I'm ever in doubt about Billy Grabarkewitz, I'll tap you."

That he liked.

"Nina said talk turkey. Talk Jack. Mr. Dodger. None better. I'd do his books for nothing," he said. "And now this, well . . . I'm here but I'm not here. Dead. My famous client. I can't deal with it."

I gave him that. He was a numbers man, not a poet.

"Mrs. Remsen said she's got problems now," I said. "Tax problems, what have you."

"Maybe yes. Maybe no. Maybe yes. The restaurant. Oh boy. Bad advice long before I came around. Now it's pay the pipe-pipe-piper."

"Is she in debt?"

"Nooooooo. Jack had great receivables. Nina's in good shape. Got her scheduled very nicely, thank you."

"Hmmm," I grumped. Mr. Sunny-day-CPA sharpened a pencil in an electric sharpener the size of a toaster. "She wasn't as cheery. Said Jack was a soft touch."

"She's right. She's right. He gave it away. Here. There. You have some. You too."

"To whom?"

"Whom. Do you know how few people use 'whom'? Well, don't get me started."

"Who touched him for cash, dammit?" I barked.

"Everybody. His friends. Ball players. The church in Pasadena. He was a very generous man."

"Too generous?"

"Too generous."

"How much to the church?"

"I can't give you a figure."

"Yes you can."

"Five hundred seventy-two thousand over thirty-eight months."

"Sheesh!"

"They're very persuasive people up there. Ever heard the saying 'Chickens come home to roost'?"

"I don't think I have," I said.

"Don't be silly. They know all the tricks. And some

of those tricky tricks can backfire," he observed, arching his eyebrows.

"Gospel?" I asked.

"Gospel according to George Pinckney, thank you."

"No wonder Nina is sour."

"It's deductible. Totally deductible."

"Doesn't matter," I said. "You throw money like that around, and people start to make presumptions."

Pinckney leaned back and calculated that one. The office was getting stuffy.

"Presumptions," Pinckney finally said. "There's no spread sheet for presumptions, now is there?"

He had me.

There was no sense in hanging around the hotel, and the desk didn't exactly break down and cry when I checked out. Celebrity funerals were big business, and my room would be relet in a minute. The Biltmore would house its share of Remsen's cronies, teammates, drinking pals, and of course Hollywood. Everybody from Peter Falk and Chuck Connors—who worked both venues—to James Garner, Charo, and Jack Lemmon. They'd sit around the lobby and the saloons like the old days and tell stories that nobody tired of hearing. There would be a lot of bittersweet laughs, and the truth would take a thrashing.

The switchboard promised to forward my calls to Joe Start's home number, and I had to take their word for it. I ransomed my rented, imported flivver from the garage and, before I aimed its lonely eyes into traffic, did a last-minute cram of my Los Angeles street map. Hill Street to Highway 101 east, better known as the Hollywood Freeway, then Highway 10, the San Bernardino Freeway, to Alhambra. Easy enough.

Downtown traffic obliged me. Stop and go, pedestrians possessed all rights, and nobody laid on the horns. It was late afternoon, and normally I'd groan at the prospect of rush-hour traffic. Ha! In Southern California it seems like every hour is rush hour. Freeway traffic is always chockablock, and the prevailing speed can go from seventy-five to five in a split second. Each automobile looks as if it is towing the automobile behind it. In the paper the other day was a story of a fellow who was stranded on a freeway divide after being struck by a car. He was there for days. Thousands of cars streamed past before an emergency vehicle stopped. The guy almost croaked, not from his injuries but from exposure.

That is what I faced as I turned off Hill onto the ramp that led onto the Hollywood. The driver behind me had the same idea, but he was in a hurry, and the next thing I knew, his door handle was inches away from mine. It was a squeeze. The ramp offered no shoulder, no relief, and no room. I panicked and hit the brakes. The impetuous son-of-a-bitch alongside me shot on ahead at the same moment I was slammed from behind by what felt like a full crew of umpires and an equipment manager. My head snapped back, and my ears rang.

Automobile collisions are like divorces. The details are crucial to those involved, but they bore the molars out of the rest of the world. Suffice it to say that the back end of my jalopy was pushed in like a boxer's puss, and the front right fender was skinned by a guardrail. The car that whacked me, a little yellow squirt of a thing, was leaking from the radiator. There was glass all over the place. And my neck hurt like the devil.

What followed was inconvenience and frustration, wind and freeway dust. I stood on the pavement like an old mope wondering whether to kick, push, or drive my car. I got no help from snarling drivers who had to edge around the mess. The young lady who hit me looked like Debbie Reynolds, cried like Shirley Temple, and swore like Tommy Lasorda. With a flapping cut lip that bled onto her white blouse, she kept sputtering that I had no right to brake on an entrance ramp.

"Shut up," I said.

It was a good two hours later that I limped onto Joe Start's street in Alhambra. It was called Grand, and it was not named after my car, which looked like a wreck but still worked. I had purchased collision insurance when I rented the thing. What a smart boy am I. But my neck was still killing me.

Had I been able to look around with any kind of ease, I'd have seen a street that looked as if it had been plucked from a midwestern small town. Two-story, half-century old stucco and frame houses with chimneys were set back from terraced lawns and sidewalks. Two kids were riding bicycles. It was all refreshingly middle class and unpretentious.

As I let myself in the front door, the phone was ringing. Much slower than you can say "whiplash," I went for a hot towel as some kind of a compress for my neck. Start's floor plan was pretty reasonable, and I soon found what I needed. The damn phone, as if it somehow knew I was there, rang throughout.

"Hello!" I barked.

"Unk! Is that you? Are you all right?"

"No. My neck's on fire. My automobile looks like a train hit it. And somebody with a flair for it wants to slit my throat."

Silence followed, then Petey did what she does best —she laughed. She giggled. She tittered. She found great amusement in the revolting situation of a relative four decades her senior and two time zones away.

"You got my message," I finally said.

"Yup."

"Whattaya think?"

"I think I've never heard you talk like that."

"You think right."

"Why don't you come home?" she asked.

"I can't. I keep seeing the image of a good baseball man dead in the front seat of his car."

"It's a maniac, Unk. Charlie Manson–ville. They'll get him without you."

I breathed deeply and swiveled my head on its axis. The hot towel was doing its stuff.

"If so, fine. Until then I'm here, and I need you, and I already told you why. The game is—"

"Don't say it."

"Whatever. You game?"

She sighed.

"What a turnabout," she said. "A few months ago I'd already be in your lap."

"Book a flight. I'll help ya forget the Manhattan blues."

"I'm already scheduled. What do you take me for, a stone? I'll be in around noon on Monday. As for the blues, we'll see."

"Atta girl."

"And what was that you said about your car?"

"Christ. That's another reason why you have to get out here. I need a *driver*. I just got rear-ended on the Hollywood Freeway. My rental heap is just that. Looks like a Zamboni machine that never made it off the ice."

Petey gulped.

"Oh, Unk," she said.

"Oh, Unk," I echoed.

8

The Reverend
Billy Harbridge

Joe Start's house smelled like the inside of an old book. Windows stuck shut, cobwebs stretched taut across lampshades, a refrigerator full of expired dates. Start lived at the *Times* and ate in restaurants; his house caught him every night like a backstop. It was a handsome place—full of unpainted woodwork, high ceilings, and a wide oak staircase leading upstairs from the center of the first floor—but it was stiff with neglect. As I walked around, the floors creaked as if they were happy just to have the exercise.

I went upstairs to check in. Joe's bedroom door was open, and from the hallway I could see that the insides were not pretty. My quarters were two doors down, a spare bedroom with a single bed and a single window. On one wall was a color poster of Jerry West, and on another wall was a color poster of Don Sutton. Both had been autographed to "Eddie." The room was obviously the former domain of Joe's kid, and Eddie Start liked his heroes blond.

The bed was mush, but the sheets were clean, even if they did smell of cardboard. A pair of lonely track trophies had so much dust on them that the figures looked my age. Any minute now I expected a bat to fly out of the shadows. From the window I could see tree leaves and buds and lots of other chlorophyll holders. With a grunt that shot a lance through my aching neck, I opened the window and got a breeze. The whole house needed a breeze. But that was okay. To a free-loader like me, the place was the Ritz. I unpacked my travel wardrobe and settled in.

While there was not a living plant or a piece of interior decorating newer than the Dodgers' seventy-seven yearbook, the house was crammed with books, magazines, and televisions. Whole walls in the living room and den were lined with volumes—sports, history, current affairs, literature. Stacks of magazines on everything from foreign affairs to pro football littered the floor like boulders. And I counted a television in every downstairs room—a red one sat atop the refrigerator—except the toilet. There were magazines there.

I nosed around a little and nursed my neck with a hot towel. I found a beaker of grapefruit juice and nursed it with vodka. In no time I was lost in peace and quiet, the house having plenty of that to spare. Grand Avenue was not Sunset Boulevard, thank goodness. I started picking through Start's library, pausing with Shelby Foote and Garry Wills, Studs Terkel, and Harry Mark Petrakis. I lingered long in something called *Toscanini's Fumble*, by a smart doctor of neurology named Harold Klawans that told me why J. Rodney Richard, the enormous smoke-throwing pitcher for the Astros, suffered a stroke.

From a bag of rock-hard bagels in the freezer and a passable crock of cheddar cheese, I made myself dinner. I went out and sat on the front stoop and munched it to the crickets and birds and other night sounds of the neighborhood—a beautiful April evening in Alhambra. I rolled the name over my tongue. I had been to the real McCoy many years ago, stayed in a Granada hotel with a balcony view of the old Moorish palace, and walked into the hills. My lover and I succumbed to the blandishments of a Gypsy boy, who for an exorbitant sum led us to a hillside cave home bedecked with copper pots, where we drank Spanish wine and listened to an old man play the classical guitar. The boy said the old man was Segovia. I sighed and put my arm around my young wife. The boy called us honeymooners. Looking around Joe Start's real estate, I could hear his Castillian lisp as clear as yesterday. There was not a soul walking on the street. Nobody to see me, an old fool, put my arm around an imaginary mate.

Start called a little later to see if I had been able to work the front-door key. I told him about my collision on the freeway ramp, and he told me where to find the heating pad for my neck. He told me to have the run of the place.

"The neighbors won't bother ya," he said. "Nobody bothers me. I wish they would."

He added that he did not know when he would get in and that I should not wait up for him. I said I had not planned on it.

"I'll cook you Sunday-morning eggs," he said.

That was news to me. I didn't even know today was Saturday.

I turned in before Joe came home and got involved in a nasty dream. It was full of people running and brawling. Somebody was driving off with Jack Remsen's Cadillac, and Preston Gomez was yelling in Esperanto about catching the bastard. Rick Monday ran out and grabbed the American flag, and there were three men on third base—Vance, Fewster, and Herman—and I had to make the call, but I didn't have any pants on.

My beef is that I rarely dream. Dreams, I believe, are the brain's ashcan. What you don't need, what does not make sense, what the mind is trying to sweep off the slate, mishmashes together while you're under. Unless they wake me, I take no significance from them. This one woke me.

I smelled coffee, eggs, toast, sausage—the whole menu. Either Start was up and cooking, or my window was getting a backdraft from Ralph's Big Boy. I also awoke to a mockingbird practicing his vibrato in the tree outside my window. Mockingbirds don't even visit cousins as far north as Chicago, so I liked his number.

I put on a bathrobe and padded into the kitchen. Start had on a California Angels apron over a sweatsuit and was working the stove top.

"Good morning," he said.

"Took the words right out of my mouth."

"That car of yours is a mess. Are you any better?"

"I'll live. Feel like Frank Howard ran over me, but I'll live."

"Eggs?"

"Over easy. Don't you sleep, Joe?"

"Not much lately. I've lost the knack. You get any?"

"Plenty, thank you. This home is like a tomb."

The eggs sizzled and soon joined a platter with hash browns, pork sausage, and wheat toast.

"This is terrific, Joe. You're a homemaker."

"I can cook eggs. Look around this place. Look like a made home to you?"

He lifted the plates and led me to a small sun porch in back. We sat down on a glider sofa that was a big seller when Snooky Lanson was belting out "Your Hit Parade." Joe cleared the Sunday papers off a low table, and we dug in. Coffee, juice, wedges of cantaloupe—we lacked for nothing. It was downright pleasant.

"Crack a few windows, will ya?" I said.

"Yeah. Great idea," Joe replied.

The outside air converged with the smells of the grub.

"Is that orange blossom?" I asked, recognizing the cloying redolence.

"That's it," Start said. "Rose planted the daylights out of this place. Now I hire a kid to cut it back. Look at that. Got a lemon tree out there. Bougainvillea, agave. It used to be quite a garden."

"What's the lavender flower I see all over the freeways—lights up the hillsides?"

"Ice plant. A succulent ground cover. It's bombproof. Been known to stop grass fires."

He went on to point out gazanias, birds of paradise, something with exotic red spikes called bottlebrush, freeway daisies, the count went on. Though he had no time, or perhaps no interest, to give to the garden, he was not ignorant of it.

"No palms?"

"Rose didn't like 'em. Neighbor over there has a

date palm. The trunk that looks like a pineapple. It's a valuable tree. Developers putting up hotels and malls always want them. If it's California, it's gotta have palm trees, so they come around and will offer as much as a thousand bucks for the large or unusual ones. Come in your yard with a back hoe, dig out a root cluster about the size of a medicine ball, and carry it off on a truck. Or sometimes they don't ask. There's a big black market in stolen palm trees."

I ate and listened. I had not had a good plate of eggs for a few days now. Old guys like Joe and me like eggs, eat them all the time and anytime. There are few pleasures comparable to meeting somebody in a delicatessen at three A.M. and having a plate of eggs. Omelets, eggs and corned-beef hash, salami and eggs, fried egg sandwiches daubed with mayonnaise. Sop up the yolk with the leftover toast. The arteries grow more clogged at the very thought of it.

"That a eucalyptus over there, with bark like a sycamore?" I asked, trying to keep him going.

"Hell, Duffy, everything out here's eucalyptus. There's gotta be over two hundred varieties in California alone. You know how they got here, don't ya? Came from Australia in the 1800s. Some bird decided there was a fortune in railroad ties in them. Trouble is, the ones they used were Tasmanian blue gums—great name for a ballclub, huh? Real fast growing, but when they put them down for ties, they split. Railroad spikes popped out of the wood like corks out of a bottle. How do you like that? Now they use 'em for cough drops, and that's about it."

"Chapter and verse, Joe. Luther Burbank would be proud."

"Us newspaper types. Know a little about everything and not a lot about much."

He got up, and the next thing I knew, the television on top of the refrigerator was on. It had to have been habit. I didn't think I bored him that much. The set remained on even though he returned to the porch with more coffee.

"This is nice, Joe," I observed. "You've got every-thing here."

He sniffed.

"I'm the loneliest man on earth, Duffy," he said.

I decided to leave that one alone. From the kitchen came a caterwaul.

"Oh Jee-zus!" it went.

"Oh Jesus," I said. From Father Devine to Oral Roberts to the Jimmies Bakker and Swaggart, airwave evangelists have never been my balm.

"I am receiving the vibrations of a man . . . who has been troubled in his neck!" said the preacher.

Joe smiled over his coffee.

"Healing is on the way," he said.

"You foul demonic spirits of infirmity," the preacher went on shouting, his volume rising, "I command you to go in the name of Jee-zus. Neck, be healed. I decree miracles today."

"Well, maybe he *is* clairvoyant," I said.

"Hallelujah! We're just gonna bind that cancer!" came the TV cry, as if on cue.

"You don't tune in the preachers on purpose, do you?" I asked.

"Not even for comic relief. I don't even know who this sleazy snake charmer and Bible thumper is. But I did want to hear Billy today."

"Billy?"

"Billy Harbridge. As in 'Billy Harbridge's Home of Hope, broadcasting live from God's House of Glass.' "

"Include me in," I said, remembering Nina Remsen's remarks about Jack's favorite pastor.

Start got up and went to the kitchen. Before he changed the channel, the voice chanted, "Oika maynay go-la go, lamba sanai, doo-be dah." It was either the snake charmer speaking in tongues or the chatter of a Manny Mota coaching third. The change of channels replaced it with a peal of trumpets and a resounding pipe organ.

"This guy got in with Remsen," Joe said from the kitchen. "He's up in Pasadena. Not that far from here. Take a listen, Duffy."

I grunted and lifted my carcass from the couch. It was comfortable but hard to get out of. My neck was still stiff. I took my coffee with me and joined Joe as he gazed up at the set. The camera lovingly panned the shining faces of a large, prosperous congregation sitting in a cathedral bathed in the sunlight streaming through a ceiling of glass. Billy Harbridge, looking every bit as beatific and coiffed as he had in the photo with Remsen, stood behind a glass pulpit dressed in a billowing black robe with velvet patches on the biceps. His face seemed to glow; either that or Joe's television had a tint problem.

"Biggest prophet out here right now," Joe said.

"How do you spell that?" I mused.

We watched. Harbridge was good, a polished vicar who'd merged his deep South patois with the glib, genial presence of a game-show host. He waved a leather-bound, gilt-edged Bible, a beautiful, costly volume that sagged slightly in his hand. After several minutes of invocations, salutations, commercials for mementos from the House of Glass, and a fawning introduction of his celebrity guest, Harbridge got down to the pith.

"We lost a true friend this week," he began. His voice lowered and his expression fell.

"Jack Remsen. That great manager of the Los Angeles Dodgers. A man who worshiped with us in this very tabernacle. Praise God!" Then Billy broke a smile. "Why, Jack used to say, 'Reverend Billy, you know I pray to that Big Dodger in the Sky' . . ." The congregation chortled; the camera dipped down and caught the smiles. ". . . 'but I think God understands.' Oh, what a great joy in life that man had. But hear me now, Christians, Jack was very close to me, and he confessed that, as with every one of us, behind that big happy face all was not always right in his life. . . ."

"Do tell, pastor," Joe said.

". . . Satan hounds us all. He looks for any opening. Here was Jack Remsen. A man *loved*. A celebrity. A *winner*. And yet in counseling, Jack told me of things in his life he was not proud of. Personal things. Things that all Christians struggle with . . ."

"Come on," Joe said, "come on."

"We got on our knees and prayed together. Praise God! And Jack learned from Scripture, from the lessons of King David. King David, as we know, had a great self-image, but he was not always honest with God and had some problems of his own making. . . ."

He went on from there, not with Jack Remsen and the personal demons of the head Dodger, but with King David of Israel. After ten more minutes of David, who had a good run but wouldn't make Cooperstown, Joe doused the set.

"Bait and switch, Billy," he groused.

"Think he knows anything?"

"Doubt it," Joe said. "But Harbridge was in there, I'll say that for him. Remsen played the church angle real hard, and Billy's show is pretty rich. Jack bought into it, Duffy."

"Personal problems . . ." I said, thinking out loud.

"Yeah, do we take the pitch or swing away on three-and-oh?" Joe quipped.

I tossed the thing around for the rest of the day. There was not a lot else to toss around. While the papers were still aflame with the Remsen murder story, not much was to be found in them. The *Times* reported the coroner's belief that a different knife had been used. Thank you. It did not report the call to Holdsworth's office, or the reference to me. Joe Start had sat on that. Detectives, including Long Jim, only said that they had received a lot of calls and several confessions, and each one was being investigated. They always said that.

That afternoon I called the Home of Hope broadcast. It took some doing. Reverend Harbridge's office had many rings of defense, and my queries were deflected like unanswered prayers. Then I reverted to the clout of the commissioner's office. It was a shameless hammer, but it worked. In no time I had an appointment with the head glazier of God's House of Glass.

Start nodded indifferently when I told him.

"For lack of physical evidence, go after the spiritual," he said.

"Maybe Billy knows what Jack was doing on Sunset Boulevard at that time of night," I ventured.

Jack scratched his head and grunted. Something was eating him. I liked the guy, and I thought he was a hell of a newspaperman and a first-rate breakfast chef, but he was kind of a grouch. A sourpuss. I've had a little experience in the area.

"Go after it," Joe said. "Remsen was a big shot. As far as I'm concerned, I'm still interested in getting the bastard who's killing those guys on the street. Haven't heard much about *them* lately."

It was a statement, and a pretty sincere one. But it was not an invitation to debate, and he went off and took a bath. Joe was okay. Not a day at the beach, but okay.

The next morning, before I returned the battered rental to the agency for a new one, I aimed it in the direction of Pasadena. At one I was to pick up Petey. From Alhambra's streets I found my way onto Highway 110, the Pasadena Freeway. According to Start, it was the oldest, and in some ways the most primitive, of this country's freeways. A dubious but significant feat of engineering, to be sure. It cuts and curves relentlessly through the deep ravine that it shares with the historic Arroyo Seco, the valley channel between Pasadena and Los Angeles. The sides of the ravine were covered with ice plant in full bloom, a shimmering magenta coat ruffling in the wind like fur on an animal. But as I wound through the parks and green areas of South Pasadena, the freeway was so narrow I was getting claustrophobia. With a waist-high concrete wall on the left and a forbidding chain-link fence on the right, I had all I could do to mind the curves and stay in my lane.

Then, almost without warning, the original freeway pulled up, stopped, and became Arroyo Parkway, a city street in Pasadena, proud home of old California money and the Rose Bowl. I passed enough banks, utilities, and mortgage offices to make me feel like I was playing Monopoly; but the street was also peppered with Earl Scheib auto-painting galleries, flower shops, and drive-ins called Fatburger.

Arroyo Parkway stopped, as Billy Harbridge's secretary had said it would, and I turned right on Holly. Dead ahead, looming in front of me like something out of Baghdad, was city hall. Not just your average pile of granite, this beige stone hall, with its dome of fish-scale tile, looked like a Moslem place of worship. Any minute I expected the imam to pop out and call morning prayers. Speaking of places of worship, Pasadena proper was lousy with them, some of the biggest holy houses I had seen anywhere.

The wide, bleached run of Holly Street intersected with the equally wide Garfield in front of city hall, and following instructions, I took a wide left and an immediate right on Ramona, and saw the low county courts building a second before I espied Harbridge's see-through palace. God's House of Glass occupied nearly a city block, and its atrium in the center looked like the world's largest hothouse.

After finding a parking space, I entered on the Euclid Street side and found myself in a bookstore—Pastor Wayne's Book Ministry, the sign said. It was a large, happy place, with bright displays and posters and stacks of books that fairly insisted on being read. A closer look told me that these were of the uplifting genre, the inspirational, testimonial, and mystical. There were life stories of Orel Hershiser, he of the gifted wing, Dave Dravecky, he of the wounded wing, and Tom Landry, he of the right wing. Nearby was a life-size cardboard likeness of Charles Colson, that born-again author and former Nixon henchman. The cutout was so lifelike I thought at first that Chuck was a browser.

"Yes, sir," said a voice across the way, and I spotted a tall, skinny man with a bald head and bifocals.

I walked over and read Wayne Bornholdt on his name tag. Pastor Wayne in the flesh, I presumed.

"I seek the Reverend Bill Harbridge," I said.

"The venerable Duffy House, no doubt," he said.

I lifted my eyebrows.

"Word passes fast around here," said Pastor Wayne,

a grin creasing his forehead a good way back. "Jackie said somebody from the commissioner's office was coming, and I knew it had to be you."

He came around the counter and held out his hand.

"I want to shake the hand of my favorite sportswriter. Right here in my own bookstore."

"I'm humbled," I said.

He laughed. Threw up a rolling guffaw from deep within his spare Nordic belly.

"I got you goin', huh? See, I used to run a shop in Hyde Park. Fifty-fifth Street and Kenwood. You bet. Back in the days of Fox and Aparicio. Greatest keystone combo there ever was. Read 'On the House' every day. Chicago *Daily News.* Jungle Jim Rivera. Landis. Billy Pierce. Hey, I know you've tried to get Nellie Fox into the Hall. Boy, do I admire that."

Pastor Wayne spoke in bursts. Pods of spittle formed in the corners of his mouth when he paused. He reached below the counter and produced a black White Sox cap, the fifties version with the diagonal interlocking Sox in front.

"That's a keeper," I said.

Wayne beamed and put the cap on his head like a crown. It sunk down to his ear valleys. He looked like a bald Earl Torgeson. There wasn't much commerce in the store, and I could see he would go on with the verbal White Sox pepper forever.

"Tell me, Wayne, did Jack Remsen come around here much?"

"Shoot, I'm no Dodger fan—ten years here and I *still* don't go for 'em. But I liked Jack. And hey, I just want to say this for the record: your piece in the *Times* on Remsen was perfect. *Perfect.* I told everybody, it was just like old times. Back in Chicago you spun one of those out every day of the week. That's the gospel truth, Mr. House."

"You're a man of taste and impeccable reading habits," I said.

He nodded in agreement.

"Was Remsen a regular here?"

"Right, I forgot. Sure, he came in often. Pastor Will can give you an earful on that."

"Where do I go?"

"Oh, right. Hey, I can't believe it. Duffy House of Chicago, Illinois, right here in my shop. See anything you like? It's yours."

I nodded and eyed the cutout of Colson but scotched the notion in a hurry. The White Sox devotee directed me into the sanctum sanctorum of the glasshouse. It had thick carpeting, low light, and muted religious pop music piped in overhead. It could have passed for the corporate office of any outfit ripe for purchase by the Japanese. People smiled, computers hummed. Secretaries who looked like Cyndi Garvey in her Mrs. Steve days lifted eyebrows at me.

I paused at the desk of one of them. Then the Reverend Harbridge appeared.

"Aha!" he said, and smiled with thick, righteous lips.

Don't believe them when they tell you people look different on TV. Harbridge looked as if he had jumped out of the set and landed in front of me. Only his flowing robe was missing, replaced by a gray business suit of the latest fashion and a yellow tie. He was a tall guy, and solid, a Jerry Reuss with silver hair. The coiffure was as big as ever, thick, unmussed, and intimidating. And Harbridge's Southern California complexion was still picture-tube radiant. When he thrust his hand in my direction, it brought along a trace of cologne, the rugged stuff worn by guys who rustle cattle. That you don't get with the broadcast.

"Welcome, Mr. House. I'm Pastor Will," he said.

I smiled and mumbled something inane.

"Convey my regards to the commissioner," he said. "I met Mr. Chambliss once. He's what the game needs."

He turned on a heel and motioned me into his office.

"Have you seen the sanctuary?" he asked. "It is impressive. I'd give you the tour, but I'm a little late."

He did not speak; he declaimed. Words bounded from his lips like stones from a slingshot. When I was a kid, I listened to Billy Sunday on the radio with my parents. Sunday had quite a following even if he did lead the push for prohibition. My dad thought he was goofy, but he liked listening to goofy.

This Reverend Billy reminded me of that Reverend Billy—same clipped delivery, same cocksure demeanor. Of course, Billy Sunday had played outfield for the old Chicago Cubs before the century turned and the Bible bug bit him. His baseball roots gave him some credibility with my dad, even though they bothered his fundamentalist friends. Back then ball players weren't considered model citizens. But when it came to the broadcast mike and pounding the pulpit as if it were the palm of his bear-greased fielder's mitt, there was none better than Sunday.

Harbridge's office was as well-appointed as he was, but it was not the furnishings that caught my eye. What did was a wall of framed photographs, some black-and-white, some in rich colors, reminiscent of the Jack Remsen gallery. Billy himself beamed in each one of them. Beaming back were presidents, entertainers, senators, athletes, and of course Jack Remsen.

I did not have much time to gawk at the images, because the good reverend wanted to get down to business. He directed me to a chair, but he stayed on his feet. Just before my tuchis hit the cushion, I noticed a framed piece of flowery needlework in the midst of the montage. 'Remember, Dog Spelled Backwards Is Still Man's Best Friend,' it said. I winced.

"What did the commissioner have in mind?" Harbridge asked.

"I'm told you have quite a counseling program here. And Jack Remsen was part of it."

He faced me full front and formed his palms in the shape of a church steeple.

"We do many things here, Mr. House. Ours is a holistic approach. We care about the body, soul, and spirit. When it comes to human character, I'm reminded of what Jesus said to Nicodemus. You know, Jesus and Nicodemus were talking, and a breeze was blowing through the trees at some distance from them.

And Jesus said to Nicodemus, 'You see how the breeze blows through the tops of the trees over there. Yet down here we don't feel any. There is always an underlying uncertainty about life—unseen, yet it is somehow always there. The breeze blows where it will, and *we* cannot always tell.' "

Harbridge lowered his hands and smiled assuredly. I didn't have a clue as to what he was talking about.

"Jack Remsen," I said, trying to get the compass needle back on the trail.

Harbridge cleared his throat.

"Yes. Jack was a dear friend. He came here for spiritual and personal needs."

"Needs? Whose needs? His or yours?"

"I'm not sure I follow you."

"Sure you do, Reverend," I said. "Jack came here with his checkbook. He laid more panes in this place than Pittsburgh Plate Glass did."

Billy Harbridge pursed his lips and all but cued the organist. He was a master at holding the pulpit.

"Jack Remsen came here with needs. But what I am about to tell you must go no further than the commissioner's office."

"Who do you think I am, Dear Abby?" I said. "Don't worry about a spill."

"Jack had a problem with self-esteem," Pastor Will confided. "You may or may not know that his mother died when he was very small. As a young boy, Jack was abused terribly by his father. He struggled throughout his life with self-image like no man I've known. To the world he was Mr. Dodger. More than that—he was Mr. Baseball. But inside himself he never believed it."

It made some sense. Remsen had come from hardscrabble folk in the hills of Pennsylvania. California was an acquired taste for him.

"He never really accepted the reality of Christ inside himself," Harbridge went on. "At times he confessed to me that he was tormented. Angry! Self-destructive. We prayed much about that together."

The pastor paused and exhaled with perfect pitch and exquisite timing. It was no time to interrupt.

"And yet he was such an exuberant man," he went on. "So full of life! A physical man. Baseball is a physical game, you know. He was a lover of the world, of people. A lover of the flesh!"

Harbridge was getting warm now. When today's video preachers start warbling about the flesh, they know whereof they speak.

"Mr. House, I only bring this to your attention because it might shed some light on the evil that transpired that night. 'Vengeance is mine, saith the Lord,' but I know we would all benefit if the killer was caught.

"The simple fact is, Jack was drawn to women. It was a thorn in his side. He could not explain it. He loathed himself afterwards. But like the apostle Paul, who also had deep sexual lust, Jack was only beginning to overcome it. And too little, too late, I fear." He lowered his head and seemed willing to let me cut in.

I paused before saying anything. I had been a fellow traveler with professional ball players for thirty years. What Billy Harbridge had just revealed didn't exactly hit me like a ton of bricks. Room service has always meant different things to different guys.

"He dipped, huh? Did he tell you that?" I asked.

"He was not cavalier about it, Mr. House. He was ashamed," Harbridge insisted.

"But on Sunset Boulevard? Did he actually tell you he went down there for the action?"

"I told him Jesus too was found among the poor and lowly of the street, among the homeless and the prostitutes."

It was time for me to smile.

"He didn't buy that, did he?" I said. "This was your game. You found a pitch he couldn't hit and kept throwing it at him. And every one had a price tag. Like an indulgence, right, Reverend? Jack had to pay up. He had to keep those big gifts coming in."

At that he looked at me as if I were the lead camera. The man had a pair of beacons, a little too fluid for my tastes, but when he locked them on you, there was no denying the gaze.

"Do you know *Him*?"

"Huh?"

"Do you yourself know the assurance of God's grace?"

I ran a paw over my mouth to buy a little time on that one. Harbridge was a fisher of men, and in his eyes I was a lunker bass. I wasn't going to bite.

"I've made my bargain with the man upstairs, Reverend. But you know what it could mean, don't you, if Jack was down there with a whore—"

"I did not say that, Mr. House. I did not say that at all. I said only that Jack was struggling with temptation. Temptation sometimes led him to Sunset Boulevard. Let no man put words in my mouth. Only Jack and his Creator know where he went and what he did after he left the stadium. Until he met up with the murderer, of course."

I lifted my palms. I did not want to press the issue. The man from the House of Glass had tapped into an unseen side of Jack Remsen. It put a whole new spin on things.

Reverend Harbridge lightly clapped his hands together. It was a benediction: my time was up.

"You know, Reverend," I said as I rose to leave, "I've never questioned the eye-on-the-sparrow line. If it makes people feel good to think that somebody is watching over them, then that's okay by me. But with what happened to Jack that night, I have to think the Big Dodger in the Sky must have been shelling a peanut," I said, apologizing to Roger Angell even as I said it.

Reverend Billy's eyes narrowed to slits the size of a mustard seed.

"Mr. House," he said, "the fires of hell are stoked by sacrilege."

9

Darby O'Brien

Having spritzed kerosene on the fires of hell, I made a clean exit from the House of Glass. There's an old axiom in the sportswriting business that whenever you talk to management, you have to take something off the top. Harbridge definitely was management; yet even allowing for what I had to skim off his spiel, his tip on Remsen's nocturnal wanderings was worth savoring. It would explain not only what Jack might have been doing down on Sunset Boulevard, but also that he had a working knowledge of the street.

Indeed, Remsen may well have hungered for more than just a soft-shell taco that night, and it might pay to talk to some of the people who sated his appetites. Then again, Harbridge had shoved me awfully hard in the direction of the street and did so when I got too close to talking cash and the House of Glass. If that wasn't the back of the hand, nothing was, and I knew I couldn't let Reverend Billy deflect me that easily.

But first I had a date with a redhead. Petey's plane was coming in at one o'clock, and I had to meet it. I also had made arrangements to exchange my ravaged rental for a new one at the airport agency. I was looking forward not only to ridding myself of this pleated machine but to occupying the passenger's seat of the new one. All that was to take place not at LAX, which was, as I stood in Pasadena, a maze of freeways away from me, but at the Ontario International Airport. The Ontario tarmac was a suburban airport located due east of downtown Los Angeles, past Claremont and Terry Larkin's house, almost to San Bernardino. My map said it was a pretty straight run from Pasadena on Highway 10, the San Bernardino Freeway, once I dropped down to it.

I drove there without incident, which is to say that nobody hit me. All around my beater, however, in automobiles of every vintage and price range, was the phenomenon of "carcooning." It is a horrible coinage, one used by local papers to describe the way California commuters cram their cars with appliances, office machines, stereos, and communication devices. I swear I saw my fellow drivers making espresso and sending fax-machine documents while they effortlessly changed lanes. The term, as offensive as it would be to Noah Webster, fit these characters.

Ontario International was smaller than its name, but fine with me. Airports are places to get out of, as far as I'm concerned. I've been in too many of them, which means I've been stranded in many more. Ontario's reminded me of airfields back when planes had propellers and you walked out on the runway to get on board. It had a no-frills parking lot and a no-nonsense terminal. Yet it was big enough to accept a silver-skinned airship from out of the dry desert sky. My deliverance was to be in the form of a sleek, freckled young passenger who scarcely needed assistance in order to fly.

From the carport walkway at the gate, I watched as she skipped down the steel steps of the ramp. You couldn't miss her: the single red braid, the oversized sunglasses, a snug T-shirt that listed the world's endangered species tucked into a pair of faded jeans that lengthened her already-long legs, and a pair of ankle-high white-and-neon-green sneakers. Women of twenty-three tend to have an inside track on good looks, and Petey was a front-runner. Not only that, but she smiled a lot, a happy, cocky smile, which she was smiling now, just lighting up an already sun-soaked runway.

I did nothing when she came in but open my arms. She was in them like a child. We hugged, and I knocked into her sunglasses and a set of earphones hanging around her neck and the cassette recorder clipped onto her belt and a copy of *The Sporting News* in her left hand. I didn't feel a thing.

Then she stepped back and grinned like Carl Erskine.

"I'm *here*, Unk," she said.

"And not a minute too soon," I said.

"Fresh arm from the bullpen . . ."

"And better looking than Clem Labine."

She stopped at that, raised a finger, and said, " 'Turn back the hands of time / Oh where oh where is Clem Labine?' "

"You've been reading again," I said, certain she'd picked that up out of the library written on the Brooklyn boys.

"Always," she said.

"Luggage?"

"Just a grip or two," she said, and turned in the logical direction of the baggage wagon.

I turned and took a step, and suddenly the horizon tipped. My foot caught something solid, and I tripped, staggered, and fell like a drunk. It was a headfirst dive with second base nowhere near.

"Whoa, Uncle Duffy," Petey said, and came after me like a good medic. Two little kids and a sailor ran up. I was a spectacle.

"What the—!" I sputtered, and then saw that my foot had been ambushed by a bloated canvas bag, bright red in color and looking like something the Cardinals would fill with scuffed baseballs. It was Petey's. I knew because I had tripped over the damn thing before. I got up and limped around like Bill Buckner.

"Anything broken? Busted?" Petey asked.

"Hip pointer. Same one I got the first time we met," I said, which was not altogether true, but Petey knew what I meant.

"You've got to stop that, Unk, or I'll have to get you one of those alert buttons that calls out the MASH unit when you've fallen and can't get up—or the Clapper."

"Don't be glib with my infirmities," I said.

In the meantime we collected her bags and between us were able to schlepp them outside and over to my zephyr. At the sight of it, Petey started laughing. She dropped her bags and just honked like a seal.

"Look at this thing!" she cried. "You weren't kidding!"

She skipped around the crinkled auto, clucking as she went, obviously amused.

"How 'bout the other guy?" she said.

"Girl. Little matchbox car. It didn't do well. She cut her lip and swore at me."

"Now what? Can you drive this?"

"Right over to the rental counter," I said. "They know I'm coming."

The whole process was relatively painless. I had the papers, and the agency ladies did not give me a hard time. The only snag came when they wanted a local address and I could not find Joe's. I knew Joe Start lived on Grand Avenue in Alhambra, but I couldn't remember the number, nor did I have the scrap of paper on which I'd written it down. The clerk said to forget it, but it irked me, and I gave Joe a call at the *Times*.

I caught him, got the number, and figured our conversation was over.

"Good you called, Duffy. Now it's my turn to give you something," Start said. "I got a tip from an old buddy of mine. Used to work horse racing in the sports section. Now he does it full-time in Vegas. Said Remsen had a girlfriend there. Serious stuff. Used all his Vegas buddies as beards and spent some solid time with this lady. Been going on a few years now."

"Got a name?" I asked.

"Would I bother you if I didn't have a name? Goes by Darby O'Brien. Gal in her late thirties. Been around the bases a few times. Course, most people in Vegas have. She's a blackjack dealer. Good hands."

"How public is this?"

"My boy says it's way inside, and not likely to get out. Those who know don't tell, and all that stuff. Even the columns don't know."

I told him I'd get on it. Then I gave him Billy

Harbridge's dope on Jack's curbside activities on Sunset Boulevard.

Start whistled into the receiver.

"A steady in Vegas, quickies in the front seat on Sunset Boulevard—what an appetite. Can't a guy take pills for something like that?"

"You're asking me?" I replied.

While we packed Petey's luggage into the new car, this one a wine-red Buick made in the U.S. of A., I told her what Joe Start had just told me.

"Why, Jack Remsen, that big sleaze," she said. "All the hype about the family and the Big Dodger in the Sky and his faithful wife of forty years—and he's gettin' it on the side."

"Another icon dashed," I said.

"I mean it, Uncle Duffy. I'm so sick of philanderers."

"Good. Nice to see you incensed again."

She slid onto the burgundy velour of the front seat, adjusted the mirror, and kicked the Buick alive.

"Let's go find her," she said.

"What? Her?" I asked, strapping myself in. "You mean the other woman?"

"You got it. I wanna hit the ground running."

"Shoot, Petey, she's in Las Vegas. That's in a different *state*."

"We're halfway there already, Unk. This is the wild west. A few hours on the road is nothing!"

"Are you nuts? This is no little junket. First we've got to get there. Then we've got to find the woman. Then we've got to convince her to talk to us. Then we've got to come back home because I didn't pack a toothbrush. And wait—for cryin' out loud—I got a seven o'clock breakfast with Grand Chambliss tomorrow."

"Great. Come on, Unk. You're the one who said the game was afoot. I say let's go. I'm ready. Been sitting in a plane for three hours, and my butt's itchy. Let's get to Vegas, find the woman, grill her, and come back. You can nap on the way. Trust me, Unk. The cavalry is here."

"You sound like . . . like Lucille Ball!" I blustered.

"Lu-cee!" she cackled.

I let her go. I'd asked her to come here, and here she was.

"This is quite a change, I might add, from someone who didn't want to come to California in the first place," I said.

"Park it or drive it, I figure. Now it's time to drive it."

"No, it's crazy," I said.

"Unk," she goaded with a grin as confident as a seal on a rock, "that's *us.*"

I insisted that we make some phone calls first. We bluffed, cajoled, and lied a little to ascertain that Darby O'Brien was a blackjack dealer at Excalibur, a new giant on the Las Vegas Strip, and that she was working until ten tonight. That was good enough for Petey. She nudged her sunglasses from the top of her head to the bridge of her nose and set off. She was incorrigible. She also had the wheel.

Before I could get my bearings—or say Rancho Cucamonga—Petey had turned north on I-15 off a spaghetti junction of ramps and soon got up to speed. In fact, I looked out my window to see if the flaps were down and takeoff was imminent. She was a casual driver, every bit as assured in California freeway traffic as I was unnerved.

We quickly sped north, past the pastel houses of Cucamonga nestled below the foothills, and headed right into the San Gabriel Mountains. We climbed out of the smog, that low-lying, nicotine-yellow cloud, bypassing San Bernardino, home of the first McDonald's hamburger, Petey informed me, pushed north again, and climbed some more. A sign said, Avoid Overheating. Turn Off Air Conditioning Next 15 Miles. That and a good deal of ear popping told us we were getting into cheap-seats altitude.

The map told us that we were in the San Bernardino National Forest. But to a midwesterner it was no forest at all. The mountains and foothills were brown and gravelly, covered with tumbleweed, scrub palms, yuccas, and some bush evergreens. It was a sort of mountain dregs, strung with massive power lines.

We did see a snowy peak or two, including Mount Baldy, on the back side of the San Gabriels. Petey admired these and said as much. But she didn't gush. She was a city kid who found beauty in crowds.

"How are you, Unk?" she finally asked, looking my way. "Besides the aches and pains, I mean. I was worried, you know."

"Appreciate the sentiment," I said. "I'm all right. I may have overstated the case. At my age I'm entitled to some hyperbole. Fact is, the blood got to me. I saw a man with his throat slit, and it got to me. Still does."

"I'd be worried if it *didn't* get to you," she said. "Ice in the veins is only good for clutch hitters and short relievers."

"Then there's you," I said. "How's your heart? You hopped off the plane with plenty of zippidy-do-da. Still the good kid I used to know?"

"Yeah, well . . ." she began, and then let it drop. Mile markers whizzed past us. The Buick was new and competent. The sun played off the hood ornament, and I enjoyed the ride.

"This is only my second time out west," Petey said. "The first time was when I was eight years old and we went to Disneyland. Dad drove the station wagon. I think we had a wonderful time."

I smiled. "Maybe I should visit Disneyland. Get a better perspective on life out here. My view has been pretty skewed so far."

"You ever think of moving out here, Unk? Like when you quit the column. Or when it's ten below on Michigan Avenue?"

"Never. Not here. Not Florida. Not Arizona. Warm weather is overrated. You need the yin and the yang of the seasons. Anyway, I like my friends and cronies better. But you knew that."

"I knew that," she said. "Just testing you."

"I admit it," I said. "I got a chip on my shoulder

about the sun states. Had it ever since I went south for spring training. And that's been a few years. What irks me is how people here give you the feeling the only news they listen to comes from the weatherman."

Petey thumped the steering.

"Paul Simon. That's good, Unk."

"Huh?"

"That's a Paul Simon line. You know, the singer. Like in Simon and Garfunkel way back when. He had a song called 'The Only Living Boy in New York,' and it had the line, 'I get the news I need from the weather report.'"

She half spoke and half sang.

"Makes it no less true," I said, wondering if anything on my mind nowadays was original.

"Petey, how can you remember something like that?" I mused. "A song lyric, for crying out loud?"

She smiled. "Me? How 'bout you? I remember one day how you dropped the names of the three Dodger pitchers Reggie Jackson tagged for homers in the sixth game of the Seventy-seven Series like it happened yesterday. Well, it's the same for me. Some things just stick to the ol' Velcro."

"Wait a minute," I said, "the Jackson stuff is important information. Baseball data. Actually, Reggie hit *four* straight homers. People forget that. He hit one in his last at bat in the fifth game. Then he walked the first time up in game six, and the rest is history. Hit them all on the first pitch. Remember?"

"How could I forget?" she said. "I was ten years old at the time."

She gave me a sideways look that managers reserve for pinch hitters who swing at the first pitch.

On she drove, and on we talked. We caught up and filled in. She updated me on what was going on back home, from the politics of my condominium association—she was tending the flat for me—to city hall and the ballparks. She gossiped and told questionable jokes. We had never had any trouble jabbering. I'm not sure Petey would have trouble talking to anybody. She bounced ideas off me like cooked spaghetti on a refrigerator door. Some stuck, some needed more heat. She was four decades my junior and then some, but oh, how she had made up the time. Her fine mind never slept.

I responded to all this verbal acuity by drifting off. It was intentional, and I asked Petey's permission. An afternoon nap on a slightly reclining overstuffed seat in a humming automobile driven by an able navigator is one of the nontaxable luxuries of our time. Eastern California and the dry lakes and joshua trees of the great Mojave Desert would have to pass by without my review.

A nudge woke me. I opened my eyes to afternoon shadows of the desert. All around me was sand and sagebrush. Just ahead was Las Vegas, Nevada.

"Chips ahoy," Petey said.

We stopped for gas, bathrooms, and something to drink. By my watch we had been in the car a little over three hours. Added to the three hours Petey had spent in the airplane, she had done her share of traveling. You wouldn't have known it. She got out of the Buick, stretched, and inhaled the hot, dry desert air. She looked as if she had done little more than walk the dog.

"I got the tank," she said, and attended to the now slightly dusty Buick. She was inexhaustible.

Highway 15 comes in on the south end of Las Vegas, running past McCarran International Airport. We had a map, but we didn't need it. I'd been here a few times, and I don't remember getting lost. Petey chose to exit the freeway into downtown, turn onto Las Vegas Boulevard, and then slowly make her way to the strip.

"Pardon me while I gawk," she said. "This is a virgin run for me, Unk."

Of course, she had seen it all before on television and in the movies. The strip and its neon landmarks were as familiar to her as the faces on Mount Rushmore. Probably more so. In the flesh, or I should say in the naked glare of its nonstop light show, Las Vegas was just as garish, just as dazzling, but more tawdry than its screen image.

"My God," Petey said, craning her neck. "The town architect hasn't got a subtle bone in his body."

She rattled off the entertainers—from Wayne Newton to Robert Goulet—ballyhooed on the billboards.

"No Liberace, no Sammy Davis, Jr.," I said.

"Alas," Petey sighed.

We paused in front of the Mirage to watch its manmade volcano spit steam and fire. It was remarkable, the first volcano that you can not only set your watch to, but which is courteous enough to slip into remission after a good blow. Petey oohed and ahed. Inside the Mirage, its sign said, were Siberian tigers. Farther ahead Petey's eyes lifted at the white stone Roman walkways leading to Caesar's Palace. I told her about Cleopatra's Barge, a gin mill where the saloon floats instead of the patrons.

"Holy Cecil B. deMille," she said.

Our destination was up the boulevard a ways in the form of a place called Excalibur. It was the newest and biggest casino in town, Joe Start had said, and he was not inventing. As we neared Tropicana Avenue, it loomed before us like something out of Disneyland and *The Tales of Robin Hood*. Between a pair of thirty-story high rises was a spiked burst of red- and gold-roofed spires, towers, turrets, and stone battlements. A moat and covered drawbridge ran in front. No commoners would take this fortress.

We opted for the parking lot and the back way, and after we entered, stopped short. Besides the brisk smack of the air-conditioning, we were bombarded by a decor rife with old-English pageantry—murals, coats-of-arms, armor, and weaponry. Castle walls and parapets, dungeons and iron gates. It was all authentically medieval yet crafted out of space-age materials.

Petey gazed around her with a slightly bemused expression.

"I got it," she finally said.

"Huh?"

"This place is a cross between a Denny's Restaurant and the Vatican."

She was winding up.

Old England gave way, however, to Excalibur's casino, a gambling den the size of three jousting fields.

Machines and tables and gamblers were everywhere; the secret of Las Vegas lay before us as obvious as the sword in the stone.

"Incredible," Petey exclaimed.

"Where do we start?" I wondered.

We made our way over to the registration desk, passing several miniskirted cocktail waitresses and cigarette girls in Maid Marion hats.

Petey snickered.

"This is the only place," she snapped, "where they can say, 'Cigars? Cigarettes? Codpieces?'"

I let her have that one.

It was not a problem for someone to direct us to the area of Darby O'Brien's blackjack table. I have a friendly face, and I lie well—"I'm her uncle"—and the Excalibur folks smelled nary a rat. Petey and I strolled casually among the dozens of tables, where the action was steady but not frenetic. We eyed the dealers' badges, but nobody paid any attention to us. Each time I have set foot in Las Vegas, I have got the immediate impression that this is a city in which you can easily go ignored. If you prefer to that is. There are simply too many other fish to fry.

"Over there," Petey said.

She nodded at a one-dollar table just to our left. The dealer tagged "Darby" was thirty-eight if she was a day, an iced blonde with a desert tan. Blackjack dealers, both the male and female of the species, remind me of veteran relief pitchers. They've seen almost everything. They've won a few, and they've been rocked for a few, but they're still around. Crows have left footprints, and gray hairs, most of them premature, have moved in for the duration. The fingers are stained from too many cigarettes. The lids are heavy, and the look is even.

But not this dealer, this Darby O'Brien. Even with the severe button-down reserve of a blackjack dealer, she was a looker, a fresh, beautiful woman who was as fetching from two feet as from twenty. When she smiled, a smile she used from time to time, the proportions held up, the glint of dark eyes, great skin, perfect teeth on lightly coated lips. Give her the voice of Anne Bancroft, and men would fly into fog for her. Perhaps Jack Remsen once had.

As Petey and I closed on her table, she never lifted her attention from the four players before her. A few yards away stood a pit boss, that flinty creature who trusts no one. He paid little mind to O'Brien.

I slid onto an end chair and bought twenty dollars worth of chips. The house did not shudder. Darby dealt me in without a pause, her long, impeccably manicured fingers with clear-varnished nails and no jewelry moving with a perfect rhythmic fluidity. She kept up a chatter, a low, almost imperceptible call of the game. She smiled slightly at my indecision, a smile you give a pup. Her hands fanned the table, kissing cards onto the felt surface, moving from player to player, working the shoe, effortlessly giving and taking chips. I admired the rhythm of the dealer's art—much more, to be sure, than the allure of her game.

When her cards ran down, and she began the shuffle of a new shoe, I said, "Miss O'Brien?"

She measured me in a single glance. It was masterful.

By then Petey had taken a position next to me. She shielded my words from the rest of the table.

"I'm with the commissioner of baseball's office," I said, low enough for only her to hear. It was the only way I could move her off the table.

If she was bothered, she didn't show it. Until, that is, she dropped a card. Then she smiled as if to scold herself and offered me the cut of the deck. She completed the shuffle, checked her watch, and restarted the game.

"Ten minutes," she said.

She meant twenty. My chips dwindled and I got up. Sometime later O'Brien moved away from her table, and we followed. Without the blackjack table in the way, I realized she had a set of legs that fit the rest of the package. She let us follow her into an employees' lounge, a brightly lit but spartanly furnished area of Formica tables and vending machines. She sat down and lit a cigarette. You don't see many people smoke anymore. I mean really smoke. Like in the old days, when dames held unfiltered, unlit Chesterfields in the air, and cads lunged to light them. Darby O'Brien smoked. She inhaled like a bellows and bubbled white smoke as thick as mushroom soup over her upper lip and into her nostrils before expelling it into the lights above. Somewhere Bette Davis smiled.

"Who are you?" she asked.

"Duffy House."

She inhaled again.

"The writer," she said.

"Yes. This is my niece, Petey Biggers."

"Your niece," she echoed, and pulled up a corner of her lip. Meat eaters would bite a lip like that. "Guys in Vegas always bring along a 'niece.'"

"This one did," Petey snapped.

"Look," I cut in, "we're not here to pick a fight."

"I shouldn't even talk to you," she said, and inhaled once again.

"Jack was a good friend," I offered. "I wouldn't be here if that didn't mean something."

She considered that.

"I read your piece—it *was* very meaningful to me," she said, softening some. I liked her like that.

"This is the first shift I've worked since it happened. I either work or go crazy. Nobody here knows."

"When did you talk to Jack last?" Petey asked.

"A few nights earlier," she said. "He called. During the season I didn't get to see him much. There's no time."

"And off season?" I asked.

She thought about that. Her cigarette glowed.

"I didn't have anything to do with what happened. I was in Vegas. It happened in L.A. The Sunset Slasher, for godsakes. One of those maniacs that city is famous for. That's why I moved here. What Jack and I had was something else."

I let her consider that for a while.

"The Slasher didn't kill Jack," I declared, trying to mask any doubt about it.

She vented smoke through her nostrils at that. I was getting sick of the stick.

"I can't get dragged into it. He kept me out of his life down there. I never went to L.A. Not even to sit in the stands. He flew in here by himself in his own plane. Oh, how he loved to fly that thing over here. We'd see Sinatra or Dean Martin or Rickles. Then we'd go out in a group. Always in a group. He saw to that."

"How long had it been?" I asked.

"Eight years last November."

Petey reacted to that. Darby O'Brien was certainly no one-night stand.

"Eight years?" Petey said. "And he kept you a secret all that time?"

"Don't be silly. *I* kept it. I had to for Jack's own good. What did he have to gain by embarrassing his wife? He didn't want a divorce, and I didn't want an absentee mate."

"Why, then?" Petey asked.

O'Brien smiled at her. It was a look that conveyed the gulf between them. Petey was very young.

"Why? Try this: Jack was the most generous man in the world. And the most loyal. The man was an angel to me. I have a house because of him. My daughter is getting a degree at UNLV because of him. That's just for starters. There aren't too many men I'd trust in this world. He was one of them. And he trusted me."

"Aren't you worried about us?" I asked.

"Sure I am," she said. "But Jack's dead. Whatever gets out now hurts only him. From what you wrote in the *Times*, I don't think you'd do that."

"Were you in love with him?" Petey asked.

She sighed. The cigarette was out, and her face was free of haze. My, what a face.

"Everybody loved Jack," she replied.

She looked at her watch.

"What was he doing on Sunset Boulevard?" I asked.

"Meeting somebody," she said quickly. "Jack was always meeting somebody."

"A prostitute?" I asked.

"What?" she snapped, her expression angry, questioning.

"I've been told as much," I said.

"Probably giving out tickets," she said. "Shit I don't know. Jack could be wild. He was horny and crazy and full of it. But not a street trick. Don't say that."

"Who else, then?" Petey asked.

"Where's the rub? What don't we know?" I added.

She searched her purse and extracted a role of mints.

"A lot of things—a lot of people," she said. "My first guess is money. He had plenty, and he was always giving it away. To friends. And a lot of people who weren't his friends but he didn't know it. He had money here in Vegas in my name. Used it all the time. Banker Darby, he called me. I parked a lot of deposits in my account. The dividends went on my taxes. He took care of it."

"Spending money?" I said.

"If you consider two to three hundred thousand spending money."

"In your name?" Petey asked.

"Yes. In fact, sometimes I thought it was mine. Or that it would be."

"Whew," Petey said. She looked like *she* needed a cigarette.

"It's still there?" I asked.

"No," O'Brien said. "Jack took most of it out a week ago."

"Most of it?" Petey said.

"That's right. Two hundred and fifty K. I sent it to him."

"Wait a minute," I said. "That's a hefty transaction."

O'Brien's look stopped me.

"This is Las Vegas," she replied.

"For what?" Petey asked.

O'Brien sniffed. Two silly queries in a row.

"He never said, and I didn't ask," she said.

We digested that for a while. Neither Petey nor I lived in Las Vegas, land of sixty-three–pound gold nuggets and horseshoes filled with a million dollars in cash.

Darby O'Brien probably handled a quarter of a million dollars a day the way she dealt cards.

"Who don't you like?" I finally asked. Her break time was growing short.

"You got a Rolodex?" she said. "There were a million guys who got too close to Jack. He let them. He was soft as a sponge. Try Harbridge, the preacher—always after money. Then there's Jack's restaurants . . . they weren't going good. Plenty of ex-Dodgers touched him for loans. Ever meet Bob Ferguson?"

"The pitcher?"

"The creep," she said. "He was the worst."

"Why him?"

She went for another cigarette, checked her watch, then decided against it.

"I've got to get back," she said.

"Why Ferguson?" I pressed.

She stood up and brushed some ash off her Excalibur shirt.

"He knew about me," she finally said. "I think he knew about Jack's money here. He knows a lot, and he's a leech. Everything he touches turns to crap. I heard he pissed away all his free-agent money."

"You sure about that?"

"Ask him."

As we walked out of the lounge, I told her I appreciated the time she'd given us. I gave her the number to Joe Start's house and asked for hers. She scribbled it on the back of a napkin.

"Will you go to the funeral?" Petey asked.

"No," she said quietly.

In the clattering din of the casino, she turned to us.

"I want to help, but I'm not stupid," she said. "Don't come here anymore. If Jack wasn't murdered by the Slasher guy, then nobody connected with him is safe. Nobody. Jack told you to take care of yourself, remember?"

"You too," I said.

At that she smiled slightly. She was an expert at taking care of herself. We watched as she walked off and disappeared into a sea of gamblers.

10

Bob Ferguson

Say this for Las Vegas: it eliminates the clock. When you are inside a casino, you may as well be inside a mayonnaise jar for all you know of the outside world. There is no sunrise or sunset; the only moon is the one in the lyric of a lounge singer. Drinks are always served; olives are fresh. The pull of a slot machine at four A.M. is as lucrative for the house as one yanked at twelve noon. There is no reason to pay any heed to time, or tell anybody the time, or so much as perch a clock on the wall.

All of which prompted me to ask, "What's the time?"

"We're in good shape," Petey said, her eyes jumping around the blipping, dinging expanse of the casino.

She knew no fatigue. Her head and nose were in the air like a beagle snagging a scent. The casino's cheap perfume smelled like a Chanel number to her. She wanted to roam, to watch the action, taste some of it, drift from table to table, game to game, and figure out what there was to this fabled den. She had a reporter's eye, no question. This old reporter, however, was blind to the fuss. My stomach called.

"I'm running on vapor," I said. "Let's eat."

"Here?" Petey said.

"Bet joints have good food—and cheap. They have to," I observed, remembering how the casinos once gave it away. They stocked buffet tables like feeding troughs and built shrimp cocktails the size of hay bales. The spreads were kept heaped round the clock for active rollers. Now the buffets had a tariff, but not more than a few bucks, and they were just as heaped.

We rooted around, found a floor plan, figured out which tower was which and how to dodge The Jester's Lounge and Little John's Snack Bar. We passed on tickets to the floor show, a medieval jousting derby called King Richard's Tournament. Its entrée, we read, was served without eating utensils and was meant to be ripped from the bones by hand. Our choices narrowed to Sir Galahad's Prime Rib, which I lobbied for, or Lance-a-lotta Pasta, which had Petey's nod.

"Indulge me with some red meat," I said.

Petey rolled her eyes, but it wasn't much of a roll. She liked the steer as well as the next guy. And it was on my tab.

In an hour, fed and lazy, the taste of coffee on our lips, we put the Buick back into the desert. In moments the barren landscape was a blur and the aura of Las Vegas was absorbed by the dark of the Nevada night. Still, our pulses had been quickened. Boomtowns do that to you. While Las Vegas counts a population of some eight hundred thousand now, virtually all of its folk are there because of the gaming industry. All of it bred since 1946, or thereabouts, when Bugsy Siegel and the Outfit poured blood and money onto the sand. Boomtown then, boomtown still, an oasis—why, the desert stops at the casinos' service docks—and a fragile one. Its lifeblood is so thin and the donors so transient that you cannot help but believe that it all could dry up as quickly as an East Texas oil well. There is no natural resource here. No mighty river around which industry forms, no mines, no forests, no agriculture. It is only the wager, the bet, the fickle allure of odds. If that were to evaporate, if people were to stop coming here—to *Vegas*— to gamble, if they suddenly turned insolent, unwilling to lose a large amount of money in a small amount of time, then it would all stop. The cards, the chips, the slots. The hotels, the restaurants, the shows, the lights. It would all crap out.

I preached as much to Petey as she locked her luminous eyes onto the road.

"Uncle Diogenes," she mused.

I had thought I would doze on the drive back, but I was as alert as a coyote. It was dark and cloudless in the desert, eerie and beautiful. The line of the highway was hypnotic, however, and I decided it was best to keep Petey a-chatter.

"So let me ask you: Could you live out here? In Las Vegas?" I ventured.

"You know me, Unk, I could live anywhere. I might get antsy after a while. Get sick of the neon. The baseball is minor league, though the stadium isn't, I hear. The libraries are thin, and the music runs too far into Wayne Newton territory. And the people—well, apart from a few sand rats, where do I go to find some roots?"

"This is the desert, Pete."

"But yeah, I could thrive. The action is palpable. You can cut your finger on it," she said. "Would it make me a good girl? There's the question."

"Or turn you into a Darby O'Brien?"

"Hah. Unk, you know how you always say 'Take a little off the top.' No chance with her. So cool. She dealt us the cards she wanted. I think she knows volumes."

"I'm not so sure," I countered. "Women like her see a lot, and see nothing. They survive on ignorance. She knows between the sheets, not between the ledgers."

"She had a bank account," Petey observed. "She was a laundry for him."

"Probably just branch banking. Another state. Away from the eyes of the missus."

"Why did she talk to us? Why not play dumb? Or just clam up altogether?"

"Because she doesn't know that much," I said.

"She gave us a couple names and a two-hundred-fifty-thousand-dollar withdrawal. That ain't bad," Petey replied.

We came up fast on a semitrailer rig, and Petey shot the Buick around it. I glanced at the speedometer. Eighty-five was a memory.

"Slow down, for cripes' sake," I groused.

She smiled and eased it down closer to my age.

"I liked her. And I didn't think I would," Petey said, still on the subject. "I'm not big on the other woman, you know. But that lady showed me something. Control. Savvy. Credits women don't often get."

"She's a dealer, like you said. Always in control of the table. I didn't see a single nerve ending," I said. "Except when I suggested Jack might have been after a whore."

"Surprise, surprise," Petey said. "It reflects badly on her. We girls have our pride."

"Don't start talking dirty now," I said.

With her left hand on the wheel, she reached into the backseat for a backpack. In it she found a tape cassette and slipped it into the dashboard. Suddenly we were accompanied by a decent piano, not Horowitz, but a guy named Jarrett, who was a good-enough noodler.

"Okay, Unk, where does it take us?" Petey inquired.

"On Jack's fronts. Baseball, Hollywood, the whole scene. Friends all over. Every big-league city. Hell, he flew in and out of Vegas like you and I go to the kitchen for a sandwich. What's new is the money. Moving a quarter of a million means something."

"And the two guys?"

"Harbridge. He's the preacher I talked to before I picked you up. Ever see him on TV? Built a big plexiglass palace called the House of Glass."

"God's House of Glass. I've seen him."

"Well, he's a television man of God, need I say more? And Ferguson."

"The pitcher? Right-hander. Short guy."

"That's the one. Played with a lot of clubs. Had one great year right after Messersmith opened the gates of the free-agent money. The Dodgers threw a bundle at Ferguson. Remsen liked him. Then his elbow blew out, he had surgery, and he wasn't much after that. He was a tough kid, and he worked hard, but I'll bet he never won more than ten games over three years here. He was in the park the other night."

"He was?"

"Yeah, with about a half-dozen other former players. Remsen's office is still like a clubhouse for them."

"Is he next for us?"

"Why not?"

I offered to spell Petey, but my offer didn't impress her. She kept feeding tapes into the player. We stopped once for coffee take-alongs. We kept each other entertained with stories. I talked about the old days on the West Side of Chicago when her mother was my little sister and I picked on her. Petey relished those memories and laughed like a kid. When we moved the talk to the present, she became more pensive. There was no mention of New York and what had happened there. I sensed that the sutures holding her heart intact were still raw to the touch.

"How scared are you out here?" she suddenly asked.

It took me off guard.

"Of the maniac," she went on, "what the cop said about you being a mark. . . ."

"I don't know. Alone in the Biltmore, nosing around Sunset Boulevard, I was as edgy as I've ever been. Hell, Pete, I can't run, and my right hook hasn't any pop. So yeah, I'm not sanguine about this thing."

"I'll help on that. I got myself a little leverage."

"How's that?"

"I learned to shoot. I bought a twenty-two-caliber pistol, and I can use it."

"You're joking."

"No, Unk. I ran down Jimmy Slagle, and he set it up for me. Even took practice on the range with him."

"That goofy copper? The human mosquito gave you shooting lessons?"

"Sort of. I learned at a range in the suburbs. Place was full of women. Learned everything about handling small arms and nailing a hood at fifty yards." She said "hood" Chicago-style, with a long $\bar{oo}$ as in *lewd*.

I munched on that for a while. Guns have never been currency with me. I never kept one in the house. There are too many stories of guys shooting their kids or their big toes or the family pooch in the middle of the night just because they heard a bump, and a loaded cannon happened to be next to the pillow. By my bed I keep books.

"You have one now?"

She laughed. "No. The airlines aren't big on carrying them on board. I'll buy one tomorrow."

"Ah, horseshit, Pete," I said. "We get trouble and we call a cop. I'm not crazy about sidearms. Turns you into some kind of TV cop with perfect makeup and a full clip."

"I like that," Petey said. "I'm good, Uncle Duffy. I can shoot. Stitch some asshole against a wall."

"Nice talk on you."

"Sorry," she said. "Put it this way. We've got a California-style psychopath who cuts now and talks later. He's already set his sights on you, which I take personally since you happen to be one of my favorite persons on this planet. My popper'll be small and lethal and in my purse or my fanny pack, and you won't even know about it. But it'll be there."

"My bodyguard," I said.

She lifted her eyebrows. *"Somebody's* gotta watch your old behind if you're not going to yourself."

It was close to midnight when we made it back to Alhambra and Joe Start's place. It felt like the old days on the road when bad connections kept you en route for half the night. In six hours I had to be up and off to see the commissioner. I invited Petey to come along. She declined. Finally she was whipped.

"Have a bagel, Duffy, you look like hell. What'd ya do, run off to Vegas last night?"

"How'd you know?"

"Get out of here. You haven't got the legs for that kind of stuff, you old fart."

"No, but Petey does."

"Petrinella! She's out here? That's good."

We sat in his overfurnished, Lord of Baseball suite at a table filled with danish, bagels, lox and cream cheese, fresh juice, a pot of coffee, and three kinds of melon. Grand Canyon Chambliss, former soybean pit trader and present commissioner of baseball, liked to eat. He was still in a bathrobe, a flannel number that looked as if he'd slept in it. Put Grand, a runty, bow-legged pug who reminded you of young Dixie Walker and old Don Zimmer, in a tuxedo, and he'd look as if he slept in it. Appearances weren't his forte.

He could, however, run the big-league game. In a time when owners were giving away the shop in free-agent dollars, and television was trying to call the shots because they supplied the free-agent dollars, Chambliss rode herd. The game for him was a business, one built on a pastime, to be sure, but a business as nasty as the trading pits. He was no Ford Frick or Peter Ueberroth. At any given time he had a half-dozen owners mad at him, wanting his hide. If that were not the case, he often said, "I wouldn't be doing my job."

"God, what a *loss!* What a cryin' shame. We can't afford to give up guys like Jack," he said. He didn't have to say more, but he would.

"People out here don't know what hit them yet, Duffy," he went on. "They thought losing Bogie and John Wayne was bad. Well, Jack was a prophet. He brought Brooklyn with him out here. And there's not much of that left anymore."

He could have gone on. He could have jabbered about how the game was horseshit and the players were spoiled and the owners didn't have the baseball brains they were born with and how it costs a guy with two kids fifty bucks to go to a ball game nowadays. But he didn't. He pushed food into his chops instead.

"Whattaya got?" he finally asked. "Who croaked him? This gonna embarrass the shit out of everybody?"

I ran down the tangibles: the Slasher, the victims before Remsen, the fact that Jack was sliced with a different knife. I told him a guy they think is the Slasher had talked to the police a couple of times and that he seemed sane and quite unfinished. I did not say that he mentioned how much he liked my potential. I brought up Billy Harbridge and his revelation of Remsen's proclivities for the lower-priced spread. And Darby O'Brien. The eight-year affair. The money. Harbridge again. Bob Ferguson. And Remsen's legions of friends, cronies, business associates, and hangers-on.

"Strings. All a bunch of strings, Duffy. Where are the cops leaning?"

"The Slasher. They gotta go with him. Six stiffs gives them no choice. Nothing says Jack didn't stop to get a taco and this guy creased him. Question is, was he that good? And what about the new weapon?"

"What a goddamned blot this is!" Chambliss said.

We drained the coffee, and he got up. The funeral was at eleven. His day was full until he flew out tonight.

"You're on this thing, Duffy. Extra innings. Spare no expense, you know that. But watch your ass. It just occurred to me—you're pickings for this guy."

I was touched by his concern. "Who'd want to bump off an over-the-hill scribe? Where'd I hear those words before?" I said.

"Not from me. In my book you're Sam Spade, Duffy."

"Good. My rates just went up."

It was a hell of a funeral. Even for Hollywood, where they can drape the bunting and orchestrate taps better than anywhere, it was a hell of a funeral. It had sunk in, I think. Jack Remsen, one of their true natural resources, that voluble, big-hearted, super Dodger, was dead. The fact hit Southern Californians with the force of a quake. They held each other and cried and turned out to pay Jack their respects. For an hour or so, most everything in the area shut down. Thousands trekked to Pasadena and crammed the streets near the edifice of the First Congregational Church. Millions watched the televised procession of mourners. Hollywood disgorged its stars. The governor and both senators were there. Official baseball, from Commissioner Chambliss on down, filed in. The O'Malleys, Vin Scully, and every current Dodger and a remarkable number of past team members, from the Bums in Brooklyn to the Garvey sunshine boys, trooped into the church. All stood shoulder to shoulder, glassy-eyed before an altar that was an explosion of flowers, the blue Dodger script, the red number 2. When Sinatra sang, they cried. When Rickles told soft jokes, they coughed, smiled, and cried. The priest invoked the blessing of the Big Dodger in the Sky. Koufax and Drysdale were among the pallbearers, as was Tommy York—chosen by lottery—from the team, and they carried the coffin like "boys of summer in their ruin."

Petey and I watched it all on one of Joe Start's televisions. We were not immune to the grief.

Among the Dodgers past and present we spotted at the funeral was Bob Ferguson. That meant he was in town. A few phone calls got us his address. It was on the beach, and Petey was up for an ocean drive. At midafternoon we got on the San Bernardino Freeway and followed it west until it became the Santa Monica Freeway. That would have taken us to Santa Monica, of course, had we not ducked south onto the San Diego Freeway. It was a relatively swift ride, given the traffic, and I again applauded my decision to get Petey out here and behind the wheel. She drove the Buick as if it were one of the other Mercedeses that surrounded us.

Ferguson lived in a little place called Playa del Rey, which was tucked between the Los Angeles International Airport, the Pacific Ocean, and a lot of land owned by the Howard Hughes estate. We came into it on Manchester Avenue and continued west on this wide drag of California commerce. The sidestreets were upscale, with winding white and pastel-colored condominiums, protected parking, and cyprus-tree landscaping. Sculpted ficus trees lined the boulevards, and shocking red bougainvillea poured out of overhanging arbors. No movie set could have painted a more typical California look.

It all led to the ocean, of course, that blue-white

expanse, which is the signature of this place. At Lincoln Boulevard we got our first view of the oceanfront valley and all of its "del Reys." Just to the north was Marina del Rey, the carnival of Venice beyond that, and to the south was Rancho Palos Verdes. At Pershing, according to our directions, we were getting close. It was hot, and there was little shade to be had. Palm trees don't offer that. We had the windows down, and I could have used a beer.

Petey kept on, eyeing a street sign here and there but generally looking as if she had been here before and would find the right address in no time. Across Pershing, Manchester went into a grade too steep for anything but a car. At its crest we got a shimmering view of the Pacific. I felt like Balboa, but momentarily, for I had to grab my stomach as we immediately pitched downward.

"Here it is," Petey said.

The street was called Vista del Mar Lane.

"How do they come up with these names?" Petey said.

It was a winding blacktop road built on the side of a dune. Terraced lots held expensive real estate in the form of smallish stucco houses with red-tiled roofs and balconies or patios opening to the sea. European cars were parked on inclines in the small driveways. All around were cypresses and bougainvilleas, banana palms and agave. Below was the white sand of the beach cut by a bicycle path, and beyond that the great blue ocean, perfectly calm except for the last curl of wave, stretched forever. A rumbling cigarette boat churned white waves just beyond a stone breakwater, and in the distance a few sailboats plied the wind.

Ferguson's house was in the middle of the block. It was an unassuming structure with a camel-colored stone front, louvered windows, and an attached dugout garage. The patch of yard held a couple of mature date palms. I didn't even want to speculate at the cost. My perspective on real-estate values is grounded in the 1950s, so I'm the wrong person to speculate.

I only knew that Ferguson could afford it, or he

could have. He was a .500 pitcher, good for a dozen wins a year with three different clubs, when Art Fowler taught him how to throw a sinker and turned him into a damn good short reliever. He was up there with Rollie Fingers and Tug McGraw when 1976 dawned and free agency hit the major leagues. In no time owners started throwing money from the skies like hailstones. Ferguson got enough to put him in oceanfront houses for the rest of his life.

Petey kept driving, following the curve of the lane as it led precipitously down to sea level. Down the road, at an intersection almost on the beach, was a restaurant called Giovanni's Salerno Beach. Darby O'Brien had said that Ferguson darkened the place, as did Sinatra and, of course, Jack Remsen. My eye caught the joint next door, a place called the Harbor Room Bar. The sign on it said, Open. But Don't Expect Too Much.

We parked on Pershing and found a phone in a coffee/yogurt/sandwich/bike-rental shop. I called Ferguson and got his answering machine. I told him I was in the neighborhood and that he could ring me at this number, or I'd just up and drop in. No sense in being pushy. In the meantime Petey bought me a cup of flavored Colombian coffee and herself a tuna sandwich that arrived covered with bean sprouts. She nodded my attention to a pair of young women in jewelry, blue jeans, and high leather boots at another table who were having an intense conversation punctuated with gasps, table slaps, and mortification. In the middle of it an innocent woman came in with a baby, and one of the talkers jumped up and exclaimed, "I need to hold it!" The mother, a trusting fool, let her.

"Draw your gun, Pete, if she doesn't give it back," I said.

Petey found the two absorbing to the point of hysterical. Later when one of the women complained that a friend of hers "shrinks" from her touch, I thought Petey was going to lose it.

At that the phone rang. Ferguson, sounding as cordial as a weatherman, called from a car phone to say he'd checked his messages, was on his way home, and to give him a half hour. Petey finished her sandwich, the two women in boots left holding hands, and we decided to drive around the beach and marinas a while. Near Venice we saw a guy who looked like Rasputin and held a placard reading:

$$2 + 2 = 7$$
4 is Propaganda

In Ferguson's drive was a small Cadillac that didn't look like a Cadillac at all but, according to Petey, had a price tag like one. Ferguson met us at the door. A dust mop of a dog hopped at his feet. He had been home long enough to change out of his funeral garb. Now he wore a rose-colored short-sleeved shirt with a tennis racket on one breast and a pair of sweatpants. He was short, a couple inches shy of six feet at least, but solid, with the good arms of a pitcher, the right bicep bigger if you looked closely. He was thicker now than when he pitched, the face fleshier but still landscaped with the thick downturned mustache so common to throwers of his day.

"Ay, champ and—" he began.

He took one look at Petey and lost his sentence. He fairly drooled as I introduced my niece, his stare a line drive of lasciviousness. It was a spectacle.

I jabbered about the wonders of the house and the layout, and Ferguson tore himself away from Petey's cheekbones long enough to set us up with some iced tea. We sat down on white wicker furniture next to silk flowers. The walls were loaded with pastel desert prints and smacked of an interior of the beach-house/low-maintenance school. The dog hopped all over the furniture.

"Still punchin' huh, Duffy? Out here writin' up a storm is the word. Not that I mind," Ferguson said. "Anytime you wanna come around with a pretty lady like this, well, just call up ol' Robert."

Petey took a quaff of her tea. It was a defensive move to hide the grimace.

"I was afraid you'd be tied up after the funeral," I said.

"Yeah, well, a few of us got together and cried in our beer afterwards. Yeager. Terry Forster. Duke Sims was there. We were down at Scaby's. But I can only take so much of that. Hell, Jack meant as much to me as anybody. A day won't go by that I won't think of him. But it's like losin' a big one, Duffy. You know something about that, champ. You can't sit around and chew on it. Jack woulda kicked our butts from here to San Diego." He drank some, crunched the ice, toyed with the dog, and played to Petey.

"Hey, Duffy, I don't remember you bringin' her around when you were in to see Jack. You holdin' back?"

"On Jack?"

He grinned. He was still a toothy relief pitcher: smart enough to know the situation, dumb enough not to let it affect him.

"Nuts. Where the hell are the nuts?" he said, and went off to a wet bar in the dining room. He still moved well. I remembered Ferguson as a guy who used to pitch hard no matter if he was one run up or six runs down. Give him the ball and let him bust it. He returned with a salad bowl full of cashews and delivered them to Petey. She smiled.

"Once knew a girl named Pete in Port St. Lucie," he said.

"Or was it Lucy in Port St. Pete?" Petey responded.

"Whoa!" Ferguson said. He sat down on a footstool.

"I won't mess around, Bob," I said. "I'm with the commissioner on this. We all think the Sunset Boulevard maniac killed Jack, but we're not taking anything for granted."

"Why you want to talk to me?" he asked.

"You were at the park that night. I'm interested in everybody who was there."

"Fine. You better put in some long damn hours. There's guys all over with clubhouse passes, thanks to Jack. You know the scene."

He stretched and did some leg lifts. I looked for

some body language, maybe a little irritation. I didn't see much.

"Ever hear of Darby O'Brien?" I said.

He looked at me, then at Petey. He stopped the calisthenics. He leaned over near Petey and grabbed a cashew. He rolled it over the knuckles of his right hand until it reached the pinky, then flipped it into the air and caught it with his tongue. Hours of boredom in the bullpen cultivate amazing talents. Petey nodded admiringly. Given the chance, she would eat Ferguson for lunch.

"Know her well. How 'bout you?"

"She doesn't speak well of you."

He snorted.

"Jack's Vegas poon," he said. "I know about her. Don't like her and never did. Tough broad. Got her hooks in his wallet and never let go. I told Jack she must give great head."

Petey stiffened. She'd killed men for lesser remarks.

"What'd he say to that?" I said before she could attack.

"Don't remember," he said. "So what is it—you here because I was in the ballpark the other night, or because the O'Brien bitch fingered me?"

"You tell me."

"Fuck you."

"Hey," I said. "Jack Remsen was murdered, remember?"

Ferguson got up, tossing the dog halfway across the room as he did. The little bugger came back for more.

"Don't give me that shit. I was a fuckin' batboy for the Dodgers when they first came out here. You ever know that? Guys like Wally Moon and Podres were my heroes. Put Jack in there too. When I went free agent and the Dodgers came after me, I died and went to heaven. Been here ever since. And you're fistin' me about Jack being murdered? Hell, I'd take the bastard who killed him apart with my own two hands if I ever caught him."

I nodded, gave him some breathing room.

"So with that out of the way, what about Darby
O'Brien?"

"She worked him. He had money in Vegas. She ran
it. Real businesswoman. I told him he was crazy to let
her anywhere near his bankbook. She knew I knew.
And that's why you're here. No bald ass surprise there,
champ."

"She says Jack took out a big check just a day or so
before. Quarter of a mil."

He laughed at that.

"Oh, she did, did she? Well, if I were you, I'd look
right back in her direction if there's somethin' missin'.
The bitch oozes scratch. She's a dealer, remember?
Show me a dealer who ain't nuthin' but a bust-out."

He looked over at Petey again. She put a nut between her teeth and held the pose for him. He winked.
Six runs down and he was still hurling.

"You seem to be doin' all right," I said, looking
around.

"Thank you. I don't advertise. People just get mad.
But I got my bank CDs and my tax-free municipals, and
I live a simple life. Fish a little. Get a bikini and go down
to Baja. Take time to smell the roses. Not bad for a forty-
seven-year-old with a busted rotator, I'd say."

I stood up. He came over and put his arm around
my shoulder. "I'm sorry I jumped on ya, champ. I'm a
little edgy, and you rubbed me a little raw. All's for-
given, huh?"

"You're as good as your last outing, Bob," I said.

"Three innings, one hit, no runs. That's it. Against
the Giants in Candlestick."

Then the dog clutched my leg and started hump-
ing. Ferguson grabbed it by the neck and put it in the
liquor cabinet. We could hear its yap as we walked to
the door. He came with us to the front steps.

"My boat's headed south tomorrow, and I want you
on it," he said to Petey.

"Business," she said. "I'm busy with business."

"I'll keep on ya," he said. "Old pitchers never die,
they just lose a few inches."

He got a big laugh out of that one. A jogger with

three Dobermans under leash loped by. The sky was magnificent. A breeze had picked up.

"We'll get back if we need you," I said.

"Just bring your escort, champ," he said, and winked Petey's way again. He was as subtle as a spitball.

We had to wait a few minutes to get out of Ferguson's driveway. The Buick was blocked by a pickup truck that was agreeably moved by a Mexican fellow. A larger flatbed truck had been maneuvered onto the side yard. A landscape crew was digging out a good-sized date palm, and as they did, its leafy crown quivered in the sky.

11

In Memoriam

I've always enjoyed the sight of two fingers pointing in opposite directions. Take Leo Durocher, or Alston, or Lasorda, and think of how many times they stood chin to chin with Augie Donatelli or Doug Harvey or Nester Chylak and pointed, just stuck a big finger in the other guy's nose and wagged it like a hot poker. With blue commentary. Nothing that fiery came to mind with Darby O'Brien and Bob Ferguson, but at least they were pointing. And in this case, with the grief of Jack Remsen's demise far outplaying the motive for it, Petey and I needed a lot more of that.

The drive back to Alhambra gave us time to throw those two around. First impressions are just that; when you're pressing a murder probe, they're even worse. I wanted to get back to the detective. Long Jim Holdsworth would have an opinion, maybe a footnote or two. I didn't have to wait long. The light on the answering machine was blipping when we walked in, and the first three messages were his. They were curt. The old pivot wanted to huddle.

"Where you been?" he said when I called. He was in no mood. The receiver growled in my hand. I gave him my itinerary.

"Let's compare notes," I said.

"Stay put," he said.

Alhambra was in his delivery area, Holdsworth said, and he'd swing by. Before he did, Petey had time to put Joe Start's kitchen in gear. She made a run to the market and came back with several sacks. It was early evening, and she was hungry again. In no time she was cleaning greens and frying chicken. She had me working on avocados—no easy task for one whose life has been centered on the potato—and slicing tomatoes and onions.

"California. Fresh produce. I can't stand it," Petey said.

Her vocabulary went foul as she attempted to find what she needed in Start's kitchen.

"Don't knock him. He makes good eggs," I said.

"And only eggs, I bet."

Just about then Joe walked in, and Petey put another chicken in the pan.

"Mr. and Mrs. Betty Crocker," he said.

But he liked it. His walls finally had an aroma between them instead of a smell. The chicken sizzled and spattered, water boiled for pasta, a head of lettuce was ripped to smithereens. Wearing Start's Angels apron, Petey hummed around the kitchen like a shortstop, occasionally throwing a hip or pinching a giblet and telling me when I was screwing up. She liked being around geezers. Maybe there was something wrong with her.

We ate at Start's dining-room table, something he apparently had not done for years. We had to move piles of books, magazines, and mail just to set the damn thing. Midway through the white meat, Holdsworth showed up. I'd say he darkened the door, but not out loud. He joined us without pause, offered his immense paw across the table when Petey was introduced, and sat his long carcass down. He looked creased around the edges, like a manager in the midst of an eight-game losing streak. He was grayer than I remembered. Yet in seconds he was shoveling food onto his plate like a big kid at summer camp, and a measure of his vigor returned.

"I didn't know black guys liked fried chicken," Petey said. Holdsworth eyed her, caught the levity, and welcomed her into the club.

I recapped our file on O'Brien and Ferguson, including the missing money. Holdsworth listened and licked his paws and seemed interested.

"But you could waste a lot of time doggin' the man's dubious acquaintances," he began. He said it slowly, gnawing on a thighbone like it was a friend. I noticed Petey. She was fascinated by Holdsworth. Throw her into a crowded room, and she would gravitate to the person who looked least like she did.

"Except maybe for that missing quarter mil," Holdsworth continued. "Old rule of homicide says there's a broad in there somewhere. Me? I look for the dough."

"All right—" I began.

"But later," Holdsworth continued. "Right now I got a game to play with the boulevard boy. He's the only killer in town, far as I'm concerned."

"Thank you," exclaimed Joe Start. He'd been sitting like a court reporter on the end of the table.

"No offense, Mr. Duffy," the policeman said, "but if we get his ass, we clear up five homicides. Let the Dodger man be in there, that's fine. But I gotta get the knife man off the street."

"Thank you," Start said.

Holdsworth looked at him.

Start came on. "I'm as big a Remsen fan as anybody. But when it comes to murder, it's one man, one vote. There's no clout in the morgue."

"The prick's been callin' in regular, you know," Holdsworth continued. "Says he misses you, Duffy."

"Get outta here."

"No joke. You should hear this cat. Talk, talk, talk. Crazy like a fox. Somethin' about him that's wrong, real wrong, but I can't nail it. Says he hates old guys. 'Clean 'em out,' he says. Like some crazy-ass cleaning lady goin' after roaches.

"That's why I'm here. 'Cept for the chicken. The big stadium deal's on tomorrow, and my man's gonna be there, I know it. He's like that. Playin' with us like he did after I took you to the scene the other day, Duffy. Calls maybe two or three times—last time he got me—

and tells us who we got on the case. Where we been. Get this: says he ain't seen 'the sweet old pooch in the baggy pants' lately.' That's how he said it, and he meant you, 'cuz my trousers are tapered."

Nobody smiled.

"They do that, you know," he went on. "The real crazy fuckers like to come out after a while. Toy with ya. Like to put the ball out where you can slap at it, then pull it away."

"You mean the memorial for Remsen?" Petey asked.

"You got it. I say he's gonna be there. And we're gonna be there. And you, Mr. Sweet-Old-Baggy-Pants-Pooch, are gonna be with us."

He got plenty of guffaws at that, but not one from me.

"Wait a minute," I said.

There was no way I wanted any part of the Jack Remsen Memorial Service. I had registered my sorrow. I had bowed my head when the coffin was lowered. Let the stadium gates be draped with black and purple bunting and let the players wear black bands. A special memorial service in the infield of Dodger Stadium smacked of being a Dodger dog-and-pony show, and I didn't want any part of it. Petey said I was being "elitist,"—a word I don't use—that the fans deserved it and that they would do the memorial justice. Hell, I still didn't need it.

Until Holdsworth said I had no choice. For an hour after dinner that night, he laid out what his people had planned for me. Bait. I was slasher bait. Oh, they'd have the stadium covered, Big Jim said, and Holdsworth himself would stay with me, and we'd both be shadowed as we moved about. But we would walk about in public areas, in the concourses and the stands. We would be as visible as vendors, but not vulnerable. Certainly not vulnerable, Holdsworth said. When he said it twice, I *knew* he didn't believe it.

• • •

The next morning came soon enough. It was Thursday, a rare day off in the Dodger's schedule, and the memorial service was scheduled for one o'clock. Petey made a quick exit that morning, and returned an hour or so later as quietly as she had left. I knew where she'd been, and I hesitated like an indecisive parent before saying anything. Then I reconsidered. I didn't like the idea of her packing a pistol. I knew California had a mandatory two-week waiting period before you could get lethal steel in your mitts. Maybe that had waylaid her.

"So, did Annie get her gun?" I asked.

"No problemo," she said.

"Huh?"

She lifted a blue-metal roscoe out of her purse. It lay in the palm of her hand like a rat.

"I thought there were laws against getting one so fast," I said.

"There are," she said, and didn't volunteer her scam.

It had turned overcast and windy, so I put on a sweater under my sport coat. Petey wore a windbreaker and swung an oversized leather purse on one shoulder. Leather and lethal. Her hair was pulled back into a ponytail, and she wore her jeans and sneakers. She looked like an undercover cop. And now she could shoot like one.

Holdsworth and the ever close-to-the-vest Sam Kimber showed up at eleven, and we made the drive to the ballpark. Long Jim wanted plenty of time to set up, to coordinate with his other men, to walk us through the concourses. Petey had never been inside the place, and I knew she wanted to explore.

We parked near the Dodger offices far down the third-base side and hooked up with a dozen other detectives in summer suits. They all looked like something out of an old *Untouchables* episode, the old TV show that always gave me a hoot because it made a big hero out of Eliot Ness, who wasn't. It was sort of like making Sandy Amoros into Willie Mays. Anyhow,

Holdsworth seemed to be top dog. When he talked, the plain suits hopped.

Petey hied herself to the box seats and surveyed the green Dodger playing field, a diamond she had seen only on television.

"Great sight lines," she gushed.

The stadium, I realized, was older than she was, so the glories of Sutton and Wills and Dusty Baker had the sepia tones of history to her. Ebbets Field and Brooklyn might just as well have been the Colosseum in Rome, for all she knew.

"Give me the tour, Unk," she said.

"Stay with me, Duffy," barked Holdsworth.

Petey glared at him. He exhaled impatiently.

"Go with Sam," he said, and nodded Kimber in the direction of the front office. A few minutes later Petey reappeared with a set of credentials—"P. Biggers, LAPD," which had a nice ring to it—dangling from her windbreaker. I gave her a few directions, and she set off jauntily for the inner sanctums.

Holdsworth and I lingered near the press box, his command post of sorts. Though he did not carry one, Holdsworth's crew had hand-held radios. At any given time, he said, he could talk to someone in just about every part of the stadium. We watched as the place began to fill. It was a scene that would have made Walter O'Malley's teeth gnash. It was only proper that the memorial be a free event, so there were no tariffs for parking or admittance. The masses simply drove up and walked in the Taj O'Malley and, except for a small roped-off area, sat anywhere they wanted. Thousands of cars and thousands of heads, and the cash register never rang once. A few concession stands were open, and they offered a limited menu. In my mind it wasn't a beer and hot dog kind of occasion, but what did I know?

It wouldn't be a capacity crowd, but an honest guess put twenty-five thousand mourners in the stands. Not bad for no game. The infield was dressed with a platform of the sort Billy Harbridge would use to save souls. Harbridge, in fact, was on the program. There was a group of string players from the Los Angeles

Symphony, which I thought was a nice touch, a color guard, and a kid's choir. And, of course, the players past and present, the current O'Malleys and the Dodger front office, Jack's widow, a Cardinal of the non–National League persuasion, and a good number of politicians and entertainers.

Things got going pretty much on schedule with the crowd forgoing the Dodger Stadium tradition of showing up in the second inning. By that time Petey had rejoined us. She'd had a good run of the clubhouse and Remsen's office. "Everybody was down there," she exclaimed. "I saw Koufax talking to Jack Nicholson. I bumped right into this chick, and it turns out to be Linda Ronstadt." She was starstruck.

Holdsworth snapped her out of it by nodding for us to follow him. We were to play it loose and nonchalant, moving around the concourses and appearing as if we had a genuine interest in the proceedings. Other eyes would watch our flanks and scan the crowd.

As Vin Scully's comforting tones echoed through the stadium, we went down to the loge level just behind the third-base gold seats. Except for the absence of the usual numbers on the scoreboard and uniformed players in the dugouts, you would have thought the event was a pregame ceremony. From time to time the crowd clapped, then went silent. Plenty of people moved through the concourses, to use the bathrooms or whatever. The food stands were doing more business than you'd expect. Jack Remsen himself probably would have eaten his way through this thing.

In any case, in Holdsworth's opinion there were too many people moving around. He bitched about it. But what did he expect? This was Dodger Stadium, and enough people to populate a decent suburb had shown up. Only a skeleton crew of ushers worked, and they were not enforcing the usual game-time rules, which kept people moving and at a distance from the last row of seats. So there were clumps of loiterers, pockets of mopes, knots of gawkers. Any one of them could have held a psychotic.

Holdsworth touched my sleeve, and we moved

again. From third over around to first, then behind the plate, then up a level. The Dodger Stadium concession areas run behind the seats in the lower levels and are open to the field. You can leave your seat, buy a Dodger Dog, and still see much of the field area. We stood in those areas, very much a part of the masses, able to see and be seen.

Still, it was not very productive, if you'd asked me, but Holdsworth was not asking. The crowd looked pretty Dodger-like: polite, dressed in Dodger blue, seeded with plenty of gray and blue hairs of Remsen's vintage, most of them anxious to beat the traffic out of there, but not very menacing. If the Sunset Slasher was among them, his sick and vicious aura was not coming through.

I paid some attention to the show. The strings played Ravel's "Pavane for a Dead Infant," which was pretty classy given the fact that Jack Remsen's musical tastes ran from "Volaré" to "My Way." The kid's choir was actually a little-league team from Glendale, and they sang "Take Me Out to the Ball Game." The ceremony's centerpiece, after a few words by many people who all said pretty much the same thing, was a video. Of course. This was Hollywood, after all. The Dodgers had gone to the film vault and put together a Jack Remsen feature. It played on DiamondVision as loud and colorful as Jack himself. It was, even in the opinion of a print man, good stuff, much better than the old Ebbets Field footage the Dodgers ran here during the ninety season. The Brooklyn newsreel film rings hollow out here. Sure it is Dodger history, but the boys had *B*s on their caps. They were no more a part of Los Angeles than were lemon trees in Brooklyn.

The Remsen video brought the stadium alive with his hollering, his raspberries, his dust-kicking, spittle-raining umpire brawls, his butt clopping, his charges from the dugout after big wins, his hugs and high fives with every Dodger from Campanella to Pedro Guerrero. He smoked cigars with Al Pacino, sang a duet with Dean Martin, told jokes to Phil Silvers. It was as if Jack had never left, that this was just a birthday party, and the robust, lovable, head bum of the Dodgers was going to come waddling out of the dugout any minute now with the starting lineup and a bellyache or two.

My bladder called about ten minutes into the film. There was a men's room just beyond the concession stand, about forty yards away.

"We got a man in there, but Sam'll go with ya anyway," Holdsworth said.

"No, he won't. Not to the damn water closet," I said.

"I will," said Petey.

"This is a lot of malarkey, Jim," I said. "I'm in plain sight."

The detective was not going to argue the point, and Petey and I started off. In this particular area were assembled the Dodger stalwarts, the eccentrics and collectors, the retirees in Brooklyn flannels, the girls in wacky Dodger hats, the old-time Bums outfits. One almost expected to see Shorty Laurice and the "Dodger Sym-phony Band" from Ebbets Field. There was the disabled fellow in the wheelchair festooned with player pins. "I will not buy or sell, only trade," read his sign. There were the old ladies with handmade Dodger dresses.

It was a motley crew, and one common to most ballparks with any character to them. The older stadiums seemed to have the best characters—from the bleacher preachers to the mascots with illuminated noses—and if the franchise was smart, they patiently accommodated them. Most of us have lives outside the ballyard. Some of us do not.

"That's discrimination for you," Petey said as she eyed the sign on the women's room.

CLOSED FOR REPAIRS. THE DODGERS
ARE SORRY FOR THE INCONVENIENCE.

"Use mine," I said.

"Women have been prosecuted for that," she said. "I'll go back to the one by Holdsworth—if I can make it."

With that she let me go the last twenty yards to the men's john on my own. I began to step through the crowd and hadn't taken but a few steps when a woman in a blue satin Dodger jacket dropped her handbag in front of me. She was a large lady, tall with a good set of shoulders, maybe fifty or so, wearing slacks—something women her age never used to wear—and running shoes. Her hair was cropped short beneath a Dodger cap. She was a fan, and one, no doubt, with a set of lungs that could make a bad case of rabbit ears worse.

"Oh *drat*," she said.

I was contemplating the last time I'd heard the word *drat* and whether or not I should help this husky female retrieve her belongings when I was suddenly shoved from the side. Blindsided is a better word, knocked nearly off my feet and into the door of the temporarily closed women's room. Except that it wasn't closed. It gave way like a café door, and I went through it like a bounced drunk.

"Hey!" I managed, which was all that came out until I was pushed again.

My rouster was the woman in blue, the big Dodger fan, and with hands the size of Carl Furillo's, she threw me onto the cold, deserted terrazzo floor. That one hurt, and my shoulder throbbed, but the pain was nothing next to the realization: I was looking into the homicidal eyes of the Sunset Slasher. I was sure of it. And those eyes belonged to a she, a bull of a woman, 220 pounds if an ounce, a female Al Ferrara who was coming on me like a boot on a dog.

"Now you're gone, old Buck," she growled, a growl that rumbled out of her throat.

I rolled and scrambled, then reached out for the leg of a scaffold left in the middle of the room. It was a good move: the scaffold shifted on its casters and caught the woman's shoe. She lurched awkwardly, and I flopped like a fish beneath the scaffold's crossbars.

It all happened in seconds—it always does when your stint on earth appears threatened—but that was too long. The Amazon regained her balance and came at me. She kicked me in the kidneys, and I saw white.

"Let's go, Buck. Try to run out this time," she snarled as she reached for me through the bars.

"Hey! Stop! Help me!" I yelled, because yelling and flailing were about the only defenses I could pull off.

She grabbed my left leg, twisted it, and damn near wrenched it out of the hip socket. I cried out and kicked with my other leg. If she didn't slit my throat, she'd pull me limb from limb like an old turkey. I didn't know which was worse. All I knew is that the doors to this killing toilette stayed shut, and I faced this crazed strongwoman alone. I kicked out again, and she lost her grip. The scaffold cage was the best thing I had going for me, and I'd spit and bite and claw with every old breath I had in me before I'd let myself become a statistic.

My resistance took time—enough, I was to learn, for Holdsworth to panic. His instincts were true, for when he saw Petey returning without me, he got on the radio to his man in the men's room.

"You got him, Les?" he rasped.

"No. He ain't in here," came the reply.

"Shit!" Holdsworth bellowed.

"What?" Petey exclaimed.

"Where is he?" Holdsworth yelled, going for the concourse.

It took Petey two seconds to react. She sprinted past Holdsworth and into the crowded concourse. When she got to the clump of collectors and eccentrics, and didn't see this one, she stopped dead, then gasped.

"The women's room! The closed one!"

During their deliberations my blue lady managed to reach inside the scaffold—her forearms made Garvey's look emaciated—and get ahold of my belt, of all things. She grabbed it and pulled it like Dutch Rennert ringing up a called third strike, and I was ripped from my cage like a doomed chicken. At the same time the crowd roared, the stadium rocked. The video had apparently come to an end, and in the din I was about to do the same.

"Buck, you worthless drunk," she snarled, obviously not talking to me and just as obviously not caring.

She looped that same viselike forearm around my neck and pulled me to my feet like an inflated doll.

"Hey! Hel—!" I croaked, but could get nothing more out.

With a sweep of her torso, she moved to one of the stalls, but not before she had reached into her pocket or her handbag or some kind of arsenal and withdrawn a butcher knife. It was a big one, with a blade the size of a sickle. I kicked and struggled and tried to elbow her, but frankly, I had little left. I shook. I cried out. I think I lost control of things I usually control. I felt more fear than I have ever felt before. I did not want to die, and I was about to.

With a swift kick of her foot, she opened a stall door. As she did, the room cracked in two. The air exploded in a sonic shock, and my attacker lurched ahead, pitching us both forward, and then, just as awkwardly, she pulled back. Suddenly the noose around my neck loosened, and she teetered backwards. As she did, the arm wreathed on my collarbone pulled away, and her hand, still clutching the knife, flashed past my face in a last attempt to slice my gullet.

It went high and outside instead, and my right ear went white hot. I reached up for it and spun around to see the woman writhing and rolling on the floor. A few feet away Petey stood with a smoking pistol. The crowd outside was still cheering, standing now, applauding through its tears. There were plenty of tears. And my hand, now warm and wet, was full of blood.

12

Mexican Blues

The woman's name was Charlene Householder, of all things. *Householder?* No Houses in my lineage had been shortened from Householders, as far as I know, but it was too close for comfort. She was also nuttier than Jimmy Piersall on one of his bad days. At least, one of her personalities was. She had several, each one more antisocial than the next. She threw a half-dozen faces at Jim Holdsworth in just his first half hour with her. That took place in a maximum-security hospital room, for Petey's slugs had stitched her in the back, one lodging near the spine and nearly causing some nasty damage, and one in the shoulder. Householder, who was fifty, and in better shape than two guys in their twenties, was a big, tough crone, and she survived the pistol's small bullets like a catcher shaking off a foul tip on the instep.

But, good Lord, she was goofy. When she wasn't trying to bust out of her bed restraints, she babbled. Holdsworth said he had barely advised her of her rights to remain silent when she filled one side of his tape cassette. She confessed to every Sunset Boulevard slashing and gave Holdsworth chapter and verse on each one. Every old-timer was her ex-husband, she said, the guy she called Buck. Good old Buck. She ranted about his leaving her, looting her, saddling her with debt and back taxes up to her biceps.

Fact was, Holdsworth later learned, her husband was a diminutive, likable fellow who ran a vacuum-cleaner repair shop and liked the grape. He died on Sunset Boulevard when his liver gave out. And his name was Benno. His demise cracked Charlene into little psychotic pieces. Buck, it seems, was Mrs. Householder's father, and he was a gambler who had run off and left his wife, Charlene's mother, in a hole of debt. It was Buck's bad deeds that had somehow tattooed themselves onto his only daughter's psyche. Holdsworth, however, didn't have the time or the inclination to delve too deeply into that. No doubt some screenwriter would.

The detective was more interested in ironclad evidence that would put his cases to bed. Householder's voice with a towel over the receiver matched that of the caller. Her butcher knife checked out, and a share of her wardrobe contained stains of old men's blood. She lived on Duff Street and was known on the Boulevard. "Big Char," they called her. Known she was, but not suspected, because she was a woman. Serial killers are supposed to be men, loners in panel trucks.

It all checked out—except for Remsen. Though she tried, Big Char couldn't tell Holdsworth a thing about Jack's murder. She didn't know if she sat in the front seat or the back, if he was parked next to the laundromat or the taco stand. She claimed only that the deed was done with a different knife, though she didn't know what kind or where it was.

"She knew that 'cuz it wasn't hers, dammit," Holdsworth said to me.

Then he added, "Five in the can. One big one still open. Now entertain me with your suspects."

Entertain nothing. I was flat on my back in a hospital room. I felt like hell, like I'd been on the wrong end of a collision at home plate. Charlene Householder had thrown me around like a tuna. My already sore neck was worse. My shoulder was nearly separated. I had contusions on my ankles and fluid on my knee where I'd thwocked the scaffold's crossbars. And finally, my ear had been nearly sliced off. More stitches than they put in a baseball kept my pink flap from joining the van Gogh pile. The bandage made me look like a fresh mummy, a foot soldier just back from the front. The sawbones wanted to admit me overnight, but I said nothing doing. What I needed wasn't on the infirmary's menu.

Not only that, but camped outside the hospital were the microphones and the cameras. The second-string crews, because the heavy hitters were all over Mrs. Householder. The word got out that it was my ticket she planned on punching, and I became a big deal. The only phone call I took, however, was from Commissioner Chambliss.

"You're okay," he said. "That's good news, Duffy."

"Hear, hear," I muttered.

I didn't have the tongue to jabber. My painkillers were kicking in.

"Get me outta here," I drawled to Petey.

A few hours later Petey and Start got me through the back door and back home. A *Times* reporter rode along and tried to squeeze out some color. I had left most of mine on the bathroom floor. Petey talked, and I nodded. Whatever was in my bloodstream turned my knees to jelly and my brain to mush. I perked up only when the reporter asked Petey if she had seen Detective Holdsworth shoot the suspect.

Holdsworth? I mouthed.

"Right behind him," she said, a little too quickly.

That night I read about myself on the front page. All it told me was that any cover I'd had as an operative was now blown from here to El Segundo. I'm a news-writer, not maker. I reclined in Joe Start's La-Z-Boy and felt every bone in my body. They disapproved of the assaults they'd sustained out here in avocado land. They cottoned only to the fact that I was self-medicating with Jack Daniels. It is unwise to mix booze and painkillers. Never do it. Unless your ear hurts like a son-of-a-bitch and images of Amazons with tempered blades keep flashing before your eyes.

"You're going to be one stiff old peckerwood tomorrow," Start said. "Need some under-the-counter analgesic? I got a pretty liberal local pharmacist."

"Nah," I slurred. "At the House house we do it the old-fashioned way. We earn it."

I did slurp some soup Petey had assembled, and it went down well with the sour mash. For the rest of the evening, I stayed awake, but groggy, and the three of us talked of Houses, Householders, Holdsworths, and other worthy horrors. I must have rambled, for I remember saying "That was before your time" more than once. I remember hearing Petey tell Joe a story about her mother. Heard it, but didn't see it, for my eyes had shut, and I was on a vast concourse somewhere above the stadium of conscious life. Old men and young were up there, teenagers with boom boxes and air-pumped sneakers, clowns reading poetry, and vendors selling everything from Pee Wee Reese bats to Mike Brito's speed guns. Pastor Wayne and Pastor Will were up there too, at a booth selling indulgences. And a large lady in a Dodger-blue jacket called me home.

I have no idea of how I got to bed, and when I awoke, I had no idea how I was going to get up. I could move my neck neither to the right nor the left, and I couldn't move much below my neck. Which in one sense was good: if I held my head perfectly still, the timpani somebody was beating inside it stayed at a low rumble. I didn't know if that was due to the pills or Mr. Daniels. I took a quick inventory of my carcass: the hot ear, the thick neck, stiff shoulders, bruises the size and color of eggplants, but good legs. Hey, my old flippers had done okay. They kicked like hell when it counted. On balance I felt damn pleased to open my eyes and find myself still in the land of mockingbirds and eucalypti, not facing up to that Big Doug Harvey in the sky.

I must have lingered like that for a while, before I heard the bedroom door quietly open.

"You still among the quick, Unk?" Petey asked.

"No Maury Wills, but I'm alive," I said.

She came in with a glow and sat on the bed. Then she grinned.

"What's the chuckle?"

"Your ear. You look like a kid who just got hit with a snowball," she said, and thought she was pretty cute.

She was.

"By the way, thanks for taking pistol practice," I said.

She smiled and bowed slightly.

"Next question. How'd Holdsworth get the gun?" I said.

"He took it. He was incredible," she said. "As soon as he saw what went down, he said, 'The gun registered?' I said sort of. I mean, the gun guy predated my application. He liked me. Holdsworth snatched it out of my hand, and that was that. He came by this morning and laid the situation out for me. Said when there's no fatality, the department's shooting investigation is pretty routine. I think he saved me a lot of grief."

I shook my head. Saved by an illegal handgun. The NRA could have a field day with that one.

"Big Jim's been around. He give you the pistol back?"

"Nope."

"Good," I said, but weakly.

"But he gave me another one. Much better. Nickel-plated. A real angry little thing."

I would complain about the new, revised, treacherous Petey, but I don't look gift horses in the mouth.

"What else is happening?" I asked.

"You and your date are all over the news. Holdsworth is positive she didn't ice Remsen, and he wants everything we get from now on. And Darby O'Brien called."

"Whoa," I said, feeling jolts of pain as I tried to sit up. "Back up on that one."

"She said she saw you on the news. She also said she thinks she knows where the money went. She wants to show you something. Said it was important, and she had to do it in person. The woman sounded pretty stressed, Unk."

"She didn't tell you what it was?"

"That's all she would say. Except she asked if we'd leaned on Bob Ferguson. I got the impression he leaned on her."

"Where did you leave it with her?"

"She'll meet me at the Santa Anita Racetrack this afternoon."

I moaned.

"You're not going to meet her, Unk. Not while you look like Pete Reiser."

"Way before your time," I said.

She winked and took off, only to return a few minutes later with a tray.

"Joe made this up for you," she said.

It was buttermilk and some of the horse pills he'd suggested last night. It was an old trick, he said, because buttermilk lays a base in your intestines so that the drug doesn't eat up your stomach lining. Our generation knows buttermilk intimately as a liquid, not just an ingredient in pancakes, so it was no hardship to chug it down. I laid some additional base with a bagel and cream cheese, and after waiting for some close cousin of codeine in the horse pills to flood my system, I started to feel ambulatory again.

Any hope of getting much done was scotched by the telephone. Somehow my whereabouts got out, and every newsbird in the land wanted me on the horn. I talked to a few of them, including Harry Steinfeldt back in Chicago and Pat Moran down in San Diego. But I kept it short. I don't like the star treatment, and I put off any "bait" talk. My line was that I was in the wrong place at the wrong time. The lady liked my looks, that's all. Hell, if I was going to do any more work on the Remsen file, I had to get back into the low lights.

Then I made a call of my own. The Cubs were in town for a weekend series, and that meant Red Carney was lighting up Southern California. Carney, my old friend, raconteur, bacchant, and star of the Cubs broadcast crew, wouldn't forgive me for not checking in. Even in my battered state, I looked forward to hearing Red's guttural tones.

"Holy cow, Duffy! I hear you ran into Ma Barker," Red bellowed.

"Ooze some sympathy, will ya Red, for cryin' out loud."

"Aw, c'mon, Duf. We all held our breath when we

heard about it. You're a living legend, you know that. But shoot, if all those newspapers couldn't kill ya, there's no way a whacked-out broad could do the job."

"She would have if it hadn't been for Petey."

"Petrinella! How is that lovely, lovely young lady? Hey, wait a minute. Whattaya mean? The papers said the cop saved your neck."

"Don't believe everything you read, Red."

"Holy cow!" he yelled, loud enough to penetrate the gauze over my right ear.

"Tell me all about it. I want every detail," he said, making social arrangements.

"I'm not much company for the time being. You'll be the only possum out tonight."

"And the big ones do walk at night," he assured me.

At noon Joe Start turned up and helped with the phone. With the slasher case closed, he was taking some time away from the newsroom. He needed it. I felt like shit. He looked like it. Nevertheless, when he saw me limping around with my lopsided head and my neck crooked, he went to his bedroom and returned with one of those foam-rubber neck braces.

"Put this on," he said. "Doctor gave it to me just after the missus left."

"I thought you took it *off* when she left," I said.

He didn't laugh.

A little while later Petey headed out for Santa Anita.

"Watch yourself," I said.

She patted her purse.

I fussed with the brace, feeling like I was on the wrong end of a hemorrhoid doughnut, but I had to admit that it kept the head stationary and put my brain's timpani down to pianissimo.

Sometime in early afternoon Start took a call from the Dodger clubhouse.

"Ike Benners, Duf," Start said. "He wants to talk to you."

Benners was the Dodger trainer, a likable, quiet

young guy who had a reputation for not chirping on injuries. Company man. A trainer can have gamblers all over him. Knowing who can play or who's at half speed improves your line considerably. The smart ones don't open to anybody.

"Got a player who wants to talk to you, Mr. House," Benners said. "Just you."

"Who?"

"Tommy York."

"Can't he use a phone?"

"He won't talk on the phone."

I told him I'd get down there as soon as I could. The Dodgers-Cubs game was under the lights, so the players would be in at midafternoon. There'd be a big gate and plenty of attention on the Remsen-less Dodgers.

"Busy day on the farm, Joe," I said, telling him about York.

"Surprise you, Duffy? Did you have the slasher taking out Remsen?"

"On my lazy days, yes. Madmen are easier to figure out than schemers."

We made it to Dodger Stadium, a place I now looked upon a little less kindly, in cut time. With my neck brace and my head dressing, I looked as if I needed an usher to wheel me to the invalid seats. Instead, we got a pass to the clubhouse. There we ran into Nobe Kawano, the clubhouse czar. He pointed at my ear and cupped a palm over his.

"Come in, Tokyo. Come in, Tokyo," he said.

Start snickered.

"This is the horseshit I get," I said. Nobe nodded like Pat Morita.

Tommy York, the aging rookie project who was still taking treatments on his groin, was waiting for us. Ike Benners gave us his office. Start stayed behind.

"Whew boy, Mr. House, I heard you got mugged up. I heard right. A lady done that?"

"That was no lady," I assured him. "So how's it goin' with you, Tommy?"

"I'm still here. Without Jack, who knows for how long? He say a injury can't beat you out. You heal up and you get your job back. But now we got Allie. He gonna honor that?"

He spoke quietly, as much out of fear as courtesy. He was referring to Doug Allison, the Dodger interim manager. The heat from York's session in the whirlpool made him sweat, and he wiped his head and neck with a towel.

"Can you play?"

"Can't go sideways. Hit it at me, I got it. . . ." he said, and left it at that.

If he couldn't move laterally, I knew, he probably couldn't stride in the batter's box. For a guy who made the team with his bat, that was trouble. Unless he healed, Tommy York was back in the bushes.

"Whattaya got?"

"Maybe nothin'. Didn't wanna bother you, what with your condition."

"Don't worry, kid," I said, "it's all in the name of Jack."

"You got it. 'Member that long game? Jack pinch-hit me in the tenth."

"Popped up."

"Shit. So I come in the video room back here. Look at the tape and see what fooled me. We can do that real quick 'cuz they tape the game while it's goin', and you can check your at-bat out. And I come back, and there's a dude back here. One a Rem's old players. You seen him around. And he give me a note and say to give it to Skip for him."

"Who was it?"

"Don't know. Short guy. Played 'fore I come around."

"So what did you do?"

"I give Rem the paper. He look at it and look at me and shove it in his pocket. Didn't like it, like he didn't like nothin' about that night."

"You didn't look at the note?"

"No, sir."

"And Jack didn't say anything to you about it?"

"No, sir."

"And the fellow who gave it to you, was he around after the game?"

"Not that I seen."

"And you don't know who he was?"

"Seen him before, as I said. Don't got a name on him."

"And nobody else was around?"

"Not that I seen right then and there. So I wish I knew who it was."

"That's easy enough," I said.

We got up and went over to Remsen's office. It had been untouched since that night and was off limits now. I appealed to Nobe Kawano. He went in with us, and Tommy York scanned Remsen's photo wall.

"Him," York said.

He pointed to a glossy of a former Dodger relief pitcher, one Bob Ferguson.

I thanked York and wished him luck. He'd need it without his Chinaman. I also asked Nobe if I could borrow a Dodger yearbook. A 1978 edition. He had one, and you would have thought I'd asked him to part with his '81 Championship ring.

"What's that for?" Start asked as we left the clubhouse.

I told him York's story.

"The more I hear about Bob Ferguson, the more I wanna know," I said.

"Note coulda said, 'Bring back Podres,' " he said.

"And it coulda set up a meet," I said.

"That's a leap."

"Let's make a phone call," I said.

In the pressroom I dialed Holdsworth's beeper. It took him only a few minutes to respond. I was beginning to like those gadgets more and more.

"Whattaya got, Duf? And how you feelin'? How's the ear?"

"I'm functional. Forget about the ear. What I got is a question. What did your bloodhounds turn up with

Jack on Sunset Boulevard that night? Anybody see him? He hit any watering holes?"

"That's a question. He was seen. I don't remember where. You wanna wait, and I'll case it for ya?"

"Won't break the line," I said.

It didn't take him long. Holdsworth had a brain.

"Got it. Okay. He was found at Lucile. 'Member? But we got two people put his Cadillac around Hollywood and Sunset. That's down a few blocks. Just two. Ain't much. It's a lot of streets come together there, Duffy. Plenty of white Caddies gonna be there even at two in the ayem."

"All right," I said.

"Why, you got something?"

"Not yet. Go back to your paperwork."

I hung up and turned to Start.

"Well?" he said.

"Holdsworth said he's got a pair of witnesses who put Remsen's car on the Boulevard in Hollywood. I say we try to put Ferguson there too. Do some old-fashioned legwork."

"You up to it?"

"No. But your pills are helping me fake it."

I adjusted the neck brace and hobbled off. In the distance of the playing field, we heard the crack of some early batting practice. It was Tommy York. He was hanging frozen ropes all over the infield.

We drove out Elysian Park Avenue to the Scorpion Tire Company and headed west on Sunset. It was a familiar turn for both of us. We passed gamey lounges with no doors and a toothless clientele, Hispanic bars with Hawaiian vocal groups, and package-store taps with plenty of screw-top bargains to go. By the time we could spy the white letters of Hollywood on the hillside, the saloons got upscale and Anglo.

We pulled up at the seven-corner intersection where Sunset met Hollywood as well as Hillhurst and Virgil. It was a messy junction of streets, a visitor's nightmare, but it also had a few joints that held promise.

Start parked at a meter.

"Here's the problem," he said. "You walk in, and

you draw a crowd. A guy with a neck brace and a headful of tape. They'll call you by your first name."

"So you wanna try?"

"I was afraid you'd say that."

"Put it this way, Joe. I flushed your slasher out for ya. Getting that bastard—er, that bitch—was important to you. Now it's my turn."

"I'll try that one first," he said, and swung out with the yearbook under his arm toward a place called Circle West—Dancing and Cocktails.

By now it was late afternoon, and these places would be attracting the head-start weekend crowd. Or maybe not. I wasn't sure how folks drank nowadays. I watched Start lumber in. He looked harmless, somewhat preoccupied, like a guy who'd left his sunglasses lying on a table. It was the perfect cover.

He emerged a few minutes later, shrugged his shoulders in my direction, and went into another place, called the Guatalina Nightclub. No luck there either. He tried two more, came out looking just as vacant, and went into a place called Oyster Burns. It had a lot of Irish clovers, shillelaghs, and beer steins on the windows. Start stayed inside a lot longer. I figured he was having a beer, the son-of-a-gun.

He finally showed his face and came over to the car.

"Base hit. Guy there knew Ferguson. Said he comes in and hangs out and wags his tongue at the waitresses. But not that night, as far as he could remember. He said check across the street. See it? Rudy Garcia's Blues Bar. When he gets stale in Ireland, he goes to Mexico."

"I'm comin' with you. I need a beer."

"Good. I'm gettin' sick of the beat."

We crossed Sunset and ducked inside. I liked the place right off. The walls were maroon and had sombreros hanging all over them. Big, floppy, *siesta-mañana*, badges?-we-don't-need-no-stinking-badges sombreros. A scarlet papier-maché parrot hung with one claw on a swing in a corner near a big saguaro cactus with a sombrero on top. The place had Tijuana in the fifties written all over it. It also had a dozen or so early imbibers, some young, some older, some Latinos, some lawyers.

The jukebox was playing a blues instead of a mariachi band, thank goodness. A makeshift but empty stage promised the real thing later on.

Start and I slid onto the stools and ordered something domestic. The young Mexican barkeep brought us Dos Equis. Take that, gentlemen. After a slug that hit the back of my neck like a runaway ice cube, I flipped the Ferguson photo in front of the kid. He shrugged the old *No comprende.*

"Quien?" Start asked.

"Rudy," the kid said, hinting at a fellow in the shadows.

He was on his way over anyway.

"Mr. Garcia, I presume?" I said, looking at a guy who was Davey Lopes's twin right down to the scouring-pad mustache and the sleepy lids. He wore a blue T-shirt that read, Bring Back John Mayall.

He looked at me and gawked at the igloo on my ear. He nodded as if I were a horse and my teeth looked good.

"In Mexico we slice 'em off the bulls," he said.

"Hooray for Mexico," I said.

"It hurts. Don't mind him," Start said.

Garcia put a wet finger on Ferguson's pic. "That's Roberto. That what you want to know?"

"You know him?"

"Very good. Good customer. Comes in and I don't got a bottle of tequila that's safe. I like Bob."

"He been here lately?"

"That's what I said. He gets tired of the chi-chis across the street, he comes over here."

"Last Thursday night? The long game night? The night—" I said.

"Like I don't remember? Like I was in Chihuahua?"

I sucked on my beer. For a blues-bar owner, Rudy Garcia was no picnic.

"Bob came in, and he wants the TV on. There was no band, no business, so I turn it on. Maybe see Terrio. Adonis. But he's long gone by then. Bobby wants to know how it comes out, so him and me watch the game.

Long game and Bob's bitchin' that he wants it over. He pitches relief, and he's complainin' about the relief pitchers. He don't care. He says a game goes past ten, and the guys sleepwalk. Me? I'm closin' at one-thirty, so I don't care. We both don't care. So he takes off. Some night. That what you want to know?"

"When'd he leave?"

"Before I closed. That's when. If he didn't, I was going to lock him in, 'cuz I was out. How 'bout you? You the guy from Chicago? Ever been at the Checkerboard? Muddy Waters?"

I grumped over my glass. He was talking junkyard-dog territory. The beer was good but gone, and Garcia didn't offer a refill. I nudged the glass and belched, but Garcia didn't budge. His muchacho behind the bar slept.

"I never heard of a Mexican blues bar," I said.

"Yeah, well maybe you need a new ear," he said. Start pinched a grin on that one.

"Jack Remsen ever come in?" Start recovered.

"Never. He digs Sinatra," Garcia said.

With that Garcia was handed a phone over the bar, and he turned away from us.

"What's the Checkerboard?" Start asked.

"Where'd John Mayall go?" I replied.

"Let's get outta here," Start said.

We had to fight Dodger Stadium traffic to get back to Alhambra. Freeway traffic was stacked up like a refugee march. Going nowhere. It was the slowest trip I've taken since Wilma took me on a tour of Pennsylvania quilting country. Start didn't seem to notice. In the meantime I filled him in with what we knew of Ferguson, of Darby O'Brien, of Billy Harbridge, of Jack Remsen's alleged midnight proclivities.

Finally we punched into Alhambra's city limits and got back home. I wasn't feeling so hot. The ear throbbed. The car seat did no good for the shoulder. I needed some more of Start's medicine.

First I played back the phone machine.

"Unk," Petey said, calling in from Santa Anita. "I been here two hours, and she hasn't shown up. Said she would meet me at the big fountain in the kids' play area. I've covered that, the betting windows, the wine sheds, the johns, even the horse paddock. Nothing. Zip. Bye."

There was a pause, a beep, and a second call.

"Unk. I been stood up, and I'm outta here. I can't get to Holdsworth. I can't get to you guys. I smell a rat here, and I'm tempted to go and find her. Where the hell are ya anyway?"

After another beep the message was short.

"That does it. I'm on my way to Vegas. Catch you later."

13

Adonis Terrio

To Petey the desert highway was the Bonneville salt flats, and she was Craig Breedlove. That's speculation on my part, because she never revealed her pace. But I'm sure she tore, injected gasoline into those cylinders like perfume on a vamp. What she did divulge was that she got to Las Vegas just as darkness fell. Then again, with all that neon, how did she know?

Finding Darby O'Brien took some sleight of mouth. She said that when she called the casino and was told that O'Brien had the day off, she passed herself off as a favorite cousin who wanted to surprise Darby by showing up in her driveway. It wouldn't have worked for me, or Start, or Holdsworth, but it worked for Petey. Home phone number and address. No one picked up the phone. That left a visit to the home.

With directions from a Unocal oil jockey who wanted to teach her how to play keno, Petey found her way to a cul-de-sac of white stucco tile-roofed bungalows a few miles east of Liberace's Museum in East Las Vegas. They were slight one-story bargains, ticky-tacky Spanish style.

Petey eased the Buick down the asphalt street. It was dark, dry, and deserted. There were no sidewalks. The cactus and rock gardens that made up front yards came right to the curb. The stones cooled in the night air. Somewhere a lot of displaced snakes and scorpions complained about progress. Drapes were closed. Each

house had an attached wooden carport, and some of
those held small foreign trucks. She spotted O'Brien's
drive and a yellow two-seater sports car parked close to
the house. The place was shut tight, however, and was
as dark as a doghouse. A white shade covered the front
window. A stranger would have guessed the owners
had left for Seattle.

Petey parked two houses down and cut the engine.
She saw no one and had the feeling no one saw her. So
much for the warmth of a neighborhood. She walked
soundlessly up the drive, feeling the radiant heat of the
concrete. Trying the front bell was silly, she decided,
and she followed a narrow walk around the side. She
was careful not to rattle a three-foot cyclone fence that
marked the property line and continued into the backyard. The house next door was as dark as O'Brien's.
Maybe the whole block worked four to midnight at the
tables.

The walk led to a small patio, which wasn't much
more than a slab surrounded by more rocks and crushed
stone. On the slab was an aluminum chaise longue,
O'Brien's tanning bed, no doubt. There was some light
back here, but it came from colored Chinese lanterns
hanging over the rear neighbor's porch. Someone giggled far in the distance. An air conditioner kicked on.

For a moment Petey stopped and hugged the
house's back wall. She'd found a dark house among dark
houses in a desert neighborhood. Her informant was
nowhere to be found. She shivered. Then, she said, she
checked her guts. It was B&E time.

She edged over to the back door. She'd break a
window, maybe a basement pane, or glass in the door
itself. Then she noticed the screen door. It was ajar. She
opened it, and it screeched, as screen doors do. Her
heart pumped, and she held her breath. Then she saw
it. The inner door was cracked. Petey nudged it, and it
swung open. She was now more terrified than ever. And
the pistol came out. It shook in her right hand as she
slipped into the kitchen.

·   ·   ·

If I was kidding anybody about my ability to bounce back after my washroom grapple, I wasn't kidding myself. I was drained by the time we got back to the house, and my body throbbed like a bass drum. It was as stupid to have spent the afternoon gumshoeing as it would have been to pitch batting practice to Tommy York. Not that many minutes after I swallowed another pill and ate some leftover soup, I sat down to watch the Dodgers and Cubs. I never made it past the starting lineups. Slept like a man without a conscience.

It was black inside except for the digital clock on the microwave. Petey pressed the back door shut and waited for her eyes to adjust to the lower light. The place smelled vaguely like a cheap air freshener, a No Pest Strip. When she snapped on the stove light, she saw the mess. A Formica-topped table was strewn with papers—thin catalogs, bags, mail. A canister of sugar had been overturned on the counter. She banged her knee on an open sink-cabinet door. It was open because the waste basket had been overturned, and there was trash all over the floor. Yogurt containers, cottage cheese, frozen Mexican dinners, empty cranberry-juice cans.

Even to a relative amateur like Petey, it was obvious the place had been tossed. She chewed a divot on the inside of her cheek. When the refrigerator started, she jumped. She had seen too many maniac movies to enjoy this. With a palm braced against the wall, she felt her way into the dining room. It too had a smell—a stuffy, mealy smell. It needed fresh air badly.

Just inside the room Petey's shoulder grazed a credenza, a tall piece of furniture with a glass front. But it was the electrical cord hanging on the side that Petey went for, and with her free hand she found a line switch. She tripped it, and an interior bulb lit up glass shelves full of china harlequins. Some of them were pretty good. A few were gifts from Jack Remsen. But Petey never saw a one of them, for the light also lit up Darby O'Brien.

Petey gasped. O'Brien was sitting at the dining-room table, a piece that matched the credenza, her head in her arms like a schoolchild taking a nap. Her lush blond hair covered her face, looking as if someone had tossed a full wig on the table.

"Darby?" Petey whispered.

She didn't move. Petey held her breath. The hot bulb in the cabinet blinked. Trembling, her heart beating in her throat, Petey stepped to her and with two fingers moved O'Brien's hair away from her face. Her dark eyes were closed, but her mouth was agape, and her tongue hung out of it like a fresh sausage. That, and the dried spittle and a chair full of urine, was the smell. Darby O'Brien, her once-pampered countenance now cruelly contorted, was very dead. Her neck had been broken. A finger on her right hand was fractured. Petey shuddered at the sight of her.

Just then Petey felt herself losing it, and she clutched her throat and sunk to one knee.

The phone didn't wake me, nor did concern over the safety and whereabouts of my niece. But when Holdsworth called, Start shook me out of dreamland. The detective had two problems: he couldn't scare up Bob Ferguson or Darby O'Brien. Before he went out looking for them, he wanted to know if I had any tips. I gave him what we learned from Rudy Garcia. I told him about Petey and Santa Anita. Holdsworth didn't like the latter one bit. Said she had no business going free-lance. His ill humor pricked me up. Made me forget the hurts. And made me worry.

Petey's queasiness passed—this was no time to add her broth to the stew—but she stood back up without much more a blush in her cheeks than O'Brien had. Yet in those moments Petey used her head and knew that she had to get what she could from the scene. She saw that O'Brien was fully dressed in slacks, a blouse, wearing jewelry. She had never made it out of the house this morning. Her purse lay upended on the table in front of her, and its contents were everywhere. Petey put her pistol back into her own purse and pawed through the pile, the wallet, makeup, papers, and keys. Someone had done it before her, someone who wanted more from O'Brien than her last breath, and Petey had no idea if what was searched for had been found.

She held each scrap of paper up to the light. O'Brien was a list maker, but none of these lists went further than the grocery store. Petey searched her wallet, finding her date book. The entry for this day was blank except for a single word: "Returns." For Petey, however, that clicked.

With the light of a lamp on an end table, she made a careful sweep of the rest of the house. Minus the corpse, it resembled the surface of the dining-room table. An indoors dust devil couldn't have made more of a mess. Cushions, books, cassettes and discs, clothing, and shoes lay everywhere. O'Brien's bedroom, which featured a giant unmade canopy bed with satin sheets, was even worse. The closet had been looted, the dressers ransacked. Petey paused among the rubble, then she spotted what she was looking for. Lying just under the bed were two shopping bags from someplace called Boulevard Mall.

For some reason the bags had not been rifled, and Petey dug in. O'Brien liked a place called Victoria's Secret. This last haul hadn't even been taken from the boxes. Petey sorted through the merchandise. O'Brien had a taste for silk camisoles and satin chemises, kimonos, and pajamas. She was a slippery lady in more ways than one. It was all slinky, expensive stuff, garb of someone who apparently did more than eat cold pizza in the bedroom.

Petey kept her opinion of the wardrobe to herself —but did check out the sizes—and hunted for the sales slip. Sales slips, she explained later, are a woman's Dead Sea Scrolls, a Rosetta stone of things done and things to do. Women keep them like diaries. Use them as bookmarks. Scribble on them.

Darby O'Brien was no exception. On the back of

this one she had jotted down a list. Names. A whole column of them. And at the top was "Ferguson." It was all Petey had to see. She stuffed the paper into her purse.

Dousing the light behind her, she made her way back into the kitchen and called me.

"She's dead, Unk," she said, whispering it into the receiver like a conspirator.

"Talk up, Petey," I barked.

She couldn't, or wouldn't, she said, and went on to tell me what she'd found. She was breathing hard as she spoke. She was one spooked, but gutsy, kid.

"Call Holdsworth. I'm getting the hell out of here," she said.

"No, you're not," I said. "You already made a very traceable call to this number, and your mitts have probably printed up the place like a finger painting. You leave now, and you're an accessory."

"Shit," she said.

"Sit tight," I said. "I'll call Holdsworth and tell him to get to one of his people in Las Vegas. He can do the blocking for you when they get there."

She agreed. At least she said she did. Waiting for the police in a dark apartment with a stiff in the next room wasn't her idea of romance.

"You okay, Pete?" I asked.

She hesitated on that one.

"A lot better than the blonde," she finally said.

She got home, she said, at three A.M. I didn't meet her at the door. But she was running on premium and was downstairs not much after eight. Before she even began to recap the night, she slapped Darby O'Brien's sales slip on the breakfast table.

"Take a look at *this*," she exclaimed.

"Backtrack," I said, and listened patiently as she regurgitated every detail, right down to the way she invaded the house to the temperature of Darby O'Brien's forehead. The cops took a better look at her neck, Petey said, and it appeared to them that she had been strangled. They did not suspect Petey, or even make an effort to punch any holes into her glib account of why she was inside the house in the first place. Holdsworth obviously had some clout, she said.

"So now take a look at Exhibit A," she said.

The back of the sales slip had eight names on it. All of them were written in longhand with the same cursive that had signed the front side. And there was Ferguson right on top.

"He gets around," I said.

I told Petey of Rudy Garcia and what he told us. As I spoke, the Mexican connection suddenly made more sense, because the rest of the names on O'Brien's list were Latin. None of them meant anything to me except the last one.

"Terrio. Adonis Terrio," I said.

"El Phenomo," Petey said.

I got up and refilled my coffee cup. Petey, who looked a little frayed around her red edges even with her morning verve, ate a banana.

"What in hell could this be all about?" I wondered out loud.

"Darby was gonna tell us," Petey said. "As she said on the phone, 'I think I know where the money went.'"

Now it was my turn to plow the fields. I felt up to it even though my ear was getting sloppy. I had an appointment with the doctor this morning, and as far as I was concerned, it was time to get rid of the gauze. In the meantime I made a call to the Dodger clubhouse. I didn't know the new skipper, Doug Allison, that well, but he was Remsen's guy, and he'd hear me out. I told him I had to sit down with Terrio. I didn't tell him why. He didn't balk.

"Let me get you to Juan," he said.

That was Juan Cassida, the Nicaraguan coach who rode herd over the team's Latin players. For years the Dodgers had worked the tropical leagues for talent, from Manny Mota to Valenzuela, and then tried to make them comfortable once they got there. They did that with coaches such as Preston Gomez, Mota himself, and now Cassida. Part of it was simple communication, part of it was cultural baby-sitting. Life in Southern California as a Dodger was a lot different from that in a village in Mexico or Puerto Rico. A whole lot different.

Through the juice of a plug the size of a hot pepper, Cassida agreed to a meet that afternoon.

"Lotta people wanna talk to my boy," he crowed.

Before that, however, I had to make a stop at the infirmary. My ear was getting a little gamey, and it needed a less conspicuous bonnet. I was sick of looking like a walking Q-Tip. Petey stayed behind to get herself together, and when I returned just after noon, I had a new look. Instead of the battlefield bandage, the right ear, which in its naked state looked like the butt end of a trussed turkey, was covered with a modest flesh-colored patch. It hugged my wattles and allowed wispy strands of white hair to fall over it like straw on a rock.

"Nice," Petey said. "You look like one-half of an android, but it's nice."

"Let's go," I said.

Terrio wasn't slated to pitch that night, but he was in the park early. Only twenty-one years old, with an arm that had a great grip on the brass ring, he couldn't get to the ballyard fast enough.

This time Petey and I parked near the players' gate beyond left field. We followed the tunnel beneath the stands and into the clubhouse. It was not yet two o'clock, and the biggest racket in the place came from washing machines and the stereos of the clubhouse boys. To my one good ear, they sounded about the same.

Juan Cassida met us with a handshake and a leaking grin. He was holding a tuna can into which he drained his cheek juice every so often. Juan was about sixty pounds over his playing weight and with knees that knocked, but he was okay. In his salad days he had had the build of Johnny Roseboro, the grin of Pepe Frias, and the mustache of Pancho Villa. He'd made a career out of being a left-handed banjo hitter. Pitchers took him for granted just long enough for him to slap a quail down the third-base line. Got to second standing up, happy as the worm in the bottle.

He pointed at my ear patch and grimaced.

"*Ai caramba,*" he said.

Petey, who was becoming a pain in the neck on this thing, snickered.

Cassida surveyed her. "*Señorita,*" he said, with enough sauce to make it illegal.

Standing behind him all this time was a stick of a kid in a nylon Dodger sweat suit. He was a tall bean, but no more than 145 pounds dripping. Dark curly hair cropped close, skin the color of cocoa. And he was young, past his curfew no matter what the time. Joe Nuxhall as a rookie looked older.

"Ay, Adonis, *que bonita,* eh?" Cassida said, stepping aside.

Petey offered a good handshake and tried to calm them down. Terrio shook it meekly. Cassida waved us into the deserted Angels locker room and pushed some chairs together. Terrio sat a half step behind Cassida, his smile wide but his teeth questionable. A front tooth was ringed with gold, and another was missing. His skin glistened, and his complexion was laced with angry clumps of acne. I had the feeling I was making him miss geography class. An Adonis he wasn't, but with a 92 MPH fastball and good control, nobody in Dogtown was being picky.

Cassida figured we were here to talk baseball, and he joked and spat. He chirped in Spanish to Terrio. The kid's English was limited to "7UP" and "Pepsi."

"I want Adonis to look at something," I said to Cassida.

"He already looks," Cassida said, with an eyebrow lifted at Petey. Terrio grinned.

I pulled the list of names out of my pocket. It was a fresh sheet of paper; I had printed out the monikers myself. Cassida took it and looked it over. He spat into the can. It was a concentrated stream, for Cassida had suddenly lost his glee.

He muttered to Terrio.

"Estes—quienes son?"

Petey knew some Spanish, and I hoped she was tapping into the patter. He passed the sheet to the young ball player. It might just as well have been an immigration notice, for Terrio's expression went blank, then green. The kid was ice in front of power hitters and forty thousand fans, but the names on that piece of paper rattled him.

"What do you want from this?" Cassida said quickly.

"Who are they? What's he got to do with them?" I asked.

Again Cassida spoke in Spanish. Terrio replied. Cassida spoke. Terrio replied. There was no levity. No banter. The pitcher squirmed. The look in his eye was that of a kid explaining high jinks to his father.

"Stay here. I come back," Cassida said, and he took Terrio with him back into the Dodger locker room.

Petey inhaled.

"Hit a vein, Unk," she observed.

A few minutes later Cassida reappeared. He'd left his chaw and his tuna can behind. He didn't sit down.

"Okay. What's this shit all about? The murder? This about Jack? Tell me what you know, man, I ain't shittin' around now."

"We aren't either, Juan," I said.

I went on to tell him our status. I also told him we were one step ahead of the police.

"It does have to do with Remsen. That's for sure," I added.

It was his pitch. Cassida chafed, looking like an edgy coach with a 3–2 pitch and the runners going.

"You scare the kid pretty bad. Hell, you scare me. But he's a boy, and he don't know nothin' but to be a Dodger, be like Fernando, you know? That's his hero from when he's barefoot. So now you got these people, these names, they in his village. Tido Dali. His *tio.* Calls him Tio Tido. Big, bad man. A family all bad. Adonis say they work with Colombians now. Colombians come to

California through his village in Mexico. You understand?"

"I think so," I said.

"He's scared now. As soon as he make the Dodgers, Tio Tido make contact. Call him up, say, 'Adonis, you're my boy.' He can't say nothing to turn him down. Not from the village like that. Now Adonis—he's the hero, you know? They all know him now, and they all his big friends. Adonis, Adonis, that's all you hear.

"And now you come with that list, and his name is on it. No, he says, those people are criminals. Not him. He don't do nothing with these people. Why should he? He think that you come here because you think he— Adonis—killed Señor Remsen, you know? That's how loco he is in there right now."

"How bad are they," Petey asked, "this Tio Tido and that bunch?"

"Mucho. They would kill your mother," he said.

"The Colombian thing. He know any more about that? Are his people dealers or what?" Petey asked.

"He don't tell me more except that Tio Tido is rich. Cadillac man. How you get rich in Adonis's village, huh?"

I pointed to Ferguson's name.

"What about him?" I asked.

"Bobby? *I* know, Bobby," Cassida said. "Played on my team. Adonis—*he* don't know Bob Ferguson. But look at this, okay? All these names—Spanish. Bobby's Anglo. That say something to you? Figure it out, man."

"But how and what?" I asked.

"Talk to Ferguson," Cassida said. "Look him up."

He clapped his hands and looked as if he wanted out.

"What did Remsen have to do with this?" Petey said.

Cassida shrugged and wouldn't commit. I tossed it around some, rubbed a contemplative hand over my chin.

"Tell Adonis he has nothing to be scared about," I said finally. "We're not the police, and we don't want him."

"Too late now," Cassida said. "He shakes like a little puppy back there. You don't know Mexico. You don't know his village."

I folded the paper and tucked it into my sport coat. I wasn't sure where to leave it now. We'd come to the ballpark and scared the bejesus out of the Dodgers' best young arm. If pitching is control and confidence, Adonis Terrio might never get another fastball over the plate.

"Now for one more thing," Cassida said. "Tio Tido and the whole village—they all coming to town. Sunday. Cinco de Mayo, you know? Big festival, big celebration in Little Mexico. Same day Adonis starts for us. Afternoon game and all his people are here. He got a ticket list that long. Full of *compadres*."

"The same ones on this list?" I asked, patting my breast pocket.

"That's right, man—for sure some of them. Adonis—he think he's a criminal now."

With that Juan Cassida, acting *tio* to a fearful, unnerved rookie from a small village in Mexico, signed off and shuffled back to his charge. No *adios*, no *vaya con Dios*. No more playful sallies with the pretty señorita. We had not made his job any easier. He had cinched ours.

14

Cinco de Mayo

Holdsworth was waiting for our call. The big front-court man just about jumped up to the phone wire and picked it off.

"I want a huddle with you both," he said.

No more clubhouse gumshoeing, no more solo runs across the desert.

We went to his place, police HQ on Los Angeles Street, and we were swept upstairs quicker than you can say Detective Lieutenant Arthur Tragg. The sea of desks and telephones that was Homicide reminded me of an old city room. Holdsworth's was covered with paper, reports from his detectives on one case and one case only, he said.

He started right in.

"We put a full-court press on Ferguson. He's been a busy boy. That quarter mil. Put it on deposit long enough for the check to clear, then took it out in cash. Few days ago.

"But that's all we got. We ain't seen him. House is shut up. Dog's gone. Cars are gone. We think he took off in his boat, and we ain't found that either. Gone. No trace."

He stood with his big paws on his hips. Shirtsleeves, a watch with hands, wing tips minus plenty of leather on the soles.

I unfolded the paper with the column of names. He took it while looking at me. At my ear patch, that is.

"Played with a cat from Indiana, said that's how they got their nickname. Hoosiers, you know?"

"All right, Jim, let's have it," I said. The ear was starting to itch lately. It was itching right now.

"Said in the old coonskin days they had a lotta fights. Big, full-court fights in the saloons, and them liquored-up guys used to bite each other. Bite each other's *ears* off, he said. And when the fight was all over, they used to pick up the remains off the floor and hold 'em up in the air and say, 'Whose ear? Whose ear?' And it stuck."

Then he broke out a belly laugh and slapped the desk and carried on. Petey was right in there with him. High old time with the two of them.

When he had composed himself he went to the list.

"Fruits of Darby O'Brien," I said, "courtesy of Petey."

Petey waited for a nod.

"Say thank you," Holdsworth said, glancing up at her.

"Huh?" she said.

"Prowlers found in dead folks' houses are usually held as suspects," he said.

Petey withered.

Holdsworth returned to the paper. I told him what Adonis Terrio had said about Tido Dali and his clan. I threw in a little description of the effect the names seemed to have on Adonis. Holdsworth exhaled a low whistle.

"Gotta hand it to you two. We got a dozen men and women on this. Good cops. As thorough as you can get. And none of them come up with something like this."

I shrugged. "I'm just an old one-lobed scribe, Jim," I explained. "With a good legman."

Petey beamed, a cocky, green-eyed grin. There was no erasing this one.

"Let me get my dope people in on this," Holdsworth said, and went for the phone.

"While you're at it, boot up Ferguson's bank account," I said. "I think he's broke."

Petey's eyebrows perked.

The information Holdsworth wanted was not long in coming. He jotted notes on my paper as he talked to his source.

"Bingo," he said, hanging up. "Dali's a major courier. My people and the DEA here and in Mexico know him real well. Been on him for months now. They run the stuff. Colombians land it in Mexico, and Dali's people mule it into Arizona and L.A. Big time. Our people say these are some of his big guys, relatives mostly. He keeps it in the family."

"The kid involved?" I asked.

"Terrio? No, not that they seen. Related though. He's got a swell bunch of relatives."

"Your drug people know Ferguson?" Petey asked.

"Only from his Dodger days. If he's in with Tido Dali, it's new territory for him."

Holdsworth swiveled in his chair. "Let me try Breggen," he said.

He played with the phone, finally got someone, then hung up and waited. A few minutes later he got a return call. Again he scratched some notes. He hung up and turned to us.

"Okay. That was Fast Kenny, my money man. He's been on Ferguson's finances. Our boy is mortgaged up to his teeth. Took out a half mil on the beach house and hasn't made the interest nut in three months. Plastic is maxed. People with markers are lookin' for him. My man don't know where the scratch went, just that Ferguson owes a lot of it."

I nodded smugly. Petey shot a glance at me. I returned with my best editorial posture, cracked my knuckles in front of my belt, and verbalized my handle on the scam.

"That's our link. Ferguson went to the Mexicans for a deal. Big do-or-die roll, as far as he's concerned. He went to Remsen for the downstroke. Jack, the soft touch, got the cash from Darby, his banker, like he always did. Told her where it was going too, I'll bet. Then somehow he found out about what it was really for and raised hell. Cost him his life."

"Darby's too," Petey said.

"I'll buy it," Holdsworth said.

"So now we only have one hope," Petey quickly added.

"What's that?" said Holdsworth.

"That the delivery hasn't been made yet," she said. We all chewed on that for a moment.

"Cinco de Mayo," Holdsworth said, his Spanish impeccable.

If you were a rich uncle in town to see your sister's kid pitch for the Dodgers, you'd make a time of it. At least we hoped Tido Dali thought that way, that he and his compadres would come a day or so early to celebrate the biggest day on the Mexican calendar. But nobody knew where they would celebrate. Los Angeles has a massive Mexican population. The barrio of East Los Angeles is a city in itself. Cinco de Mayo, Holdsworth assured us, would be a hundred festivals in dozens of places: parks, street corners, shopping malls, downtown at the Pueblo de Los Angeles, backyards, on the hoods of automobiles.

For his part Adonis Terrio wasn't saying another word. Cassida said the kid was scared witless. He complained to Doug Allison, who got on the horn and chewed me out. I gave him his nickel. Allison was a baseball man in a tough spot, and I was tampering with his meal ticket.

Holdsworth did no better within his network. Dali was already in the country, he learned, probably in Los Angeles, but also possibly in San Diego. He had depots in that city. Nobody had a clear line on him. For all of the concern he supposedly posed for U.S. drug watchers, they didn't pay much attention to him when he went country hopping. At least, not as much as we wanted them to.

I racked my brain and cast about. I called Joe Start at the paper and had him work on it. I called politicians and librarians. I called Manny Mota, and Manny said, "What the hell? I'm from Santo Domingo, Duffy." I called my Mexican cleaning lady back in Chicago. She said I was loco and that I should hurry up and get back to town because she was sick of cleaning what she'd already cleaned.

Then it hit me: go to the main bean in the pot. One of the biggest piñatas in Little Mexico was still Bombo Carillo, everyone's favorite Mexican Dodger since Valenzuela. Wherever Bombo was, there'd be a party. The kind to draw Tio Tido.

It took me a while, no doubt because Bombo's a busy guy. But I finally got him. The background noise was something awful, and he chattered through a margarita as thick as a malted, but I finally got him.

"Cinco de Mayo? Ay, man," he said. "Bombo be one place: Obregon."

"Obregon?" I asked.

"Obregon," he repeated. Then he told me to come around, ride in his car, shoot off some firecrackers. Then I lost him to a lot of laughter and limes.

Eugene A. Obregon County Park was a small neighborhood patch of green grass and pine trees just off Brooklyn Avenue in East Los Angeles. It was quiet, leafy, and surrounded by residential side streets, with two ballfields, a swimming pool, and a sandy playground with a *caracol* and *calumpias*. Picnic tables were scattered about, but couples with little Jorges and Carmens preferred to sit in the grass and munch corn on the cob or takeouts from the "Mariscos, Tacos, Burritos" truck parked in front. It made sense, Holdsworth said, that a park like that would come alive on Cinco de Mayo.

It also made for a headache. This was a pocket park, a neighborhood niche crammed with families and thousands of kids. It wasn't a warehouse or a wharf, a dry arroyo or a deserted canyon road. It was the perfect place for a drop if you were the dropper; it was a nearly impossible place to stake out. But what choice did we have?

Sunday morning came chilly, like the cool of a desert rock before the sun hits it, and Petey and I headed out. The day reminded me of when I was a youngster, waiting in parking lots as a Boy Scout on Sunday morning to be transported to adventure outside the city. For us city kids then, urchins who climbed up the elevated tracks and ate the sparks of passing trains, the adventures had been tame.

We had time, so we skipped the freeway and drove city streets south out of Alhambra, past its twin icons—automobile dealerships and Chinese churches—into Monterey Park until we hit Brooklyn Avenue. It is the same Brooklyn Avenue that becomes Macy Street for a brief time downtown before it turns into Sunset Boulevard. Brooklyn is a street, however, as different from Sunset Boulevard as Boyle Heights is from Bel Air.

As we followed it into East Los Angeles, I swore it could have been lifted right out of Mexico City. Crowded, sensuous, busy, the smell of *chorizo* in the air, its sidewalks thick with people. The curbs were clogged with trucks and vans offering goods on their tailgates—coconuts, watermelons, cassette tapes, tube socks. Music crackled from speakers nailed over the doors—"Diskoteca Brooklyn." Brilliant technicolor murals that need not apologize to Diego Rivera adorned brick walls next to moody, gang-banging grafitti. It was a true barrio.

"God, you can *feel* this place," Petey said as she pumped the brake and jockeyed the Buick through the bazaar.

We went south on Carmelita and met Holdsworth at the edge of the park. It was not yet nine, and the grounds were mostly empty except for a few crews setting up a bunting-draped soundstage between the ballfields, and others readying vending trucks and concession stands. Cinco de Mayo at Obregon was an all-day affair, a festival, a Mexican Fourth of July, a Latin Mardi Gras. In a couple hours the park would be full of flags, banners, mariachi bands, deafening sound systems, craft displays, dogs, vendors, picnickers, and people, thousands of people. Bombo Carillo, of course. Tido Dali and clan, maybe. And perhaps a visiting Anglo, a former middle reliever on a mission.

We followed Holdsworth in his unmarked car to Sunol Street and into the parking lot of a two-story office building directly across the street from the park's main entrance. This was a neighborhood social-service center, closed today except to us. Once we'd parked, we got out and Holdsworth eyed Petey.

"Chiquita," Holdsworth said, then touched his finger to his tongue and hissed.

Petey was in uniform. Her hair was frantic and gelled, her makeup—coal black eyeliner, three shades of eye shadow—laid on like greasepaint. Hoop earrings the size of drapery-rod rings clanged from her ears. Barely covering the upper deck was a white sleeveless blouse gathered at her décolletage but coming up short of her belly button. A pair of icy black Capri pants hugged her gams like Saran wrap. Because she wanted to get around, she wore *huarachis* instead of heels. And a big white purse, which she hugged.

Petey wasn't a cop, and Holdsworth didn't want her in on this. But he knew if he told her so, she could and would work the park on her own. I know *I* couldn't have stopped her. As a compromise Holdsworth paired her with one of his detectives. She was a young investigator named Germany Smith, and she was a stunning kid, a twin of Rita Moreno in her *West Side Story* days. Together Petey and Germany looked as if they had just flown in from Rio.

"Don't wear the jacket," Holdsworth admonished. At the last minute Petey had grabbed a Lakers jacket from Eddie Start's closet. "Gangbangers start things over jackets," he continued. "Stay out of sight and wait for Germany. And do what she tells you to do.

"Be careful out there," Holdsworth leveled. "They're deadly motherfuckers."

If Petey would have winked, or blown him a kiss, I'd have killed her. She nodded.

Holdsworth took me to a second-floor office in the service center, with a view. With binoculars and a two-way radio, we'd monitor things the best we could from here. Cinco de Mayo in East Los Angeles was not an ideal occasion for an old white fart with an ear patch and an eighty-inch black guy to go undercover.

"Nice little place, isn't it?" Holdsworth said, scanning the green.

"Almost too nice," I said.

"Don't know who Eu-*gene* Obregon was," he went on, "but there was a famous Obregon in Mexican history, you know. Went against Diaz. Became El Presidente for a while."

"Is that right? I think I missed him."

"Yeah, well, he didn't do too much," Holdsworth said, raising the glasses. "He was assassinated."

In an hour the fest got going. It was a clean, almost smog-free day, sunny as a Mexican holiday, and the little park began to hum. The bands kicked up and the barbecues smoked and the Mexican flags flew everywhere. As if on cue people flooded into the park, people everywhere, pouring out of houses and cars and covering the grounds. Most were families with small kids—little girls in lacy purple dresses and little boys in striped pants and bow ties. And babies, there were babies everywhere. There was enough breast milk out there to put out a brush fire.

"*Damn,* look at the mob," Holdsworth grumbled.

The older kids hung in clumps near the curbs, knots of teenaged girls made up like Petey and guys with sunglasses and sneers and boxy stereos that competed with the live bands. They crowded around cars, Detroit's hottest—sculpted, sleek, fast models with big tires and plenty of fiberglass. Some looked as if they'd been plucked out of the showroom this morning.

Then there were the lowriders, those customized monsters whose carriages hovered a whisper above the pavement. Holdsworth prepared me for them. "You got twenty, thirty thousand bucks in some of those jobs," he said. Indeed, they were the trophies of California's Hispanic car clubs. Most were sedans—Buicks, Chevys, Pontiacs—adorned with blinding chrome work and glittering paint jobs, interiors decorated with crushed velvet floorboards and dashboards, and steering wheels made of chrome chains.

The secret of lowriders, however, lies in trunks full of batteries and hydraulics that could raise the front and back ends up two feet and then thump them down again just as fast. They did it standing still, or in an awkward procession, lurching down the boulevard like technicolor, hiccuping turtles.

Several of them had pulled up along the curb on Michigan Street, their owners in car-club jackets hovering over them, draping the hoods with flags, enticing chippies, basking, trying to get some of their investment back in envy.

"You see that lime green lowrider on San Carlos?" Holdsworth said.

I craned to get a look, then spotted the rolling pea soup.

"That's ours."

"Criminy," I said.

"See the sheriff's car and those trustees in prison greens along Michigan? Pickin' up trash with forks. Ours too. The ice cream cart guy by the field house. He's ours. My point guard is up on the knoll. See him by the bushes? From there he can see just about everything. And two narcotics guys in the vending truck over there. Then there's Germany and your niece in Times Square down there. We got cars on Marianna, San Carlos, Sunol, and on First Avenue right behind us."

"A lot of overtime out there."

"Tell me about it. My worry is the freeways," Holdsworth added. Only a few blocks away, hooking around the park on the west and south, were the Pomona and the Long Beach freeways. "If Ferguson or Tido Dali's people make the Pomona, they're gone."

"Any sightings anywhere? Anybody telling you anything?" I asked.

"Nothin'," he said, his brow tight to the field glasses.

It was a good thing, Petey said later, that her Spanish wasn't keen. As she and Germany Smith strolled arm in arm, giggling and cracking gum, the chatter and trash talk bounced off them like bad-hop grounders. The bandsmen loved them. The vendors plied them with food. Fathers of four offered them tamales and ears of corn. Young guys with pimples lobbed scandalous entreaties. The old-timers in pointed shoes and straw cowboy hats grinned gapped teeth at them.

Petey smiled back and kept her painted eyes moving. Like every detective out there, she knew the faces of Tido Dali and his kin, and she was looking for any sign of them. And of course she remembered the look of Ferguson's mug. Germany Smith, in the meantime, had an earphone hidden beneath her coal black hair, and she talked to Holdsworth via the handle of a hairbrush.

The two of them kept moving, sometimes in my view, sometimes out. They stayed near the street, lingering in the entrance lot on Sunol and near a smaller parking lot behind the backstop on Michigan. They ate crispy *bunuelos* and sipped sodas. Only sipped. They didn't want to be in the bathroom if something broke.

Petey loved the kids, especially the little dark-eyed girls in their lacy dresses and patent-leather shoes. But in no time their dresses were stained with flavored ice or chocolate, fruit juice, or grease. Every family had food on a barbecue, and every kid had a helping in one fist. And yet the vendors, from the independents—the ice shavers with their bottles of flavoring and ice-cream sellers with their squat *helados* carts—to the big, full-menu trucks, were also selling grub like mad.

"We got one," said Holdsworth.

His radio rasped with the voice of one of the agents in the vending truck as he pointed out two men walking up to the Sunol Street entrance. Members of Dali's crew, they were in their forties, heavyset, surly and dark-skinned, one in a straw hat. They wore cowboy boots and slacks with enormous jade belt buckles. Sport shirts open to midchest. They kept their hands in their pockets and swiveled their heads, scanning the terrain like periscopes.

"Pilot fish," Holdsworth said.

My spirits rose, and I looked out at the smoky park like a losing manager who'd suddenly gotten two men on.

"C'mon, big tuna," I said.

The radio crackled again, the voices chopped, the words abbreviated, almost in code.

"Two more," Holdsworth said. "Walked past our guy on the knoll."

This pair was younger, but just as wary, eyes sweeping the crowd. Coming in from the east on Marianna Street, they moved into the heart of the park, checked the bandstand, and turned north toward Michigan. Two more *hombres* had appeared there, at the corner of San Carlos, thereby completing the triangle.

It was almost noon now, and a program of sorts had started. A hoarse but jolly emcee hogged the microphone, laughing and shouting in Spanish into a microphone that ached with static. As earsplitting as he was, he was hard-pressed to get the crowd's attention. What did was a commotion in the parking lot near the ballfields.

"Shit," Holdsworth barked, training his glasses on the fuss. "We can't have the fuckin' bangers goin' at it."

He grasped the radio.

"Whattaya got, Phil?" he yelled.

Even I understood the reply.

"Bombo."

Bombo Carillo and his Señorita Review swept onto the scene in a caravan of convertibles. The crowd rushed his way. Petey and Germany Smith were part of it, though they stayed by the sidewalk to keep from getting trapped in the middle. Carillo jumped on a hood with a heavy step and a radiant grin and waved his left arm above his head. His fans cheered and whistled. His shirt, a replica of the Mexican flag, was open, and his ample, carpeted chest was ablaze with gold. To the crowd's delight he grabbed a flag and started waving it like a revolutionary. Fireworks went off. Trumpets blared.

And behind him, reported by three separate teams of agents, appeared Tido Dali.

With Holdsworth manning the radio like a director in a sound truck, the detectives held their positions, watched their flanks, and kept watch. Dali's people now numbered a dozen, most of them staying with him as he waddled about on the fringes of Carillo's entourage. And waddle he did, for Dali was a big enchilada, at least three hundred pounds of *tío*. He wore a straw fedora and an ice-blue baggy summer suit that swished about him as he walked. He laughed, perspired, and wiped his brow a lot, and it wasn't that warm out.

Though he was not part of Bombo Carillo's group, Dali obviously enjoyed being near it. The festival was hopping now, certainly more fun and more excitement than Tido Dali knew in his village. Or maybe not. But he grinned like a fish, sang, clapped, and even jigged a bit.

Petey edged closer and got a gander at him. One of Dali's lackeys eyed her and slobbered all over himself. All the while Germany Smith stayed on her hip, relaying Holdsworth's instructions. They were to stay close to Dali, she said, keep him in sight. That was easy, because Dali followed the crowd as it followed Bombo Carillo to the bandstand. Bombo was the show as far as the people of Obregon Park were concerned. Tido Dali was just a sweating fat man.

As Bombo mugged and yipped on stage, Petey began to get edgy. Dali was a lump—a well-guarded one, but a lump nonetheless. He wolfed down a taco, tossed back tamales like Butterfingers, then worked on an ear of corn. He clapped and chattered, but gave no indication that he was doing any business.

"It's not gonna happen around him," Petey said to her partner.

"Stay here," came the reply.

"No, it's time to move," Petey insisted.

Germany Smith glared at her, yet Petey peeled away. A few seconds later Holdsworth got the word and cursed, then he told Germany to stay where she was. He wasn't pleased.

Still, nothing was going down. The members of Dali's crew who were not at Tido's elbows were content to sit like sentries on the rim of the park. And Holdsworth's people sat on them.

For her part, Petey moved south along Sunol until she reached the playground just inside the parking lot. She was now in plain view. We could almost have lifted the window and jawed with her. Holdsworth grumbled as she passed the vending truck with his men inside. Every so often Petey paused, removed a stone from her sandal, tossed a ball to a child, and checked, always checked around her. She was getting good at this stuff.

Then she went on, walking through the playground area toward the field house, following a walk as it curved southwest toward First Avenue. Soon she was out of our line of vision, and, without a wired partner, she went out of our touch.

This was now all very familiar to her, Petey realized. She'd covered this area several times during the morning, seen many of the same faces before, many of the same little boys and big boys. The craft tables and vendors were the same, content to stay in one place rather than move with the crowd. With Bombo on stage, this corner of the park had thinned. Two-year-olds and their mamas were not yet big Dodger fans.

Then a little dirty face caught Petey's eye. It belonged to a chubby kid, no more than four but as big as a third-grader. He wanted another ice cream, and he wanted it bad. *"Helado. Helado,"* he whined, first at a lone vendor, a shaggy, emaciated kid, huddled over a beat-up ice-cream cart near the sidewalk, then at Petey. Petey would have ignored him, preferring not to stuff the pillow any fuller, had not the vendor snarled at the fat little boy. Just waved his hand and told the kid in universal lingo to get lost.

That was a new one, Petey thought. Usually these guys will sell ice cream to diabetics. So Petey fished a buck out of her purse and slipped it to the kid. He beamed and returned to the vendor. Again he was rejected. *"No mas. No mas,"* growled the skinny vendor. The kid cowered, about to break into tears, but then turned and bolted for another cart. Petey scowled at the guy, but moved on.

At First Street she went north along the edge of the park, eyeing the traffic, finally coming to a small employee parking area near Carmelita. It was nicely landscaped with pines, cedar and arborvitae shrubs, and white-barked ficus trees. Though there were cars parked everywhere, this side of the park was less crowded and less noisy than the areas near the bandstand.

Petey was about to double back and return to the crowd when she spotted a kid with a puller, a Slim Jim, the long strip of metal used by cops to unlock locked car doors. Only this kid wasn't a cop, and when his eyes met Petey's, he bolted from between two parked cars and ran like hell. She sprinted after him for ten yards, then stopped, content to have interrupted the little felon.

As she stared down the street at his heels, the snout of an expensive yellow car pulled up at the corner of Carmelita. Petey took notice of it, and for some reason it registered. She ducked down behind a shrub and watched as the car passed slowly by her. She held her breath. It was Bob Ferguson's pint-sized Cadillac. Driven by the artful dodger himself.

"Where'd she go?" Holdsworth shouted into the radio.

His vending-truck detectives in the parking lot had lost her.

"Get out and get on her," he barked.

Then he got Germany Smith and told her to forget Dali and get over here.

"I don't want her on her own," he said.

Petey watched as the Cadillac slowed, nearing Sunol. There was no space for it to park or pull over. Its taillights glowed. Petey edged closer, staying in the shadows of the cars parked along First. She was frantic for backup, yet she did not want to expose herself to

Ferguson's rearview mirror. His car was no more than twenty-five yards away from her.

Just then a vendor with a *helados* cart appeared and moved toward the car. It was the same cart, the same vendor who had spurned the little fat boy with Petey's dollar.

Suddenly she knew, and she ran for it.

At the same moment Holdsworth's two detectives spotted the Cadillac.

"We got the pitcher!" they snapped into the radio.

Holdsworth spun around, and with massive strides he went for the door. I followed him, lagging badly.

In seconds Ferguson, dressed in jeans and running shoes and looking like he was about to put a couple of T-bones on the grille, had popped his trunk lid and was out of the car. With a single motion he and the oily vendor hefted the small cart and laid it into the well of the trunk. The lid closed, and Ferguson, without pause, without a look at the spectacle of Cinco de Mayo, went to get back in the car.

"Ferguson!" Petey screamed.

At her shout he stopped, looked at her for two long seconds, and immediately knew he was discovered. To his right on Sunol Street the two sprinting detectives, their guns drawn, closed in on him. Holdsworth had made it out of the service center and was galloping behind them.

Ferguson jumped into his Caddy and jerked it left onto Sunol. Petey and the detectives ran up, one of them raising his revolver at the fleeing Cadillac. He decided against firing and collared the vendor instead. The skinny no-account was flopped spread-eagle on the ground, his nose pressed to the sidewalk until it nearly cracked like a nut.

Ferguson's Cadillac howled off in the distance, shooting beneath the viaduct of the Pomona Freeway, a block away. An entrance ramp was at Third Street, a few blocks west, and one of Holdsworth's squads was waiting there.

"Yellow Caddy. Bullshit model. In your face, three-one!" Holdsworth shouted into his radio as he got to the scene. He was talking to the unit at the ramp. It was a black-and-white, its Mars lights flashing. A few moments later its occupants relayed back.

"Got him! He's coming back your way!" the voice barked.

The marked squad had blocked the ramp, and Ferguson saw it, pulled a U-turn, and roared east on Third. At Sunol he was blocked again, and he turned north, coming back toward the park.

Just then Holdsworth's car and the two dicks in the pale green lowrider pulled up. Holdsworth slid into the front seat but told the driver to stay put. He gripped his radio tightly, waiting for a cue.

Instead, we heard it. Tires hissed and squealed, engines groaned. Holdsworth had positioned his cars perfectly, and now four of them were engaged, preventing Ferguson from access to the freeways, turning him back toward the park. In the narrow side streets that wound around us and the thousands in Obregon Park, the chase, with tires pealing and gears grinding in a terrifying racket, was on.

"My God!" Petey gasped. She clutched my arm and trembled as we knelt by Long Jim's open car door.

By then the crowd had thickened behind us, and some of the detectives tried to move people off the curbs. Yet we all stood paralyzed, hearing the two-ton hounds, growling and spitting rubber and smoke, chase their fox. By the sounds alone we could tell approximately where they were. Holdsworth's cars closed quickly on the Cadillac, forcing it to charge about, changing directions, jumping curbs, desperately seeking escape through the streets all around us.

"There they are!" someone yelled, and we craned to see a racing squad car. Two more cars had come in, Holdsworth said, about six in all. He decided not to join them. He held the radio near his lips, spoke into it every so often, but mostly listened. His face, his entire skull, was rinsed with sweat.

Just then we saw the Cadillac show itself atop an incline to our right. It was a gleaming, rich car, one hardly prepared for this kind of run. It hurtled down First Avenue, past Bonnie Street, and again with the awful howl of rubber on asphalt, it was gone.

"Just give up," Petey breathed.

She was shaking now, her fingers viselike on my sleeve, hoping against hope that Ferguson's lethal flurry would cease.

"Keep him from the park, dammit," Holdsworth growled. It was more a plea than a command.

Just then we saw the yellow Cadillac appear, this time to our left. It had circled and was now screaming eastward, coming over the bluff of Marianna, following the street southeast along the edge of the park. A bouncing, sandy brown unmarked car was only yards behind it. The two cars were coming in our direction, like roaring, unpredictable animals.

On its own the crowd edged fearfully back into the park. Holdsworth swung around in his seat, watching them come, bracing for the worst. Petey and I crouched in the shadow of Holdsworth's squad, our heads just high enough to see the onslaught.

In the fury of the moment, we did not pay heed to our right, the area across Sunol Street where First Street jogged left and rose precipitously as it went away from the park. Land adjacent to the service center had been dug out into the hillside at the base of the street. The area had been bulldozed for expansion of the center and formed a deep ravine so that the houses on the next block appeared to be on a cliff, high in the air. A cyclone fence surrounded the lot and a lone construction trailer inside. And directly next door, now completely exposed, was a shack of a house, a leaning hovel with a blanket on the roof to cover missing shingles, a rotted porch, a yard full of trash and lacerated cacti, and two limping dogs with infected ears. On the porch stood an old guy in shorts, a bronzed and ample bare belly, and a Dodger cap that he was swinging like a flagman at the finish line of the Indianapolis 500.

Just then Ferguson's car flew by us, his speed frightening, the brown police car bearing down on him. As he approached the intersection of Sunol, another unmarked car approached from the north. That squad car braked frantically and slid sideways into the intersection, forcing Ferguson to veer right to avoid it. First Street, however, jogged left as it inclined. The yellow Cadillac did not recover and did not make the turn. Ferguson's car spun on the gravel and turf next to the street, jumped the curb, and left the pavement, soaring through the air, brushing the top of the cyclone fence and hurtling into the construction site.

The car bounced madly, raising a cyclone of dust and stones, tilted on two wheels, and rolled over. As it did, its trunk opened like a toilet seat, and the *helados* cart bounced out, hitting the gravel upright and rolling on its own as if it were fleeing the action. At that the Cadillac slammed into the construction trailer, caving in its sides in an explosion of metal and glass and dust.

Then, like the aftermath of a dying Roman candle, it was over, deathly quiet for a second, before the crowd heaved, and cops and onlookers, and Petey and I, rushed to the mangled auto. As we did, passing through the hole in the fence, the wild old coot on the worm-eaten porch next door whooped and coughed and waved his cap like he must have when Sandy Amoros grabbed Berra's liner in the Series of '55.

We didn't share his glee. At Holdsworth's elbow we approached the car where it lay on its side, the driver's door to the ground. Ferguson had remained inside, but he had been bounced around like a line drive in the corner. Now he was lifeless, his skull fractured, his neck broken, and his face sliced open by parts of the windshield and anything else in the cockpit with an edge on it.

There was blood everywhere. It covered him, coating his powerful, once-talented hands like scarlet gloves, and dripped onto the seat. It ran red. The real stuff always does.

15

Boxscore

"Hey, Duf, when a guy says, 'Lend me your ear,' you don't wanna take him seriously!" Red Carney said.

He got a good chuckle out of that as he slobbered over his porterhouse.

We'd finally gotten together, this time sharing a booth at the venerable Musso and Frank Grill in Hollywood. We sat in wooden seats that had been around longer than mine and reveled in the artistry of the grill man. He was just over our shoulder, plying his trade on dozens of steaks, chops, and slabs of salmon and swordfish sizzling over a live fire. With a great pair of wrists, he kept the flame down with a wet broom of parsley.

It was late evening, several hours after the event at Obregon Park and the conclusion of the Cubs-Dodgers game. The Dodgers had lost. Adonis Terrio had pitched terribly, wild and unsettled; finally Manager Allison yanked him in the middle of the fourth. The announcers, including Red, said it looked as if the kid's mind wasn't in the game. Little did they know.

"So when are we gonna set a date, pretty lady?" Red went on, playing, of course, to Petey. "You get better lookin', and I keep gettin' better. What a pair."

"But you're married, Red. For sixteen years. Four kids," Petey said. She was buried in a plate of lamb chops. Her appetite was remarkable.

"I know, you want me all to yourself," he said.

I let them talk and nibbled at my swordfish. It

sounded good, and the imagery was right for my wounds, but I wasn't doing it justice. I didn't have the stomach to eat. My bones hurt. The painkillers I'd ingested were riling the blood. I could have used some more buttermilk, but Musso and Frank, as old as they were, didn't stock it.

"For what it's worth, I never liked the son-of-a-bitch," Red started. He meant Bob Ferguson, and he didn't have to explain. "Bitched about everybody else when he lost. Took all the credit when he won. It's just a cryin' shame what he did to a man who treated him like a son."

"Jack treated everybody like a son," I said.

"How'd the guy lose all that money, for cryin' out loud? He made *millions* goin' free agent," Red blustered. He was off the air, but his sound level hadn't sunk a decibel.

Petey started in. "He spent it like it was never going to stop coming in. They're all like that."

I nodded. My stomach was upset.

"According to the cops, he lost a bundle in a restaurant franchise deal," I added. "Then he tried to get it back playing the stock market—"

"Options," Petey said.

"—and lost even bigger. The drug deal was a crapshoot to get it all back."

And a coke deal it was. The runaway *helados* cart was lined with several kilos of cocaine. It was good stuff, Holdsworth's people said, that Ferguson was probably going to sell directly to a dealer. If all had gone according to plan for him, he would not have held the stuff for more than a couple hours. And made a couple-million bucks.

"I got a question," Petey said, turning to me. "How'd you know he was broke? You knew it all the time, didn't you?"

I pushed the fish around my plate.

"Nope. Only when we pulled out of his driveway. Saw the landscape crew. A guy who's sitting okay doesn't sell the palm trees out of his front yard."

She stopped her fork in midair.

"Of course," she said. "Of course."

"What? Palm trees? What in hell is this all about?" Red demanded.

Petey waved him off and started pumping catsup on her hash browns.

"Aw, don't do that to 'em," Red whined.

Watching the two of them eat was killing me. I looked up and saw the army of Latin waiters bringing raw steaks to the grill man.

"How'd Jack get in the middle of it?" Red wanted to know.

"He had to sooner or later. He was a soft touch, but he kept his ears open," I said. "We don't know for sure, but we think the kid told him. Terrio."

Petey cut in.

"You should have seen the kid's face when we showed him the list of names with his uncle at the top. He just about shat."

"He was still doin' it on the mound today," Red said.

"And what he saw was a copy," Petey said. "The original had his name underlined. Little arrows around it. And we wondered why."

"The list you got from the floozy?" Red said.

Petey snarled at him. "Floozy!" she muttered.

"Well, she wasn't Mother Superior," Red said.

"She was all right. Her problem was that she dealt one too many hands," I said. "She sent me off to the preacher while she tried to shake down Ferguson."

"Just wanted a cut. A few points out of the gross," Red said. "They're all the same out here."

He sat back and wiped his chops. The meal had raised a sweat on his perpetually flushed mug.

"Ah, that was masterful," he said. "My compliments to Frank and Musso."

He eyed the long wooden bar, and his kidneys fairly glowed.

"Now we wet it down some, whattaya say?" he said.

I knew he wanted to make a night of it. The Cubs had the next day off before they opened in San Diego. Red had no curfew and no wake-up call.

"There's something wrong with ya, Duf. Besides that ear of yours. Hey, just kiddin'. Huh? How 'bout it? You two are heroes. You get the bad guy and break up a big dope ring."

I winced.

"One for two," Petey said. "Turns out they never got the Mexicans. The guy with the ice-cream cart was just a stiff. They'd given him a hundred bucks to make the pass. Ferguson made the money drop before that. Probably just before I saw him. The cops never recovered it."

"Yeah, sure, but come *on*, everybody knew what they were there for," Red said.

"Only Ferguson was caught in the act," I said. "What you gonna charge the *muchachos* with? Overeating at Cinco de Mayo?"

Red grumbled about that.

"Well, you can't win 'em all," he said. "And you still didn't say what's eatin' ya, Duf. So what's eatin' ya?"

"It's been a bum trip, Red. Springtime in California and all I've seen out here is blood in the flowers."

Petey turned to me, about to say something, when Red started in.

"You know, I always love comin' out here," he said. "The Dodgers are a hell of a franchise. And I'm a guy who always loved Brooklyn. But they are, Duffy, you gotta admit that. Three million people with ticket stubs can't be wrong. And that beautiful ballpark they got out there. And they always beat the brains out of the Cubs.

"So a guy like this Ferguson comes along, and he thinks he's a big shot. He does something just unbelievable like that. What's the world comin' to? Why didn't he just take his free-agent money and get the hell out a long time ago? Huh, Duffy?"

He looked around for something wet.

Petey answered him. "This is Hollywood, Red," she said. "A cruel place for has-beens."

She had something there. More than she knew.

"Remember the movie *Sunset Boulevard*?" I asked.

"Of course," Red replied. "Gloria Swanson. Now there was a beauty."

"And William Holden," I said. "Gloria Swanson played a faded movie star trying to make a comeback. Name was Norma Desmond."

"I can see her now," said Red.

"And William Holden said to her, 'You're Norma Desmond! You used to be in silent pictures. You used to be big.' And she said back to him, 'I *am* big. It's the pictures that got small.'"

"There you go," Red said. "There you go."

I sat back in the booth, and Petey swung her arm around my shoulder. My ear itched, but I couldn't scratch it.

About the Authors

CRABBE EVERS is the pseudonym for the partnership of William Brashler and Reinder Van Til, a pair of boxscore devotees who admire the poetry of Franklin P. Adams and have spent long hours at the feet of Duffy House.

WILLIAM BRASHLER is the author of eight books, including his novel about baseball in the Negro Leagues, *The Bingo Long Traveling All-Stars and Motor Kings*, which was made into a popular motion picture. He has also written biographies of Josh Gibson and Johnny Bench. He lives and works in Chicago.

REINDER VAN TIL, a long time book editor and freelance music and art critic, has published a book on regional history and numerous magazine articles. He lives and works in St. Paul.

CRABBE EVERS has also written two other Duffy House baseball mysteries, *Murder in Wrigley Field* and *Murderer's Row*.

TO SPEAK FOR THE DEAD
by Paul Levine
author of *Night Vision*

Miami trial lawyer Jake Lassiter "ex-football player, ex-public defender, ex-a-lot-of-things," is defending Dr. Roger Salisbury, a surgeon and womanizer charged with malpractice in the death of wealthy Philip Corrigan. But the dead man's daughter insists that the doctor and his sexy stepmother conspired to kill her father -- and wants Lassiter to prove it.

Can Lassiter really defend his client for malpractice and build a case against him for murder? Turning for help to the wisdom of his old friend, retired county coroner Charlie Riggs, Lassiter hopes to get the evidence he needs from the dead man himself. But outside the courtroom, he soon finds more trouble than he ever imagined possible -- murder, missing persons, grave robbery, kinky sex, and deadly drugs -- as he searches Florida's steamy streets and tropical swamps for a cold-blooded killer.

"Move over, Scott Turow...*To Speak for the Dead* is courtroom drama at its best." -- Larry King

TO SPEAK FOR THE DEAD
by Scott Turow
Available wherever Bantam Crime Line Books are sold.

AN352 -- 10/91